Praise for *An Unclean Place*

"In crisp, riveting prose, Barbara Barrow explores the fluid boundaries between love and obsession. *An Unclean Place* is a simmering, sinister backyard thriller: trust shape-shifts into malevolence, those most familiar to us become monsters—and reflect back to us how easy, how quick the descent."

—Melanie Finn, author of *The Hare* and *The Gloaming*

"With confident prose and vivid characterization, Barrow unravels a world of secrets that turn fascination to obsession, love to dread. A worthy cousin to Donna Tartt's *The Secret History*, *An Unclean Place* affirms that monsters hide in the most ordinary places, people."

—Jen Michalski, author of *You'll Be Fine* and *The Company of Strangers*

Praise for *The Quelling*

"Instantly achieves page-turner status…insightful, vivid renderings of circumstances and events contribute to a collective narrative greater than the sum of its parts."

—*Foreword Reviews*

"Complex and strange, *The Quelling* is a marvel of a debut… Barrow paints the sisters Dorian and Addie with tenderness and keen psychological intuition."

—Jen Julian, author of *Earthly Delights and Other Apocalypses*, winner of Press 53's 2018 Short Fiction Prize

"Ferocious, tender, astonishing…[*The Quelling*] brims with terrifying insights and the eerie intimacy of dreams."

—Anca L. Szilágyi, author of *Dreams Under Glass*

"An unusual, involving novel, enticing and imperfect and entirely readable."

—Katharine Coldiron for *The Inquisitive Mind*

AN UNCLEAN PLACE

Lanternfish Press
21 S. 11th Street, Office #404
Philadelphia, PA 19107
lanternfishpress.com

Cover Design: Kimberly Glyder
Cover Art: Alex Eckman-Lawn

Printed in the United States of America.
27 26 25 24 23 1 2 3 4 5

Library of Congress Control Number: 2022940074
Print ISBN: 978-1-941360-73-6
Digital ISBN: 978-1-941360-74-3

An Unclean Place

Barbara Barrow

LANTERNFISH PRESS
Philadelphia

Also by Barbara Barrow

The Quelling

An Unclean Place

For D.H.

Part One:

Atlanta, 1992–1993

Chapter I

Spring 1992

THE POLICE CAME for Ms. Ella, our eighth-grade teacher, in the middle of Bryce's report on Franklin Delano Roosevelt.

It was a warm day in June. Bryce wore an Insane Clown Posse T-shirt—a neon burst of grinning faces on his chest—and kicked the base of the podium with scuffed-up Doc Martens as he delivered the report. We listened, our stomachs rumbling, to his sullen rendition of Roosevelt's 1936 "I Hate War" speech. Ms. Ella sat behind us, in the back of the room. We could feel her eyes on our backs and sat up as straight as possible.

"I hate war," Bryce mumbled, "the nation hates war, even my little dog Fala hates war."

The door opened. Our principal, Jean, stepped into the classroom with a police officer, a man in a blue uniform that said *City of Atlanta* on the shoulder. His radio emitted a fuzzy belch of static.

Bryce stopped. We all stared.

"I need to speak to Eleanor Hallstrom," the officer said.

We turned in our seats, following his gaze. Calmly, Ms. Ella lifted her hand. She was wearing a gray blazer over the white Philadelphia Eagles T-shirt we knew so well. As usual, she had freshened her makeup after lunch, so that her sharp brown eyes were ringed with liner, her small lips a bright red.

"One moment," she said. "Bryce, go on."

"Um, okay," he said. "Keep reading?"

"Keep reading."

We turned back to the front. He stumbled his way to the end while the officer waited, his radio crackling every few moments, Jean shifting nervously beside him. We sat transfixed, not daring to look at each other. When Bryce was finished, Ms. Ella put down her notepad, picked up her bag, and strode through the doorway, past the officer and Jean, her high-tops squeaking, not looking back. Jean gave a quick glance around the room and pulled the door shut.

Dawn ran to the window first, then Tracy and Kayla. The rest of us followed, and we formed a little semicircle in front of the glass. Bryce, who was the tallest, pulled up the blinds. We peered through the magnolia tree outside the window, straining to see past its haze of white blooms, and spotted the squad car parked below.

"He just put her in the back," Bryce said.

"What's she doing?" asked Tracy.

"Just sitting." Bryce craned his neck. "The officer is writing something, in the front."

Outside, the engine started, and the officer pulled out of the driveway, pausing by the flaking wooden sign that read *Stillwater Alternative School: A Private Academy Nurturing*

Today's Youth for Tomorrow's World. He did not use the siren or speed away as we had seen police cars do in movies. He simply signaled left, drove past the apartment complex next to our school, and disappeared.

We stood, stunned, and stared at the empty driveway. On the windowsill, in the shade from the magnolia outside, stood a papier-mâché statue of the ancient Greek priestess Cassandra, a statue Dawn had started but never finished. This Cassandra was urgent but incomplete, a woman with raised and gesturing hands, but no eyes. We looked out into the new, strange world and the Cassandra looked back at us, her empty face frozen in perpetual, unuttered fury.

We heard a choking sound, a kind of growl, and we turned. Dawn had moved away from the window and was sitting on the floor against the wall, underneath the long, taped-up sheets of Ms. Ella's handwritten notes, the ones that Amber had worked on all year. Dawn's face was bright red and her hands were shaking. Her feet, too.

"This is because of Amber," she said.

"We don't know that," said Tracy, but we all looked at Amber's desk, empty now, Amber still missing, as she had been for days.

"Amber snitched," Dawn repeated. "She must have. I'll kill her."

Chapter II

Ms. Ella had come to us in late September of the previous year, when the magnolia blooms were closed and the tree was a dark, rustling green. None of us knew who Cassandra was then.

There were sixteen students in our class, and she was our third teacher of the term. The last one, Bud, had stormed off after just three weeks, to go to a "real school," he'd added, as he was saying goodbye.

When Jamal asked him what a real school would look like, Bud took off his glasses and jammed his hand through his hair. For starters, he said, it wouldn't be in a house.

It was true that our school looked like a regular house, a giant brick house with white shutters on a residential street. Parents routinely missed the turn on Open House days and had to turn around, squinting at our wooden sign. But once you came around the circular driveway to the back of the school, past Jean's jaunty black Porsche Roadster, you saw the big playground in the back, in the bottom of a hollow, and that helped.

This playground was made up of items donated by parents and churches. A red boat sat at the front of the playground, the boat where Kayla fell and broke her arm in the third grade, and behind it a tire maze snuck its way across the dirt, each tire getting bigger and bigger until you reached the creaking swing set in the back. This playground was surrounded by woods that had once sheltered Dawn during one of her violent rages, when no one, not even Amber, could come near her. To the right of the playground was a soccer field, slushy with mud and runoff that came down the gulley when it rained. To combat this, Jean ordered a truck to come every few weeks and dump wood chips into the wettest part of the field, and all of us, the older and the younger kids alike, would run outside and trample the pile until the mud was covered up and the air was filled with the sharp scent of pine.

One afternoon, when we were trampling out the wood chips, the kids from the apartment complex next door came out and threw rocks at us. The ringleader, Caleb, a muscular boy in Kris-Kross jeans, told us that our private school was sloppy.

"Why don't you go to Peachtree Middle like everyone else?" he said.

We didn't know, and that evening Amber asked her father, who gave her a long, complicated lecture on Reaganomics. When Caleb and the boys came again, she said,

"It's because of the defunding!"

"Because of the who?"

"The defunding. Reagan took the education budget for defense."

"But you pay to go there anyway, and it sucks." He gestured at our school, its shutters badly in need of new paint. "You wouldn't pay to go to public school, which also sucks. Right?"

"Yes," Amber said, blushing.

"Y'all stupid," said Caleb.

His friends nodded gravely.

By then, we were used to people not taking us seriously. Friends and relatives never tired of asking our parents about Stillwater at birthday parties and luncheons and fundraisers and after church.

"But what about grades?" they asked. "Extracurriculars? Aren't you worried about them adjusting to public high school next year?" Or: "What about personal responsibility, shouldn't they be learning that?"

Our parents shook their heads and changed the subject, or spent the rest of the meal locked in long, wearying debates. Sometimes they got out the brochure that explained the language and policies we used at our school: one primary teacher for all subjects, to foster personalized learning; holistic progress reports instead of grades; "exploratory time" instead of recess. They quoted from the "Stillwater's Philosophy of Growth" brochure.

"It's about the *radical growth of the whole individual*," our mothers might say primly, lifting their forks to their lips.

"It's about the radical growth of tuition!" our uncles or godfathers or grandfathers might quip as we sat restless, waiting to be excused.

So when Bud thundered off to go to a "real school," none of us were surprised, and when Jean walked into the room the following week to announce our new teacher, we all figured she too would disappear after a month or so. We all knew, from Bud, how measly the salary was, how hard it was for Jean to find teachers who would stay.

The new teacher followed Jean to the front of our classroom, a large, airy room, the only one on Stillwater's neglected second floor. She seemed a little older than our mothers, in her forties maybe: a white woman with tanned skin and greyish-brown hair cut into a shag, and strong wrists, wrists we would later see in handcuffs, and a watch that glinted when she wrote her name on the board. We saw, when she did this, that she was left-handed. She wore a red tie-neck blouse, khakis, and brown loafers, and her eyes were alert and slightly impatient, as if we were already displeasing her. She looked right at us, and we straightened up in our seats and looked back, waiting.

"Class, meet your new teacher," Jean said, in the strained, high voice she used at parent-teacher meetings and orientations. "This is Ella."

"Ms. Ella," the woman said.

Jean moved her fingers nervously. She had done puppet theater before opening our school and her fingers always moved unconsciously along the strings of remembered marionettes.

"Of course, it was probably different at your previous school. But here, we like to be on a first-name basis. It helps lessen the hierarchy between teachers and students."

"I know it does," the woman said, still looking at us and not at Jean. "But I want you all to call me Ms. Ella, always. It's a sign of respect."

We nodded, to show we understood.

"Good. I can take it from here," Ms. Ella said.

Jean was still smiling, a bit too brightly.

"Ok," she said. "I'll leave you to it!"

The door shut behind her. Ms. Ella pointed at Jamal, in the front row.

"What's your name and where are you from?"

"Jamal. I'm from southwest Atlanta."

"And you?"

"Wei. From Stone Mountain."

"You?"

"Amber. From Decatur."

She moved over to the next desk, where Dawn sat drawing, her strawberry blonde hair loose around her shoulders, her dark eyebrows furrowed in concentration. Ms. Ella grabbed Dawn's notebook, turned it around, and peered at the page.

"What the hell is this?" she demanded.

"Give it back," Dawn said, reaching.

"What's this? An elf?"

"It's not an elf, it's Link," Dawn said. "From *The Legend of Zelda*. Give it back," she said, reaching again.

"Ms. Ella, she has permission to draw," Amber volunteered.

This was true. Dawn was considered artistically gifted; our school counselor, Chuck, said she should be able to draw whenever she wanted to, a privilege that none of the rest of us enjoyed. He said it would help her behave.

But Ms. Ella still held the notebook out of Dawn's reach.

"Video games will rot your brain." Ms. Ella ripped the page out of the notebook, crumpled it, and threw it in the trash. She handed the notebook back to Dawn. "In my class, you pay attention and take notes when I speak."

Dawn said nothing, but her face was red, and for the rest of the class she stared down at the notebook. An angry tear made its way down her cheek. She did not bother to brush it away.

The rest of us sat up straight and answered quickly when Ms. Ella pointed at us. She made her way around the entire room, and then she went back and said each of our names on her own, by memory. When she was finished, she said, "Let's start with our first history lesson. Get out your books."

We were silent. Clumsy Brandon looked at skinny Amber and skinny Amber looked at clumsy Brandon and we all looked at Jamal, the smartest kid in our class, whose mom had gone to both Spelman and Emory Law School, a bookish boy with wire-rimmed glasses and a flattop. Jamal raised his hand.

"Ms. Ella. We don't have textbooks."

"Textbooks are biased," Amber added.

"I know that. I don't care about textbooks," Ms. Ella snapped. "In history class we read primary sources. Where are your primary sources?"

Tracy raised her hand.

"What's a primary source?"

"Jesus Christ," Ms. Ella said. "They treat you like babies here. Let's start over."

She wrote PRIMARY and SECONDARY in large letters on the board, lectured us on the distinction, and quizzed us afterward. When we all had written the right answer, she looked at her watch.

"I need a cigarette," she said. "Already."

She found some of Bud's old worksheets on American colonial history in the supply closet, handed them out, and disappeared onto the fire escape.

As soon as she left our room, Dawn got up and marched over to the trash can. She rescued her drawing and returned to her desk. A few minutes passed while she smoothed out the page, dabbing at the smudged pencil with her eraser. Then she said loudly, "I hate her."

"She's not so bad," Jamal said. "She's better than Bud. She knows her stuff."

"I hate her," Dawn said again.

"Listen to you!" Ms. Ella said, behind us.

Unheard, she had slipped back into the classroom and was strolling past Dawn's seat. She picked up the drawing again, folded it, and slipped it into her pocket.

"Hate is a strong word," she said. "My advice? Quit doodling, sit up, and pay attention. You might learn something. You might grow up. Or do you want to stay a little kid playing games forever?"

Dawn ignored her and stared straight ahead.

That night, when our parents and grandparents and caregivers asked us about the new teacher, we just said that we'd introduced ourselves, and that Ms. Ella wanted us to read primary sources.

Only Brandon told his father, over the din of his younger sisters, that the new teacher seemed a little bit strict. He had to repeat himself because the oldest sister kicked the youngest in the shin and ran away. His father bent down to console her.

"You know," he said, wearily, "I'm starting to wonder if strict is such a bad thing."

We were a little in awe, we know now. She was different. She wanted us to call her Ms., and when something wasn't up to her standards, she got mad, like men got. That was something, we thought.

The next morning when we arrived at school Ms. Ella was waiting for us at the front of the classroom in a fresh, white button-down shirt and black slacks, her foot tapping. She had taken down the attendance awards and ribbons on the bulletin board and wheeled in the old wooden podium from the storage area by the fire escape. She stood behind this podium now and pointed at a row of cardboard boxes on the floor, underneath the whiteboard.

"Make a line," she said. "Each of you come up here and pick one."

"What are they?" Jamal said.

"Books. Primary sources. My own books. From my own house."

We lined up behind the boxes. Jamal was first, and he had trouble choosing, so Ms. Ella asked him a series of questions.

"What hobbies do you have?"

"Kickball."

"What do your parents do?"

"My mom's a public defender."

"What kind of films do you like?"

"Action and adventure."

"You like heroes? Quest stories, stuff like that?"

"Sure."

Ms. Ella consulted the boxes, withdrew a copy of *Gilgamesh*, and handed it to Jamal.

She followed the same process for the rest of us. We each received something different, depending on our answers.

Kayla said she liked Halloween and gory movies, so she received a copy of Edgar Allen Poe's short stories.

Tracy liked flirting and makeup and boys; Ms. Ella gave her a copy of *Pride and Prejudice.*

Bryce was into punk rock and ICP and profanity; he received a volume of poems by Charles Bukowski.

Wei's extended family was in Boston, and he'd always wanted to visit; he received Benjamin Franklin's *Autobiography.*

Mousy, nervous Amber liked to write; Ms. Ella handed her a copy of *The Yellow Wallpaper and Other Stories.*

Some of us still have these books. They are dog-eared and battered now, our names still scrawled on the inside front covers in our proprietary adolescent handwriting, as if we expected someone to take them away from us.

"Do I have to read all of this?" Tracy said, staring down at her copy of Austen.

"You *get* to read all of that and write a report. It's a privilege. You're going to do some critical thinking here, all of you. Under my direction. You don't get this kind of personalized attention in public schools."

"Why not?"

"There's too much overcrowding. There are too many students and not enough teachers. And everyone has to learn for the tests. The teachers don't have time to teach, because of all the testing and assessment. I worked in public schools up north in Philly for fifteen years before I came down here and it's the same everywhere now, in this country."

Tracy was silent, and so were we. We were not used to hearing our school favorably compared to any other, and we stood caressing our books, reflecting on this new idea.

Dawn was next. She marched up to the box, grabbed a book at random, and turned to go, but Ms. Ella made her stop. She took it out of her hand.

It was a copy of Aeschylus's *Agamemnon*. On the cover was a weathered statue of a long-haired woman in robes, her muscular shoulder exposed, her mouth parted. Her expression was urgent and terrible. *Cassandra* was printed in capital letters across the pedestal.

"This is an old chesnut!" Ms. Ella said. "From my freshman year English class. You'll like it," she added, smirking. "It's full of vengeance and doom. You like doom."

Dawn snatched the book back and sat down, trembling.

Ms. Ella explained the assignment. Every morning, that whole week, we were supposed to read our books and take notes. We would have our other subjects, math and science and civics, in the afternoon, and then we would write our reports over the weekend. On the following Monday and Tuesday, we would come up to the podium and deliver our reports. When each student was presenting, we were expected to listen carefully and ask good, thoughtful questions.

"Be curious about your work," Ms. Ella said. She pointed at Dawn. "Even you. Especially you. As a matter of fact, you're going to go first."

"I don't have to do anything I don't want to do." Dawn's voice was low, malicious.

Ms. Ella leaned over Dawn's desk so that her forehead was inches away from hers.

"Then you'll face the consequences."

"What consequences?"

"Try me and find out."

Dawn looked up at her, not moving, and they stayed that way for a moment, eye to eye, while the rest of us watched.

"I'm not scared of you," Dawn said. "You'll be here for a couple of weeks and then you'll take your dusty old books and go. Just like Bud and the rest of them."

"Will I? Is that what you want?" Ms. Ella straightened up. She was still looking at Dawn, but she seemed to be talking to all of us, raising her voice so that we could all hear. "You want me to leave because I'm going to make you work and get better and smarter, and everyone else pampers you and lets you draw your little cartoons, is that it?"

Dawn ignored her and drew for the next hour while the rest of us bent over our books. Ms. Ella moved around the back of the classroom, unpacking the rest of the boxes, filling the shelves with volumes. Soon, our room began to resemble a small library, book-filled and silent. The only sounds were turning pages, periodic coughs, and sixteen pencils scribbling.

When Ms. Ella finished with the bookshelves, she began sorting through the other boxes in the supply closet, the catch-all debris of our former teachers: tattered classroom posters, broken geometry compasses, an old laminate projector. In our periphery, we saw her pull a wooden paddle from the closet, the kind found in frat houses. It said ATTITUDE ADJUSTER in blue letters across the front. It was a gag gift, something that had been given to Danny, the teacher before Bud, and forgotten. Ms. Ella tossed it onto the empty desk beside the podium with a little clatter.

Usually, when the Stillwater teachers wanted to smoke, they went off school property, to the sidewalk across the street. But Ms. Ella used the fire escape, a skeletal black structure that faced away from the main entrance and the playground. The door that led out to the fire escape was through a grungy storage room that no one used, filled with old file boxes and broken furniture. Soon the downstairs teachers started coming upstairs to join her, slipping a brick in the doorway to keep the door from falling shut and locking. In this way, standing near the crack, we learned a great deal about Ms. Ella that year, things she never told us herself.

Kayla and Tracy, snooping during one of the morning breaks, learned that Ms. Ella had moved to Atlanta from Philadelphia, which was why her vowels sounded different from ours. Everything moved too slowly for her down here, she said. Traffic. Speech. Grocery store checkout lanes.

Brandon, going to fetch his lunch satchel off of the top of the filing cabinets one day, learned that Ms. Ella had a teenaged son, Monty, whom she called a slacker. We caught a glimpse of him when he dropped her off at school one morning: a tall kid in a gaudy van covered in anarchy symbols and graffiti.

Jamal, pretending to call his ride from the dusty phone one afternoon, heard Ms. Ella say she didn't think much of Jean.

"She's a hack," she said. "She's not familiar with the most basic tenets of educational theory. She's never even heard of Benjamin Bloom. She couldn't identify a learning outcome if it bit her in the ass."

The other teachers agreed.

During lunch on the day Dawn took the copy of *Agamemnon*, the conversation was about the news, at first. There had been a scandal with a beloved local pastor, Herky Dyer, who'd slept with a sixteen-year-old girl in his congregation. He'd tried to flee with her to Mexico but was arrested outside Mobile and brought back to the Fulton County Jail, where he was awaiting trial. Our parents had been talking about it for weeks. Ms. Ella called it another sign of the bumpkinness of the south, and the other teachers agreed with this, too.

Then we heard Ms. Ella say, "What do you do about behavioral problems here? I got a kid who's giving me trouble."

"Well, there's a counselor, Chuck," said Hank. "But he's useless."

"This school is a black hole." That was Tilda. "What kid is it?"

"Dawn Brodie."

"Dawn Brodie? Forget about it."

Tilda launched into a story we all knew well.

"Earlier this year, there was an incident with her. Someone said something about one of her drawings, something critical, and she got into one of her rages. Bud tried to talk to her. But she kicked him in the shins and ran off into the woods. She hid for hours. We had to close the school and send out a search party."

"Jesus," Ms. Ella said. "Isn't she a bit old for that kind of tantrum?"

"She's got issues. Her mom walked out on them two years ago. Her dad's a single parent. He can't handle her on his own. And he's high up at Atlantic Products. He's probably the only parent in your class who's paying full tuition. Everyone else is on a sliding scale, or behind. As long as her dad's cutting tuition checks, Jean won't do shit about that kid."

"She does want to stay here," Hank said. "Her dad told her that if she can't make it work at this school, this year, he's going to send her to boarding school up near Tallulah Falls, in North Georgia. All-girls' school, Catholic, daily religion classes, lots of hiking, woodsy stuff, that sort of thing."

"Dawn wants to stay here because Amber is here," Tilda added. "They've been best friends for years. Also, Dawn's been held back a couple of grades, for her behavior stuff. She's already older than the rest of them. She can't be held back any more. So, you have that."

"Mr. Brodie went to Catholic school?"

"He did. I think the mom did too, but they're not in touch anymore."

"What kind of Catholic school? Just religion class, or did they have the nuns, too?"

"The full deal. Boarding school, uniforms, chapel, nuns with rulers."

"Hm," Ms. Ella said.

That week we all read diligently and took notes, but Dawn did not. She sat at her desk, drawing. All through class we heard her pencil scratch. All through class we saw her bending over the page, long hair hanging in her face, sneakers disappearing under the torn hems of her jeans. She sketched. She erased. She blew the shavings off of the page. Every now and then, Ms. Ella passed Dawn's desk, stopped, looked down, and said, "What are you doing?"

"I'm drawing," Dawn replied quietly.

"Put it away and work on your report."

Ms. Ella would move away from the desk and Dawn would glare after her, face turning red. A moment later, she would bend over the sketch again, pick up her pencil, and recommence her drawing.

At lunch that Friday, we crowded around her desk and peered over her shoulder at the open sketchbook, where Link was entering a dungeon to retrieve his magical recorder.

"Why do you keep doing this?" Brandon asked.

"Why do you care?" she said. "It's my notebook." Dawn finished shading in Link's cap and blew some more eraser shavings off of the page.

On the following Monday, Ms. Ella came to the podium and gave a short speech to open our day of presentations. She talked about the importance of thinking for ourselves, of formulating research questions, of learning to express our thoughts well, of immersing ourselves in lots of subjects and debates. There was a great deal more to be said on the subject of education, she went on, and we would be hearing it from her this year. Our model, she said, was the Renaissance man: the well-rounded scholar of all things, the fully informed participant in civic life.

"The best way to become well-rounded is to immerse yourself in all kinds of topics. That's what primary source research is, an immersion in knowledge. A return to the sources. Not tests. Not worksheets. Not baby stuff. You've never been asked to meet your full potential before," she finished. "In my class, you will. Dawn, you're up."

Dawn stood up, tugged at her long black T-shirt, and walked to the podium. She unfolded a piece of paper, flattened it out on the wood, and read, stumbling a bit over the unfamiliar names.

"*Agamemnon* is the first play in a trilogy. It's about a soldier who returns home after fighting in the Trojan War. His wife, Clytemnestra, is angry because he sacrificed their daughter, Iphigeneia, years ago. She greets him with fanfare but has secretly been plotting his murder while he is away. His mistress, Cassandra, prophesies that he will die. No one listens. She prophesies that she will die too, but she goes inside the house anyway, to meet her doom."

Dawn stopped and looked calmly at us.

"And?" said Ms. Ella.

"That's it."

"That's it?"

"That's my report."

"That's your report that you copied directly out of the encyclopedia?"

"I didn't have time to read the play," Dawn said.

“Is that so? Didn’t you notice that the rest of your classmates were reading their books?”

“Yes.”

“So you think you’re better than them?”

“No, I don’t.”

“Your report was supposed to be ten minutes long.”

A red flush began at Dawn’s throat and crept up her face into the roots of her hair.

“I told you. I don’t have anything else. I’m done. So fail me, or do whatever you want to do, but I’m finished.”

“Oh, you’ve already failed. But you’re not finished.”

Ms. Ella crossed the room and picked up the Attitude Adjuster paddle.

“Bend over.”

Tracy giggled nervously. The rest of us stared. Dawn stayed upright. She turned to face Ms. Ella. Ms. Ella wasn’t much taller than Dawn, but she seemed bigger, in that moment.

“What did you say?”

“You heard me. I said bend over.”

“No. Fuck you.”

Ms. Ella moved in close to Dawn so that their chests touched.

“That tortured teen stuff might work with your father, but it’s not going to work with me,” she said, in a low, threatening tone. “You can do what I say now, or you can go home and I will tell your father what you did today. He will pull you out of this school and away from Amber and send you to Tallulah Falls where you’ll take ministry classes and serve the Lord and never, ever be allowed to draw any of that brainless pop culture shit you draw. Is that what you want?”

Dawn, speechless, bent forward over the podium. Ms. Ella raised the paddle and told us all to count.

"Count what?" Dawn cried.

"One hit for every missing minute of your presentation. You have seven hits total."

The paddle landed, with a crack, against Dawn's body.

"One!" we cried.

At first, only a few of us counted, but by five we had all joined in, even Amber. When it was over Dawn straightened up, went back to her desk, and crumpled into her seat, not looking at any of us. The rest of us were frozen and thrilled and surprised, not quite sure what we had seen.

"Next time, do your work," Ms. Ella said. "That goes for all of you. You kids need to learn some discipline." She glanced at her watch. "Kayla. You're up next," she said.

At lunch, Ms. Ella went out on the fire escape, and we gathered around Dawn, who sat at her desk. Amber put an arm around her shoulders. Dawn was so angry she could barely speak. She said, "I'm going to tell my dad. He's going to get that bitch fired."

Brandon stood up from his chair in a surge of brotherly protection.

"I'll go down and tell Jean right now," he said.

"If you tell Jean," Jamal said, "then we'll get another Bud, and we'll just sit here and do worksheets. I'm sick of worksheets."

Kayla and Tracy nodded. After a moment, the rest of us nodded, too, or looked down at our shoes or away.

That evening, Amber left school with Dawn, as usual, and the next morning they met us outside, under the magnolia tree. They said that they had gone home and complained to Dawn's dad about the punishment. But Mr. Brodie didn't react the way the girls thought he would.

Dawn started with the drawing incident, then moved on to the threats, the paddling, the cruel way Ms. Ella made us count the hits. Mr. Brodie listened to the end, and then he said, "Why didn't you finish your report?"

"What?" Tears of disbelief welled up in Dawn's eyes.

"Why didn't you finish your report?" Mr. Brodie repeated. He was a broad-shouldered, kind man, but broken by his wife's abandonment; our mothers used to whisper about him at the parent-teacher nights.

"Who cares? She hit me with a paddle!"

"I got hit with big paddles in Catholic school," Mr. Brodie said. "All the kids did. We got hit if we didn't turn in work, or if we acted up and misbehaved. Those nuns came after us. I tell you one thing about paddling," he added, twisting a clump of spaghetti onto his fork. "I did my work. I didn't mess around like kids do today. That's for sure."

"She's a monster!" Dawn cried.

"She's a monster who's going to get you in line. You'll ask her if you can make up your report for a late grade and you'll do it this week."

"No! Fuck her report. I'm not a child anymore. I don't have to put up with this."

"You'll do it this weekend or Amber goes home. Or Amber goes home," her father repeated, sternly, over both girls' protests.

"So what are you going to do?" Kayla asked Dawn the next day.

"Nothing," Dawn said. "Fuck her."

Amber took her hand.

We were quiet then. Something was happening, something tectonic, unseen. A shifting of plates underneath our feet, a slow adjustment of worlds. We looked at Dawn underneath the magnolia, and she looked at us, and we thought that Ms. Ella had come to make us right, and well-rounded. She was going to stamp out our immaturity and flatness, and she was going to stamp it out of Dawn first. She was going to show her, and the rest of us, that it didn't matter if Dawn was gifted, or temperamental, or if her father had a nice job at Atlantic Products: she was still going to read her books and do her work, just like everybody else.

Chapter III

After Dawn's report, we all thought there would be another showdown between Ms. Ella and Dawn. As we trooped upstairs the next morning and took our seats, we wondered if Dawn would draw, if Ms. Ella would scold, if they would fight. Maybe Dawn would run out into the woods to hide again; maybe the police would come. Her father would whisk her away to the boarding school in North Georgia, and she would say goodbye to Amber and to the rest of us, and that would be the end of her.

But Ms. Ella changed strategies.

She didn't say anything to Dawn that morning. She went up to the podium, brisk and commanding in a gray blazer, and announced the order of the day's reports.

"Amber," she said. "You're up first."

Amber came to the front of the room and began to deliver her presentation on "The Yellow Wallpaper" in a faint, trembling voice. She was a thin girl, taller than most of the boys, with pointy shoulders that slumped forward. She had a habit of chewing on her hair, so that strands of it hung in damp clumps around her chin. She wore a flowered purple top that looked like it had belonged to her mother or an aunt or an older cousin, and her legs under her denim shorts were lean and pale.

She read: "This story is about a woman who goes mad in a room by herself. Her husband locks her in there after she has a baby. The longer she's in there, the crazier she feels. She starts to imagine things in the wallpaper. Weird patterns moving. A trapped lady, creeping around."

Amber told us that the woman was suffering from depression because of the baby, but also that it was common for wallpapers in the Victorian period to contain deadly levels of arsenic. She told us about another book she had researched, called *Shadows from the Walls of Death*, published by a Union surgeon in 1874.

"This surgeon, Dr. Robert Kedzie, discovered that the arsenic in wallpapers was making people insane and slowly killing them, and he wanted to tell the world about it. So he made a whole book of the poisonous wallpaper samples. Wallpaper back then had a lot of botanical prints and curlicue designs and things like that. And the patterns were brightly colored."

Amber drew a flower on the board and colored in the center with a green marker.

"See this green? This was a very popular and poisonous color back then. It was called Scheele's Green after the person who discovered it, and it was made by mixing copper and arsenic. Victorians liked it because the green wallpaper designs matched the greens found in nature. But it was super deadly. Women and children sat in their parlors and ingested just a little bit of it, every day, and it slowly made them crazy, and no one could figure out why. And Kedzie's book didn't help much, either, because the book itself was so poisonous. You can't read it without gloves and a mask and protective clothing. Most libraries have destroyed it. Only a few copies exist today. I think that Gilman's story, and Kedzie's book, are about the dangers of beautiful things."

Amber sat down, and we all clapped. Ms. Ella waited for the applause to die down, then said, "Amber, that was an excellent presentation."

"Thank you." Amber looked down at her desk.

"It was an excellent presentation because she was interested in the story and did her own research, without being asked," Ms. Ella said—gesturing at Amber, but addressing the rest of us. "She went above and beyond. She did the assignment, but then the assignment raised new research questions, and Amber investigated further to answer them."

She glanced at Dawn, held her gaze for a moment, and went on.

"This is why I'd like to appoint Amber to be my research assistant, to stay after school and help me with some important tasks. Amber, would you accept this position?"

Amber's eyes went wide. She nodded.

"This will be a serious position, after school, with many responsibilities," Ms. Ella added.

"I understand."

"Good. Now, let's get back to work," Ms. Ella said. She called Jamal to the podium.

We kept looking at Amber while he began his report on *Gilgamesh*. It didn't seem like she'd gotten a reward; it seemed like more work, and already Ms. Ella made us work harder than any other teacher. But then again, maybe it was a reward, when you thought about it. It was recognition, and recognition gave you a little glow, a humming inner beam. We had never thought much about Amber before. She was always just a friend of Dawn's. And now, like a flare, she leapt out from the murk of us. We sat in our desks, just a few shades more invisible.

At lunch, we went to congratulate her. She was sitting at her desk, next to Dawn, biting into a bruised apple. She was so bony that her shoulder blades poked out of the back of her shirt like dorsal fins.

"Nice work," Jamal told her.

"Thanks," Amber said. "I thought your report was really good too."

"You learned all that just last week?" Bryce said. "You're smart, aren't you?"

Bryce was universally despised among us, a lanky, unwashed boor of a boy who shoved us when we played kickball and never took showers. At lunch, he mostly listened to his Walkman; he never said anything nice to anyone, so we thought he was being sarcastic at first. But then he smiled at Amber, a real smile, or his version of it—like a jack-o'-lantern baring jagged, unhealthy teeth.

Even stranger, Amber smiled back.

Dawn watched with the rest of us.

"That after-school thing sounds like bullshit to me," she said. "I wouldn't do it."

"Well," Amber said, and looked away. "You don't have to."

That afternoon, after class, we packed our things and got ready to meet our rides outside by the magnolia tree, or to head downstairs to the basement arts and crafts room.

Amber lingered at Ms. Ella's desk. Ms. Ella pulled two volumes off the shelf, a larger and a smaller one, and invited Amber to sit next to her.

"I want to show you something," she said. She ripped a page out of Amber's notebook and folded it, once. "See this? See how it makes two leaves? That means it's a folio size. Like this book." She set the folded paper next to the larger volume, so that Amber could compare their sizes. "If you fold it twice, it has four leaves. A quarto. The size of this smaller book."

"Oh," Amber said. "So, if you fold it again—"

"—An octavo," Ms. Ella said. "Even smaller. This is how you learn the different book sizes. Your *Shadows* book, I've never seen it. But it's probably one of the larger sizes."

"I want to see it."

"You can if you go to the right college. Near one of the big archives. Penn or somewhere in New York, by the New York Public Library. Or somewhere in DC, near the Library of Congress. Somewhere where you have access to all the arts and sciences. The full humanities curriculum. Poetry, philosophy, rhetoric. Much more than this dinky school can offer."

"How do I do that?"

"Work hard," Ms. Ella said. "Stick with me. Quiet people get overlooked sometimes, I know. But I see you, and I can see what you're capable of."

Dawn had been gathering her things with the rest of us,

silently, trailing behind in the classroom. Before she went downstairs, she approached them.

"What did you mean about my art not being grown-up enough?" she asked. "Is that something I could learn?"

"Sure, if you applied yourself," Ms. Ella said. "Sketch the human figure, make studies. Many great artists have done that. You can start by looking at the drawings of Da Vinci."

"I want a second chance for my Cassandra report," she said. "I want to make something for it. A statue, like the one on the cover. Like, real art."

"Your report? Forget about it," Ms. Ella said. "That ship has sailed."

Downstairs, Dawn got out her sketchbook while the rest of us pulled out our homework. When it was time for a break, Tracy and Kayla went to see what Dawn was drawing. There was no Link or Princess Zelda or Ganon on the page. Instead, Dawn had sketched the Cassandra statue from the cover of *Agamemnon*, an athletic figure in robes.

"I thought Ms. Ella said no to that project," Kayla said. "You don't give up, do you?"

Dawn gave her a long, withering look, and slammed the book shut.

Autumn came to Atlanta, in the glancing, hesitant way autumn always stole into our city, tiptoeing around heat waves, storms, and deadly tornadoes. Here and there, a few acorns fell; here and there, a tree blazed yellow and red, but the summer held sway.

Then, at last, after a few false starts, the days began to shorten, the nights and early mornings grew cool, and birds flocked overhead, making the journey south. Trees erupted into color. Pumpkins appeared on doorsteps. The air smelled of burning leaves. We pulled sweaters out of drawers, tugged forgotten windbreakers from the backs of closets.

We gave reports on the Civil War, the abolition of slavery, Reconstruction. At Stillwater, there was one teacher for each grade, in charge of all subjects, so Ms. Ella taught us a bit of everything. But history and English were the subjects where she really shone; these are the lessons we still think about sometimes, when we wander through bookstores or stop in front of historical markers.

Amber stayed after school and worked as Ms. Ella's research assistant while Dawn went downstairs to enrichment, alone.

Soon, we began to see signs of Ms. Ella and Amber's work. One October morning, we came to class to find the walls covered in sheets of long white paper, the kind that waiters put on tables at restaurants. Each of these sheets was partially filled with Amber's handwriting. We gathered that Ms. Ella must have dictated while Amber wrote. We moved around the room, studying each one, like visitors in a museum. We glimpsed mysterious phrases here and there: *Bloom's taxonomy*, *the cognitive domain*, *personal accountability*, *discipline*. Some of the phrases were connected to each other with arrows. Others had more handwritten notes jotted beneath them. We followed the dynamic motion of Ms. Ella's mind, like the arc of a swallow in flight, and thought of Amber flying somewhere beneath it, waiting to rise. The sheets were taped to the wall at the top and not at the bottom, so that whenever the door opened and another student came in they lifted gently off the wall and resettled.

Every week, Dawn asked Ms. Ella if she could stay after school with Amber and do her Cassandra statue. Each time, Ms. Ella said no, and Dawn went back to her sketches, sullenly.

One afternoon, when Ms. Ella was at a staff meeting, Dawn saw Amber leaving with Bryce and stopped her.

"Where are you going?" she said. "Aren't you coming downstairs?"

"Outside, with Bryce," Amber said. "To wait with him until his ride comes."

Their flirtation had progressed, to the disgust of us all. He'd made her a mixtape, and she'd started wearing his I.C.P. hoodie. When Ms. Ella went out to smoke, he came and sat by Amber's desk, his dirty, large hand wrapping around her timid, small one.

"How about tomorrow?"

"I can't. I have to stay up here and work on Ms. Ella's project, remember?"

"But you always stay up here. You never come downstairs anymore."

"And I have to keep staying after, until it's done," Amber said, a little testily. She slipped her new black planner, the one Ms. Ella had gotten her, into her bag. "That's how this works."

She went out, Bruce loping after her. Dawn watched them descend the stairs, her cheeks flushed.

Our first progress reports were sent home in late October.

"You're doing so well this year!" our parents and caregivers and aunts and uncles and grandparents all said.

Even if we were struggling, Ms. Ella had written out the ways we had improved in the first two months, and she had written out a short introduction to her educational philosophy, which she discussed at the parent-teacher nights and the staff meetings, using the terms from the wall. If we moved up each stage in Bloom's Taxonomy of learning, from knowledge to comprehension to analysis, we would arrive at synthesis and evaluation: the final stages where we learned to combine all the different subjects and make contributions to civic life. This couldn't be done through rote learning, Ms. Ella stressed: it had to happen through encounters with real sources, Socratic debate, and sustained, disciplined attention to our work.

"Just imagine," our parents said, leaving the reports open on tables and counters so that other people would see them. "All those books and reports and sources. I wish I had gotten to do that. All we did in history class was memorize dates and names."

Other teachers noticed Ms. Ella, too. Hank and Tilda still went out on the fire escape to smoke and talk to her, but now some of the nonsmokers joined her too, to gossip about the Herky Dyer case or ask her for advice. Fewer teachers went down to the staff room on the second floor to eat lunch with Jean now; whenever we passed by its windowed door on the way to the bathrooms, we saw Jean in there with her administrative assistant, Lulu, or with the third-grade teacher, Ada, a sour woman in khakis and loafers who was strangely loyal to Jean. Ada was the only teacher to have survived at Stillwater longer than two years. We leaned into the crack in the fire escape door, listening.

"How are things with Dawn now?" Tilda asked. It was the Friday before Halloween, and some of the teachers were dressed up: Tilda a witch, Hank a farmer, Susan and Marie, the kindergarten and first-grade teachers, in whiskers and mouse ears.

"Dawn?" Ms. Ella said. "That's all fixed."

She must have made some paddling motion with her arm, because the other teachers murmured and made little noises of recognition.

"You know, that's how I came up, too," Marie said. "It wasn't pretty. But it worked."

"Sure it did," Hank said. "It teaches discipline. And accountability."

"There's no reason you can't, down here," Ms. Ella said. "It's legal. The only thing the Georgia law says is that you have to issue a warning first, and that it can't be extreme. And there has to be a witness."

"Jean wouldn't go for it, though," Susan said. "You know she wouldn't."

"Yes, and that's the problem," Hank said. "How much control does she have over any of these students, really?"

"Exactly," Ms. Ella said. "Exactly."

In early November, Bryce's mom got promoted to manager at her restaurant, and she began arriving later and later to pick up Bryce. One afternoon, during after-school enrichment, while we were all sitting bored around some craft project,

Tracy and Kayla saw Bryce and Amber disappear into the woods behind the kickball field. Ms. Ella was in a staff meeting. The next morning, during the break, Tracy went up to Amber in the girls' room and said, "Did you go to second base with that Juggalo?"

Amber looked down at her feet.

"Don't be shy. Listen. There are things no one will tell you." She leaned in and began whispering in Amber's ear. Tracy had an older sister, Becca, who went to Peachtree High and had a real boyfriend, one who drove and took her on dates, so Tracy fancied herself an expert. Amber listened to Tracy's fuchsia-tinted, whispering lips, her eyes wide.

"Three," she said.

"Did you like that many fingers?" Tracy asked.

"I didn't mind it."

"The point is to *like* it," Tracy said. "Next time, tell him not to use his fingers on the inside. Tell him to try focusing on the outside part more, the part on top."

Then Dawn came out of the stall behind them. Tracy stopped talking, abruptly, but it was too late. Dawn went straight upstairs to Ms. Ella's desk.

"I have something to tell you," she said.

"Shoot," Ms. Ella said.

"But only on one condition."

"Oh? We have demands?"

"Let me do the statue."

"I'm not bargaining with you," Ms. Ella said irritably. "You better say whatever you have to say or get away from my desk."

Dawn leaned in and spoke close to her ear. Ms. Ella grabbed the paddle.

"Go get Amber," she said.

Dawn found her under the magnolia with Bryce and led her upstairs.

"Stand by the door and tell me if anyone comes up the stairs," Ms. Ella told Dawn. To Amber, she said, "Bend over."

Dawn took her place in front of the door. Her face was a strange color: flushed and triumphant. Kayla and Wei were in the storage area, and they told us that afterwards, Ms. Ella gave Amber a long speech about her education and her future.

"It's normal at your age to want to talk to boys. But you have a bright future ahead of you. A lot of girls your age, they get sidetracked, sometimes knocked up before they even get a chance to complete their education, see the world. I've been there and I've seen it happen, a million times. So go have lunch with your little boyfriend if you want. Listen to music, go for walks, kiss, hold hands, whatever. But don't mess with your future."

"I won't," Amber whimpered.

"I mean it," Ms. Ella said. "No one else is looking after you. So I have to do it. Don't I?"

Amber didn't answer, so Ms. Ella repeated the question.

"Yes, you do," Amber said, at last.

Two things happened as a result of that day.

The first was that Dawn finally got permission to do her Cassandra project. But there was one condition: she had to finish it by our end-of-the-year class trip.

The graduation trip was a Stillwater tradition. Every year, the eighth graders got to go on a trip as a celebration before they moved on to high school somewhere else. It was one of the few expenses already covered by our tuition money and one of the few traditions our parents' friends spoke of approvingly. In past years, teachers had taken the eighth graders to Charleston, to Nashville, to Huntsville, but Ms. Ella wanted to take us to Washington, DC, farther than the others had.

"You need to follow through with the things you start," Ms. Ella told Dawn, out on the fire escape. "And if you don't, you get paddled. That's how this works. You want projects, you get the accountability, too. You can't have one without the other. Without the discipline, you lose."

"I lose what?"

"This opportunity," Ms. Ella said, "to improve your character. To become the artist you want to be."

Dawn began work on the Cassandra that very afternoon, after school. She had her drawings already and went down to the enrichment area to collect arts and crafts supplies. Over the following weeks, she shaped a base out of wire coat hangers, forming a jagged outline of Cassandra's body and a bell-shaped dome for her skirt. Then she tore some newspaper into long strips, dipped them in papier-mâché, and made the core of the sculpture.

Each afternoon it grew, little by little, a two-foot-tall figure in the window, and every morning we stopped to look at it. The eyeless gray Cassandra prophesied, her arms raised in warning, her robes, cut from a white pillowcase, trailing from her body. Even without eyes, there was something sinister and sad about the face, something about the contours and the position of it that struck you when you looked at it. It was an improvement from Dawn's old sketches, and we told her so.

"Just wait until I'm finished," she said.

The second thing was that Amber stopped going with Bryce. She didn't go downstairs with him while he waited for his ride after school the next day or listen to his mix-tapes in her Walkman. Instead, she worked harder on Ms. Ella's research, helping her write out remarks for the next parent-teacher meeting. Two days after the paddling, Bryce passed her a note in class, but during the morning break she got up and threw it in the trash. He put his head in his dirty hands and looked hurt.

Only once did Tracy hear Amber and Dawn arguing, in the restroom, but they stopped when she came in.

"What's up, sluts," Tracy greeted them.

They nodded at her. They had both been crying, Tracy said. A moment later, they left.

It was around this time that Amber's parents separated, and Amber started spending even more time at Dawn's house, weekends and most weeknights too. The girls arrived together, every single morning, and stayed after school with Ms. Ella every afternoon. We grew used to the sight of the three of them, working, their heads bent as if in prayer. We said, "It was all a phrase," and agreed that the paddling had straightened Amber out.

Soon after that, Bryce started going with Tracy, who wasn't as smart as Amber, but then no one expected much from him, anyway.

Chapter IV

LOOKING BACK, we understand that all the paddling and scolding Dawn and Amber received only seemed unremarkable to us at the time because they seemed unremarkable to Ms. Ella. Our moods were weathervanes that spun with the currents of Ms. Ella's voice: if she was excited and laughing, we were excited and laughing; if she was loud and upset, we were loud and upset; if she was quiet and still, we were quiet and still.

It is only now, looking back from a distance of almost twenty years, that the police officer's appearance in our classroom takes on that lurid tabloid palette, his movements grainy and slow in our memories, like the dramatic reenactments on the true crime shows we watch when our kids are asleep. Menacingly, he appears again and again in the doorway, filling it with his massive frame, throwing a long, dark shadow into the classroom.

In the weeks and months after his arrival, everything in Ms. Ella's class darkened under that shadow. The reports. The books. The papers on the wall, and Amber's research project, and Dawn's statue. It is hard to disentangle those things from the dark rumors that flew around afterwards, to remember something pure.

But there was something pure. Ms. Ella had promised to make real scholars of us, give us an education that people would take seriously. And for a short time, in the school year of 1992–1993, she did.

It started during class, this awakening of pilgrims. But she won her real converts after school.

Stillwater's after-school enrichment program, like most of its classes, was eclectic, a mixture of student-centered activities and bonding games. Sometimes we worked on vision boards; sometimes we did trust falls. Sometimes we sat in a circle and shared our feelings, passing around the talking stick. There was no real plan or organization; we did whatever the enrichment staff scrounged up for us to do on any given day.

Naturally, when Ms. Ella formed her little group with Amber and Dawn after school, we were curious to see what all the fuss was about. Jamal remembers Amber scribbling away on her research project while Ms. Ella and Dawn sat side by side, looking at an art book from Ms. Ella's house.

"This is Edmonia Lewis, *The Death of Cleopatra*," Ms. Ella said. "Marble. From 1876. At the Smithsonian in DC. Other artists used to depict a romanticized Cleopatra before her suicide. But Lewis shows her at the moment of death. She pushed the envelope. She was bold. Revolutionary."

Dawn leaned in.

"Why is she smiling?"

"Why do you think she's smiling?"

Dawn looked at the sculpture for a while.

"She's happy?"

"And filled with asp venom," Ms. Ella said. "It was a shocking facial expression, in its time."

"I wish I were that talented."

"Then you have to work at it. Talent matters, of course, but so does effort. You have it in you to make great art. But you've got to push yourself more. Be disciplined. Be ruthless. You absolutely have the talent to make something as bold as that if you put the hours in."

Together, they looked at the Cassandra on the window-sill. Dawn had thrown herself into the project at first but had stalled after a few weeks, content to work on her regular assignments and put off the statue for later. Its eyeless head blazed in the sunshine that flowed through the magnolia branches.

"For example: you have to finish that," Ms. Ella said.

Dawn fell silent and kicked her legs restlessly.

"Hey," Ms. Ella said. "What's up? Look at me."

"My mom was the one who used to make me do my assignments and stuff like that," Dawn said. "My dad tries. But it's not the same."

Ms. Ella nodded.

"I hear you," she said. "Your mom walked out. And that fucking hurts. I know it."

"Yeah," Dawn said.

"But I'll tell you what. Your mom walked out because she had problems of her own, and she didn't know how to deal with them. So she dumped them on you and your dad.

Always remember that those problems are her problems. They don't have to be yours."

Dawn wasn't looking at Ms. Ella anymore, but she was listening.

"You deserve to live the life that's ahead of you as fully as you can," Ms. Ella said. "You have potential. So use it. I see your potential. That's why I'm hard on you. Do you understand that? I want you to succeed. Your mom walked out. But I'm not going to walk out. I'm here to stay."

Fall gave way to a bare-treed winter. The sun was still bright, but snow flurries dusted the grass in front of Stillwater and the magnolia shone with ice. We heard branches cracking and splitting in the woods, looked out at the birdless sky. The heating ducts lumbered and grunted, spat gusts of hot, musty air.

More of us began to linger upstairs after school. First Jamal stayed, then Wei. By the time we returned from the holiday break, in that long, bleak stretch of days between New Year's and Easter, Kayla and Tracy and Brandon had started staying after, too. Bryce was still upset about the Amber incident, though. He always left right away.

We worked on homework alongside Amber and Dawn. But we also talked to Ms. Ella about things. Our families. Our assignments. The news.

"How's your sisters, Brandon?" Ms. Ella might ask. Brandon would look up from his copy of *Invisible Man*, his large body hunched over the desk.

"They're good," he said. "But the youngest one won't go to sleep. Keeps me up late."

Ms. Ella nodded.

"They do that, at that age," she said. "You're a good big brother to help out your parents. But make sure you take care of you, too. Get your work done."

Brandon nodded and sat up a bit straighter, self-conscious. He was overlooked at home, we knew; there was a big gap between him and his louder, more rambunctious siblings, and he never had an adult's undivided attention.

Ms. Ella listened to Amber complain about her mother, who said she was spending too much time at Dawn's house and wanted her home more often.

"She needs to learn to put your needs before hers," Ms. Ella said. "You need the best environment in order to develop your talents. Right now, that environment is with Dawn, and after school with Dawn and me. You two need to stick together. Hold each other accountable."

Sometimes we looked at college brochures together. It would be years until any of us had to think about applications, but Ms. Ella said it was never too early to start looking.

"Most of you, your parents didn't go to college," she said. "They might not know the best way for you to apply. So you have to start informing yourself. It was the same for me. No one in my family went. I returned to school as an adult learner, had to sort everything out on my own."

Dawn looked at brochures for MIT, the Art Institute of Chicago, the Rhode Island School of Design.

"I've never been to Chicago," she said. "Or Rhode Island. Or any of these places."

"You get in, and you can go visit," Ms. Ella said. "You just need to assemble a portfolio. Think of all the art you could make."

"I could try the Cleopatra. After the Cassandra."

"You could. What's stopping you?"

Sometimes, Ms. Ella asked us to find out what the lower grades were doing. Tracy and Kayla stood at the window, reporting, as the kids lined up and filed into the van.

"They're going on a trip to Stone Mountain today," Kayla said. "I saw the permission slip in the mail."

"Stone Mountain?" Ms. Ella said. "That old Confederate wet dream?"

We looked at her blankly.

"That bas-relief etching on the side," she said. "The guys on the horses. Those are Confederate leaders. The whole piece was a project of Klansmen and segregationists. It was finished in 1972. The KKK used to burn crosses on the summit."

"That's disgusting," Amber said.

"That's Atlanta," Ms. Ella said. "A center of the Civil Rights movement and home of violent racists. You didn't know that? About the mountain?"

Some of us didn't, and we felt betrayed. The Stillwater teachers had been taking us on trips to Stone Mountain for years; no one had ever said anything about the origin of the three men on the side. And they hadn't said much about the riots in LA, the year before, or about the video we'd all seen of the officers beating Rodney King, though there had been an assembly in the basement where we were all told, vaguely, to respect each other.

"It's because Jean and these other teachers don't treat you like adults, like I do," Ms. Ella said. "They don't talk to you about the real stuff."

Since then, of course, since we left Stillwater, we've had

other teachers, other mentors. We know now that Ms. Ella stepped over the line, that she did things to get in your head. If only she'd been wrong about everything, we might have written her off entirely, might not have gravitated toward her the way we did.

But she wasn't wrong about everything. We were doing better in her class, and when we spent time with her after school. She was right about things that were important, that others were afraid to say. She was right about all the things we hadn't learned, all the things that had been kept from us.

And she was right about Jean.

Over time, as Ms. Ella and Amber's project evolved, we learned more about the heated battle over our minds that took place at staff meetings and, in smaller ways, in the day-to-day life of our school. On one side was Ms. Ella, campaigning for rigorous education and what she called a "pedagogy of accountability" that would build us into civic-minded individuals; on the other side was Jean, placid, conflict-averse, with her brochures about Stillwater's "pedagogy of positivity."

"She told me yesterday at a staff meeting that we're not trying to deliver content," Ms. Ella said. "What we're trying to do is 'build community.' But of course I'm trying to deliver content! I'm trying to teach you how to think for yourselves and pay attention to the world so that each of you gets into a great college where you can realize your potential."

Being in on this battle made us feel like part of a dramatic, unfolding conflict, an atmosphere of espionage.

One afternoon in late March, Jean saw Tracy waiting with Bryce for his ride outside and intercepted her on her way back up to our classroom. She ushered Tracy into her office, sat her down under a marionette of a jester with wooden shoes. The office was on the ground floor, a giant, windowed room that overlooked the playground and the Roadster. Jean had decorated it with antique marionettes she'd brought back from her trips to Sicily and Burma and the Czech Republic. Unlike our hot classrooms, Jean's office had a window air conditioner that pumped a cool breeze into the room, and the marionettes swayed back and forth on their wires, performing spontaneous, unmanipulated theater.

"Tracy," Jean said, smiling. "How are you? How's your sister?"

"Becca's fine," Tracy said.

"And everything is going well upstairs? With Ms. Ella?"

"Yeah. I'm doing a research project on flappers," Tracy said. "I love it."

Jean beamed harder. Tracy was conscious of the way the jester's feet skimmed her head, just above her bangs.

"That's great," Jean said. "Listen, Ada mentioned that you haven't been down in after-school enrichment at all this month. We were wondering if something happened, if there was anything you wanted to tell us about."

"Nothing happened. I just decided to stay upstairs. I can do my work up there."

"What kind of work?"

"Just research," Tracy said. "Critical thinking. I'm developing my skills."

"Okay," Jean said. "That's fine. But if you ever want to come back to enrichment, you just come on down. The door is open. We miss you."

"Thanks," Tracy said.

When she told us about this exchange, back up in the classroom, Ms. Ella burst out laughing.

"You did the right thing, not taking the bait. Jean hates my educational philosophy. She'd fire me without cause if she thought she could ever get a replacement on this salary."

"No," groaned Brandon. "Then we'd get another Bud."

"If she won't let me teach what I want, then I'll start my own school," Ms. Ella said. "I'll teach it in my basement, if I have to."

"You would?" Jamal said.

"I would," she said, and turned back to her work, to show us the conversation was over.

As spring came, our last spring at Stillwater, the crocuses in the flower beds unfolding, the dogwoods heavy with blossoms, this idea grew rich with significance. One week later, Jamal sat in his mother's office, under her diplomas, and called Bryce.

"Did you hear?" he said. "Ms. Ella is for real going to start a new high school. The Renaissance Academy."

"No shit," Bryce said. "Who told you that?"

"Amber. She said that Ms. Ella wants her to help plan a new school, once she's done with her presentation at the staff meeting."

"For real? Doesn't she need a bunch of money to do something like that?"

"Amber said Ms. Ella has ideas for possible donors."

They talked about *Mortal Kombat* for a moment, then hung up.

Bryce called Tracy and gave her the news. She was on the clear phone in her bedroom. You could see all the neon circuits and wires inside, like a brain with its synapses going. Kayla was at the dresser, fiddling with the VCR. On the screen, a reporter in a giant winter coat was shivering in front of the courthouse, talking about the Herky Dyer verdict. Ten years in prison.

"Kayla, can you turn that down?" Tracy said irritably. "Babe. What did you say?"

"It's going to be in a bigger building. Bigger than Stillwater," he said. "And closer to downtown. Everyone will write reports every day. Paddling will be mandatory."

"Are you going?"

"No way. I'm not going to any school where that bitch teaches."

He launched into an angry rant, and Tracy put her hand over the mouthpiece.

"Hey," she said to Kayla. "Get this. Ms. Ella's starting a new high school downtown called the Renaissance Academy. You have to test to get in, but we would all be automatically enrolled."

"What?" Kayla said as she slid the tape into the VCR for the third time. The machine swallowed it obediently and began whirring. The opening credits of *Child's Play 2* appeared on the screen. The camera pulled back from the doll's horrifying blue eyeball to reveal his burnt head, hairless, the other eye missing, the teeth clenched and bared, the skin dripping with brown, gluey pus. Kayla paused the tape and leaned in to study the texture of the skin, the uneven craters of charred flesh.

"Ew," Tracy whispered. "Kayla, are you listening? I said there's going to be a new school, with Ms. Ella in charge."

Slowly, what Tracy had said seeped through the gore of the film and into Kayla's consciousness.

"Will there be a theater department?" she asked. Kayla was into theater and stage makeup, and Ms. Ella had told her, once, to look up drama programs at the local high schools.

"Will there be a theater department?" Tracy asked Bryce, interrupting him.

"Maybe," he said. "Who cares?"

"He says he thinks so," Tracy said.

"Shhh," said Kayla. "This is the best part."

Tracy rolled her eyes.

"Baby, I'll call you back," she said. She hung up and called Brandon. He always took the cordless phone into the living room so that he could keep an eye on his younger sisters. Whenever we called him, we could hear all four of them in the background, shrieking.

"Did you hear?" Tracy said. "Ms. Ella's starting a new school called the Renaissance Academy. It's going to be downtown and there's going to be new students and field trips. Also, there's going to be theater and performing arts."

"For real? What about sports?"

"Sports, too," Tracy said. "Definitely kickball and basketball. Maybe soccer."

In this way, news of the Renaissance Academy spread to all of the eighth graders and some of the younger students, too, so that the vision of our new school felt like a reality. It would be in one of the large office buildings downtown, perhaps near Underground Atlanta, and Ms. Ella would hire new teachers for it, one for each subject instead of one for all subjects, like we had now. That way, we would acquire the skills we needed. We would learn to speak Spanish fluently, and Brandon would go play sports at the university complex, and we would take end-of-the-year trips to New York City so that Dawn could see the Met, and to Hollywood, so that Kayla could visit film sets. Wei even speculated that the trip to DC was a part of the plan. Maybe Ms. Ella was going there for research; maybe she was going to meetings at the Department of Education. We weren't sure. We just knew that the most important thing was that Ms. Ella would keep teaching us history and, at the Renaissance Academy, she would be in charge of everyone else.

Our final progress reports were mailed home in late May. At dinner tables and birthday parties and after-church potlucks, our parents showed their friends and relatives Ms. Ella's comments, along with our long, detailed research papers, bragging that we were all flourishing in our advanced learning program. They said that instead of "banking" education we were learning to formulate questions and think for ourselves, and to write reports like these. They always saved the clincher for last: Ms. Ella had given us one of Georgia's standardized tests for reading comprehension, as an experiment, and our scores were higher than the state average.

"Hm," our parents' friends and relatives said as they flipped through our writing, impressed, and they stopped making fun of our school at dinner and started asking to see the Renaissance Academy brochure instead.

Ms. Ella gave her final presentation at the staff meeting. It must have been a success, because Kayla heard the other teachers congratulate her out on the fire escape. But Wei said that Amber got paddled for messing up something in the bibliography, forgetting to cite a source.

"It was just one," Amber cried. "I just forgot."

"Accuracy matters," Ms. Ella said. "Giving credit matters. You can't just steal other people's words."

The biggest parent-teacher conference of the year always took place in May, too. For the eighth graders, it was a big event, the one where all the details for the final trip got worked out, where the chaperones volunteered. Ms. Ella moved around the classroom, tidying chairs, straightening the books on the shelf.

"This trip is going to be good for you," she said. "You kids aren't worldly enough. You need to get out. See a bigger city. And *you*," she added, turning to Dawn, "need to finish what you started."

Dawn looked at the Cassandra statue on the windowsill. She was robed and gesturing, but still eyeless, with only the barest hint of a mouth.

"I need more time," Dawn said.

"You're a kid. You have nothing but time. You've been either tinkering with it or ignoring it for weeks. This statue needs to be done by the time we leave for the trip. By the trip," she added sternly, over Dawn's protests. "Or else."

That evening, as our parents parked in the field and made their way up to the meeting, we gathered on the fire escape, the crickets shrieking in the grass, and talked about it. It didn't make sense. Why couldn't she just finish it?

"She never finishes anything," Tracy said. "She was like that in seventh grade, too."

It was true. We remembered Dawn's half-made volcano for the science fair and the fateful report on *Agamemnon*, just months before.

"What happens when it's over?" Jamal said. "When she finishes it? Does she go back downstairs?"

We thought about that. The statue had been her way in, her reason for staying after. Maybe completion would mean the end of it; the excuse would be gone.

At the same time, it must have cost Dawn something, all of that work for Ms. Ella's attention, all of those delicate, unspoken calibrations between Dawn and Amber, and we wonder now, in hindsight, if the incomplete statue, with its hollow gaze, was a small act of rebellion in itself, a little resistance that would swell up soon and blow us all apart.

Chapter V

JUNE CAME, and the first day of our class trip, and still Dawn had not finished the Cassandra. The eyeless statue looked down from the window as we gathered by the vans at nine on a Monday morning. Our parents bustled back and forth, helping us with our backpacks and suitcases, reminding us of our toothbrushes and inhalers and pocket money. It was an overcast day, but the sun broke through in momentary patches of brightness, throwing a soft glow over the road that would take us to DC.

Around ten our things were finally loaded into the two vans. Ms. Ella clapped her hands to get our attention. She was wearing jeans and a simple black T-shirt under her blazer that day, and her hair was pulled back in a ponytail.

Amber's mom was the sole parent volunteer. This was amazing to us, because usually there were three or four, but Ms. Ella had scoffed at Jean when she suggested this.

"These kids are young adults," she said to Hank and Tilda, on the fire escape. "Why do they need two more chaperones?"

Now Ms. Speese, Amber's mom, stood beside Ella in a floral top and high-waisted jean shorts. She was at least ten years younger and wore stylish black sunglasses, like an actress.

"All right!" Ms. Ella said. "I'm in the blue van and Ms. Speese is in the white van. Eight of you go in one and eight of you get in another. Let's go."

"Shotgun!" Dawn cried, heading towards the blue van. Amber started off behind her.

"Amber," Ms. Speese said, "are you riding shotgun with me?"

"I guess," said Amber, miserably.

The vans sped away from the city and deep into northern Georgia, into the parts of the state our parents called "outside the perimeter." The heavy traffic faded, and we shared the interstate with long-haul trucks and the occasional tractor. The Blue Ridge Mountains rose before us in the distance, a string of rippling peaks surrounded by violet-gray mist. Handmade wooden signs dotted the side of the road, promising fresh peaches, fresh peanuts, fresh cider.

In Ms. Speese's van, everyone talked about the hotel. Ms. Ella had divided the class into boys and girls, and said that all the girls would be in rooms on one side of the hallway and the boys on the other, and we would sleep two to a bed. She didn't say if there would be a pool, but we had each brought swimsuits, just in case. There would be vending machines and cable TV.

"There might be HBO," Jamal said.

"Or the Spice Channel!" Bryce said, lowering his voice so that Ms. Speese couldn't hear.

In Ms. Ella's van, she and Dawn talked while everyone else listened. At first, the conversation was about the staff meetings and projects Ms. Ella had scheduled for the summer, and the art camp she wanted Dawn to attend. Then, outside Charlotte, Dawn asked about Monty.

"Why didn't he come on the trip?" she asked. "Doesn't he like to travel?"

Ms. Ella lit a cigarette.

"He's older than you guys and he has his own life. He has to work. He just started a new job at the Cheesy Slice in the square."

"Is he cute?" Tracy called out from the back.

"He's cute but he's lazy. He takes after his dad."

"His dad was a pizza cook?"

"No, dummy, he just never thinks about his future. I do. I've always been like that. When Monty was little, I used to put him in the stroller and walk him down to the library so that I could read while he napped."

"The library in Philly?"

"No. The library in Kansas. A small town in Kansas. Greensburg. That's where I lived after I got married. That's where my husband was from. He was my first boyfriend. I met him when I was sixteen. Just three years older than you guys."

She cracked the window and rested her cigarette hand above the pane. The orange embers blew away in a little shower of sparks. We watched them burst against our own windows in the back of the van.

"He repaired farm equipment for a living and when Monty came I quit teaching for five years, until he was in kindergarten. I was so bored. There was nothing to do. Nothing stimulating. You can't reason with a child, or have a real conversation with it. I was so bored I used to go watch the tornadoes come in. When the sirens came, I would send Monty to the basement with Ted and go sit on the front porch and watch the funnels forming, way off on the horizon."

"That sounds dangerous," Kayla said.

"That's how bored I was! If I ever end up stuck in a house again, doing nothing, kill me. This is what you kids don't understand. You say you're bored every five minutes. You get bored if a report goes on for too long. You get bored reading long books. You don't know what boredom is. That's what I tell Monty. When he graduated high school, he said he didn't want to go to college because he thought school was boring. Just imagine! When I was his age, I couldn't wait to go to college. As soon as he was in kindergarten I went back to school and I devoured everything they gave me. That's when I read about American history, pedagogical theory, the Renaissance. All the stuff I share with you guys."

We were all struck by this. We pictured ourselves living in Ms. Ella's house, which would be sunny and filled with books, reaching new heights of achievement. We would not be allowed to be lazy or sleep in, of course, but we would succeed at everything, and so it would be worth it. Dawn would be an artist, Amber would do some kind of thing with books and research, Kayla would work on famous movies, and Tracy would…we weren't sure, exactly, what Tracy would do, but she would be better at it, whatever it was, if she lived in Ms. Ella's house.

Tracy said, suddenly, "I don't think I want to go to college, either."

"Don't ever say that," Ms. Ella snapped. "Every single one of you is going to college. You kids need to learn to believe in yourselves. You don't know yet what you're capable of."

We were quiet after that. As we pulled into a rest stop, Dawn reached over and took Ms. Ella's hand.

"I hope you're never bored or unhappy with us," she said.

Ms. Ella yanked her hand away. "Don't do that. People will get the wrong idea."

Dawn was hurt. "I didn't mean anything bad by it."

"I know," Ms. Ella said.

Out on the open road, all the rules vanished. There were no reports or assignments to set the day's pace, no routine. Instead, there was the highway, long and gleaming, stretching before us. As dusk fell, the setting sun poured blue light on the pavement. We stretched, sighed, talked, fought, and slept in the long seats. The vans sailed down the roads, across elegant bridges that swept us over rivers, past towns that flared up and disappeared like images in a flip book.

Violence was the trail we followed, from Cowpens to Manassas. The land was filled with lingering ghosts: from the wars fought between the Algonquin Indians and the Virginia Colony settlers, from Nat Turner's rebellion and the brutal retaliation that followed, from Grant's futile frontal attack at Cold Harbor. In Arlington, we streamed out of the vans and went wandering through acres and acres of trim gravestones. We joined in the midday ceremony for the Tomb of the Unknown Soldier, where the living, with stiff faces and uniforms, fired shots for the dead. The guns burst in the green hills.

In DC we saw obelisk and flat and round monuments, reflecting pools and eternal flames, soldiers' names on black shining walls, sidewalks strewn with carnations for the fallen. We paused by the still, pacing soldiers of the Korean War monument, circled around the three bronze servicemen of the Vietnam War. We stood on the sidewalk across from the White House, watching protestors hold placards and chant.

"What are they protesting?" Jamal asked.

Ms. Ella squinted at the signs.

"The war in Bosnia," she said. "The protestors don't think the US is doing enough to stop the massacres." Ms. Ella always talked about the morning news on the trip, told us to pay attention to current events so that we could be informed voters one day. She described the genocide as we crossed back through Lafayette Square. We were fatigued by the bloody sums; tired from staying up all night talking and giggling, playing pranks on our sleeping bedmates, or making secret trips to each other's rooms. We longed to go back to the hotel with the pool and the televisions and the shower caddies and Gameboys and makeup, all of it deliciously unsupervised. Ms. Ella rolled her eyes at this.

"Have fun, be kids," she said. "But by eight in the morning, you'd better be awake, outside, and ready to learn something."

For two days, Ms. Ella was our guide through these catalogues of the dead: Ms. Ella and Dawn in front, the rest of us in the middle, Ms. Speese and Amber bringing up the rear. Then, on the third morning, as we were getting ready to go see Ford's Theatre, the site of Lincoln's assassination, Ms. Speese pointed at a stand with a sign that said SIGHTSEEING TOURS ON THE POTOMAC.

"Ella, why don't we take a little detour?" she said.

Ms. Ella looked up from her map.

"That?" She waved her hand dismissively. "That's a tourist trap. They overcharge you to put you on a boat and tell you stuff you already know."

"I think it looks nice. Look, it goes past the Pentagon and the Memorial Bridge. The first one starts in twenty minutes. We could get some pictures of the kids on the water."

To our surprise, Dawn said, "I want to go."

We all watched Ms. Ella, waiting. We wanted to go on the water too, but it seemed like the wrong choice.

"Fine," Ms. Ella said, folding the map.

She put on her sunglasses and was silent during the boat trip as we moved around the deck snapping pictures with our instant cameras. Her stillness made it hard to enjoy the motion of the water, the feeling of the breeze, the monuments we glimpsed as we floated by, the sounds of all the different languages spoken on the boat. It felt like a guilty and childish thing. When Ms. Speese asked us if we were enjoying it, we said yes, but we dampened our enthusiasm a bit, tried to show her that we weren't taking it too seriously, that what we really wanted to do was get back to the dead people. Only Dawn seemed unembarrassed. She went to sit next to Amber, instead of Ms. Ella, for the first time since our departure.

We disembarked on the wharf by the Jefferson Memorial. Ms. Speese and Amber left to go pick up sandwiches.

Ms. Ella lit a cigarette and said, "That was a waste of our time and resources. But that's how it is when people go visit places they've never learned about. They just want to do tourist stuff. Take pictures, say they've been there. They don't want to see real history. If we get the grant to start the new school, you'll understand. You'll start to see all kinds of things that other people don't see."

"You can't just work all the time," Dawn said. Her tone was light, jesting.

"Oh?" Ms. Ella said. "Absorbing the history of our nation's capital is work to you? I bring you to DC and all you care about is the goddamn hotel pool. You'd all rather go on a dinky boat ride instead of going to see the theater where the great Abraham Lincoln was shot."

We looked at Dawn, uneasy.

Ms. Speese appeared behind us with two giant, greasy paper bags.

"Who wants lunch?" she cried.

That afternoon, we went to the Library of Congress, where Ms. Ella had set up a guided tour and an appointment to see Amber's *Shadows* book. A docent in khakis and a name tag took us through the main reading room with its great domed ceiling and statues of Homer and Moses and Newton before ushering us into a small exhibition room where *Shadows from the Walls of Death* was propped open on a small table, its pages encased in plastic. An archivist in white gloves explained that this was to keep people from inhaling toxic particles of arsenic.

"Our workers had to put on special protective suits in order to handle the book," she said. "But it's safe to look at now."

We crowded around it, Amber in front, turning the pages: the patterns of blue and delicate, filigreed gold, the deadly green blossoms, the twirling gray arabesques.

"What's this quote on the front?" Amber said. She leaned in and read, "'And behold if the plague be in the walls of the house, with hollow streaks, greenish or reddish, then the priest…shall cause the house to be scraped within round about, and they shall pour out the dust that they scrape off without the city into an unclean place.'"

"That's from Leviticus," said the archivist.

Ms. Ella seemed distracted and barely glanced at the book; she wasn't at the front of the group asking questions, either, like she usually was.

Back out on the National Mall, where a group of drummers tapped a catchy rhythm and kite fliers sent pastel birds and dragons high in the air, Ms. Speese said she wanted to do some shopping. We knew better and looked to Ms. Ella for her reaction.

But to our surprise, she said, "Great, why don't you take any of the kids who want to go? I can take the rest of them to Folger Park and meet you there at three."

"What do you think, honey?" Ms. Speese said to Amber. Amber nodded and stood up without being asked. Tracy and Kayla followed.

The rest of us went with Ms. Ella to Folger Park, a square park a few blocks away from the Capitol, calmer and shadier than the Mall, encased by an antique cast-iron fence. It was Saturday, and the parkgoers were relaxing, walking with dogs and strollers, or sunbathing on picnic blankets. By the entrance, a large, square, waterless fountain rose out of the ground, flanked by benches on either side where people sat reading newspapers. Giant copper beeches and holly trees grew at intervals along the circular walkways. Southern magnolias, much bigger than the one outside Stillwater, loomed full-blossomed above us, breaking the park into shady, private clearings.

Ms. Ella led us to one of these grassy, hidden nooks, spread her sweatshirt on the ground, and sat down while we circled up to play hackey sack. She took cigarettes out of her purse but did not light one. Instead, she squinted down the path where, farther away, an older couple was out walking and a group of younger kids was playing freeze tag. Her body was alert; she seemed to be waiting for something.

After maybe forty-five minutes had passed, as we were starting to get bored with the game and disperse, she said, "Stay there," then got up and walked in between Wei and Bryce to the middle of the circle. She opened her bag, took out the Attitude Adjuster paddle, and used it to point at Dawn.

"You," she said. "Come in the middle."

"What?" Dawn's face was red. "Why?"

"You know why."

"I don't!"

"Did you finish that statue?"

"No." Dawn choked back a sob.

"Did you know what would happen if you didn't finish that statue?"

"Yes."

"Then bend over," Ms. Ella said. To the rest of us, she said, "Count."

"One!" we cried in unison as the paddle came down. Wei and Bryce were directly behind Ms. Ella's swinging arm, and they moved back a few steps to allow Ms. Ella more momentum. Then the rest of us moved back, too, to even out our circle. To an onlooker, we could have been any of the dozens of school groups out in DC parks that day, playing games, playing sports, huddling over a ball that would be sent up, shortly, into the air.

"Two!"

"Three!"

"Four!"

"Five!"

Ms. Ella waited for longer intervals between the last five, so that the punishment seemed to slow down, to become more prolonged as it went on, each slap more momentous and anticipated. It seemed rougher, more violent, than the paddlings in the classroom, more violent even than the paddling Amber had gotten just a few days before for messing up Ms. Ella's citation.

We understood that it was about the Cassandra, but it also seemed to be about something else, about the boat trip on the Potomac and the hotel pool. It was important to be loyal. That was what the paddle said.

When it was over, Dawn stood up, her face the deepest red we had ever seen it, glassy tears in her eyes, beads of perspiration above her lip. She shoved her way past Ms. Ella and in between Wei and Bryce and ran over to the other side of the park. She almost knocked over Ms. Speese, who was just returning with Amber and Tracy and Kayla.

"Dawn?" Ms. Speese said, startled. "What's the matter, honey?"

Dawn ignored her and stormed past, squirrels darting away at her approach. She disappeared into a copse of blooming redbud trees.

Ms. Ella shoved the paddle back into her bag and watched her leave with a murderous look.

"What was that about?" Ms. Speese said, turning to Wei and Bryce.

"She'll get over it," Wei said dismissively.

"Come on, kids. Let's go." Ms. Ella took out the map. "If we leave now for Alexandria, we can still see the Fort Ward Museum before dinner. Brandon, go get Dawn. Tracy, you ride shotgun and read me the map."

Back in the other van, Ms. Speese told Amber to come sit in the front seat.

"Amber," she said, "what was going on back there?"

"Back where?"

"Back there. In the park. With Ms. Ella. Just now."

"I don't know. It was probably about Cassandra. Did you know," she said, turning to Wei and Brandon in the back seat, "that if you breathed in the dust from the *Shadows* book for a long time, you would get arsenic poisoning and start to go nuts?"

"No shit," said Wei, leaning forward.

"It was a vicious cycle," Amber explained. "Women would feel ill from the wallpaper and go lay down next to the wallpaper to rest, and then more of the arsenic dust would drift down and make them sicker. And they would start acting strange, and forget things, and people would get frustrated with them because no one knew what the matter was, but really they were being fatally poisoned in tiny, tiny doses."

"Did they die?" Brandon asked.

"Eventually. But they walked around saying crazy things for a while, first. It took a long time."

"Kids, please, try and focus," said Ms. Speese. "Who is Cassandra? What are you talking about?" She glanced back at the rest of us in the rearview mirror, but we were silent.

"You're blowing it out of proportion," Amber said.

We drove on, the gray highway yawning before us.

Chapter VI

WE ARRIVED BACK at Stillwater late on a Sunday evening, giddy and exhausted.

The school looked a little smaller to us, a little dimmer, after our week of travels. The building was closed, the black shutters drawn, the playground empty and full of evening shadows.

Amber was the first one out of Ms. Speese's van. She pulled her knapsack and suitcase out of the back and started to carry them, straining, over to Mr. Brodie's new minivan, but Ms. Speese stopped her.

"Over there," she said, pointing at her battered red Camry.

"Why?" protested Amber. "I don't need anything at home."

"You're coming home," Ms. Speese said, her voice slightly hysterical. "Tonight." She steered her daughter towards the car, ignoring Amber's protests. Amber folded her lanky frame into the passenger's seat. She propped her elbows on the car door and waved at us as her mother drove past, the muffler chugging and huffing.

Dawn was standing at the back of Ms. Ella's van, waiting for Bryce to dig her suitcase out of the jumbled heap of luggage.

"Ms. Speese is upset," she said.

Ms. Ella turned from her conversation with Tracy and squinted at the Camry. Amber was looking back at us through the rear windshield. With her pale, long arms, she reminded us a little of an octopus we had seen in the aquarium the year before, on a day trip to Tennessee.

"We all know Ms. Speese exaggerates," Ms. Ella said. "It'll blow over."

Ms. Speese signaled left at the magnolia, and the Camry vanished.

None of us thought anything of it, then. We all figured Ms. Speese was tired, didn't want to hang around making small talk with the other parents, especially not with Mr. Brodie, who was older and more well-off than she was.

But the next morning, Amber wasn't in class. We all sat at our desks, talking loudly about the trip, while Ms. Ella stood at the podium, calling us to order. Then we noticed Amber's empty chair.

"Did you call her?" Tracy asked Dawn.

"I tried, last night. But her mom wouldn't let her talk."

"Maybe she's sick," Kayla said. "Maybe she got sick on the trip."

She didn't sound convinced, but then again, Amber would be the first of us to get sick, with her skinniness and vegetarianism.

She wasn't there the next day, either, but by the late afternoon we forgot about it. It was the kind of early summer day that you see on Atlanta postcards: warm, with a light breeze that swept through the trees and made their branches stretch as if joining hands with one another. Full, dewy honeysuckles, like capsized, whiskery bells, drooped from the bush in front of Caleb's apartment. Tulips shot skyward from neighboring gardens. The scent of wood chips drifted up from the field. After school we gathered outside for a game of kickball, lining up the younger kids so that each of them could take a turn. The teachers from the younger grades saw us through the windows and came out to watch, and when our parents and siblings arrived to pick us up, they got out of their cars and gathered around the field too, laughing, smoking, passing the time.

That night, a warm front moved in and brought a thunderstorm that tore through the city, splitting trees, flooding sewers, and knocking down power lines. Giant, severed branches lay in the streets. Flowers closed themselves against the drench. Worms crawled onto the sidewalks, coiling and writhing. The next morning, the younger children ran into the school wearing slickers and brightly colored rubber boots. We followed close behind, dropping our wet umbrellas on the hallway floors.

Amber was still missing on this day, the third day.

"Her mother won't tell me anything!" Dawn told us. "I tried calling, three times. She just says every time that Amber can't come to the phone. She must take the cordless into her room so that Amber can't use it."

We stared out of the windows at the endless rain. That

morning we started learning about the Second Boer War and the Scramble for Africa. Ms. Ella didn't say anything about Amber being missing from class and the after-school accelerated program, not even to the other teachers who smoked with her on the fire escape. We thought Amber might reappear later in the morning, but she was not there when Jamal gave his report on the Russian Revolution, and she was not there when Brandon gave his on the Maji Maji Rebellion. And she was not there as we launched ourselves, under Ms. Ella's guidance, into one last spell of reckoning with grisly historical death.

Soon, rumors started to spread. Wei said he ran into Amber at the drugstore. His mom sent him in to get sponges, and he rounded the corner and found himself face-to-face with Amber in the cleaning aisle. They stared at each other for a moment next to a large display of Pine Sol bottles. Amber was in her oversized World Wildlife Fund T-shirt and cut-offs, and her hair was pulled back in a greasy ponytail.

"Hey!" Wei said, surprised.

Amber's voice was low, barely a murmur. "Hey."

"Where have you been? We've all been wondering about you."

Amber leaned forward. Her eyes were red; Wei said he could see the inflamed blood vessels in the inner corners of her eyelids.

"I've been—" Amber began.

"There you are."

Wei turned. Ms. Speese was standing in the aisle with a

small paper pharmacy bag in her hand.

"Hi Wei," she said curtly. "We were just leaving. Amber, come on."

Amber followed her mother out of the aisle, turning just once to wave goodbye.

"She seemed like she was on something," Wei told us at lunch. "Like her tongue was too fat."

Then Brandon, who lived down the street from Dawn, told us that one of Amber's uncles, a stout, bearded man in a construction uniform, had turned up at Dawn's house one Sunday in his pickup and asked for Amber's things.

"I saw him go in the house with Mr. Brodie," he said. "Dawn wasn't there. Ms. Speese must have planned it that way."

Dawn knew as little as we did. Ms. Speese had never much liked Amber being away from home so much, and now she was extricating her, bit by bit, from Dawn's house.

Another day passed, then two, then the weekend came and went and the twins, Ray and Eddie, were gone. They had been with us the previous Friday, sitting at their two desks in the middle row, Ray's hair short and cowlicked, Eddie's growing over his ears, and then they went home and none of us saw them at Stillwater again. Kayla and Tracy tried calling their house, but the phone just rang and rang and went to the answering machine.

That Wednesday, Jamal disappeared. That was even stranger, because he had perfect attendance, and we thought that surely Ms. Ella would say something.

She didn't. At quarter past eight on the morning of the arrest, she came up to the front of the room as usual, in her

Eagles T-shirt and blazer, and announced that we would spend the morning working on the mission and educational philosophy for the Renaissance Academy. She had an upcoming interview for grant funding and needed to have her talking points prepared.

We looked around, uncertain. Tracy raised her hand.

"Ms. Ella, that's Amber's project."

"Now it's your project."

She split us up into groups and assigned a leader to each.

"Tracy's group, you're going to copy my notes from the left paper, on Benjamin Bloom. Bryce's group, you're going to take the middle panel, on Renaissance humanism. Dawn's group, you take the last panel, on civic responsibility."

She stood behind us and gave instructions over our shoulders as we transcribed her notes from the wall onto a series of index cards.

At ten we had our morning break, and Ms. Ella went out onto the fire escape, Dawn following, while the rest of us escaped the warm and stuffy classroom for the shade of the magnolia. We had just started asking each other if anyone had heard from Jamal, when we heard Ms. Ella's voice coming from above us. We looked up. She was leaning out of our classroom window, moving the branch out of the way.

"Enough down there," she called. "Come on. Come upstairs and let's finish our work."

When we came back up to the room Ms. Ella looked flushed and exhilarated, as if the heat was animating her instead of making her dozy, like the rest of us. We worked until noon. When we were finished, Ms. Ella pushed three of our desks together and spread the index cards out, looking each one over carefully, pausing here and there to cross out a word or fix a spelling mistake. We waited.

"All right," she said at last. "This is good. This is really good. This is going to work."

We started to drift out to the storage area, to fetch our lunch boxes from the top of the filing cabinets, but she called us back into the room.

"What do you guys think you're doing?"

"Getting lunch," Brandon said.

"We still have work to do. We have reports to get through. Come on," she said, motioning us back into the room. "Just grab a snack and come back in the room. We can eat later."

We filed back in with bags of pretzels and plastic sandwich containers in our hands. It was now a quarter past twelve; our lunch period normally ran from noon to 12:45. Ms. Ella went to her desk, freshened up her makeup in a compact, and consulted a list in one of her notebooks.

"Kayla, you're up first," she said. "Kayla and The Great Depression. Let's hear what you have."

Kayla came up to the podium and started reading. At 12:30, Tracy came up and delivered her report on flappers and suffrage. At 12:45, Brandon muttered his way through a halfhearted account of the October Revolution. At 1:00, Ms. Ella said, "Bryce, you're up. FDR. Let's go."

And that's what we were doing when the officer came.

Chapter VII

WE DISAGREE about what happened next.

Wei and Kayla remember that Ms. Ella turned to us and said in a breezy tone, "Hold down the fort," as the officer led her out in handcuffs.

But Brandon thinks she said, "I'll be back," like the Terminator.

Tracy doesn't remember her saying anything, but she remembers the way the police officer's radio crackled with static, and how he said, "Ten-fifteen" into his shoulder as Ms. Ella strode past him.

The rest of us don't remember hearing anything. Just watching her gray blazer disappear through the doorway. Now, it bothers us that we don't know her exact words in that moment, if she even said any. If we had known it was the last time we'd all be together, we would have paid more attention.

After the squad car took Ms. Ella away, another officer pulled up to the school, a lanky woman with a ponytail. Chuck, the part-time counselor, was just a few steps behind her. He was a bearded man with wire-rimmed glasses, wearing a green "Just Say No" T-shirt, and looked shabby and unprepared, like he had been in the middle of something when he got the call. He explained that our parents would be arriving soon. The officer, Officer Kelly, would be asking us each some questions down in Jean's office.

"I'm not talking to anyone," Dawn said quietly. Her face and neck looked hot.

"Your dad will be here," Chuck said. "For support."

"I told you," Dawn said again. "I'm not talking to anyone. Leave me alone."

Chuck gave her a feeble smile. "Let's just see when your dad gets here, okay?"

He led us down to the basement event room where our parents and aunts and older cousins came in, all at different times, flustered and hysterical. Lulu, Jean's secretary, greeted them as they came in through the back doors, but they ignored her and came over, immediately, to embrace us. Hank and Tilda, the second- and sixth-grade teachers, stood in the corner whispering, their students left unattended in their classrooms. Ada, the third-grade teacher and Jean's only ally, surveyed the scene with a self-righteous air.

No one knew what to do. Lulu put *Back to the Future Part III* on the VCR. Tilda found a giant bag of hot fries and opened it. Another police officer, a lean, dark-haired man, stood in the back of the room, watching the entrance. A few kids from the younger grades came halfway down the staircase, peering down at us, staring at the officer. There was a sense of general mayhem. Above us we heard the scramble of moving feet and teachers' voices, high over the noise, calling their classes to order.

Kayla's mother arrived right away, so she was the first one to be called into Jean's office. Jean was sitting in her desk chair and Officer Kelly was on a folding chair beside her with a clipboard in her lap. Chuck stood at the door, smiling blandly. Kayla and her mother sat on a loveseat next to a table with a wooden Pinocchio, who was small-nosed still, on the precipice of his lies. Kayla's mother had come straight from the utility company where she worked; her ID badge still hung around her neck.

Jean folded her hands in her lap and said, in a voice shrill with panic, "Thank you for coming in on such short notice, Ms. Russell. Officer Kelly is going to ask Kayla some questions, and Chuck is going to be here too, just to help. We don't want this to be any more upsetting than it already is."

Ms. Russell turned to Kayla and put a hand on her knee. "You okay with answering some questions, baby?"

"Sure."

"Kayla," Officer Kelly began, "did you ever see or hear Ms. Ella act in a physically violent manner towards any of your classmates?"

"Violent?"

"Hitting them. With a paddle, for instance."

"Oh. Yeah."

"Can you tell me what you remember?"

Kayla shrugged.

"Amber got punished a lot, for not doing her work. Dawn, too, for not finishing Cassandra."

"Who is Cassandra?"

Kayla mistook the question for a test of her reading comprehension and launched into a long summary of *Agamemnon*. It took a while for the officer to bring her back around to Ms. Ella, and to get her to summarize everything she knew about the incident after that point: the bad class report, the beginnings of the sculpture, the promised completion.

"She got maybe fifteen hits for the Cassandra," she said at last, "for not finishing it."

Ms. Russell broke in.

"Can I just point out how unacceptable this is?" she said. "Paddling? These kids are thirteen years old."

Jean started to speak, but Officer Kelly stopped her.

"Please, let me do the talking," she said.

She looked carefully at Kayla. A few moments passed. When she spoke again, it was in a quieter register.

"Kayla," she said, "in all the time Ms. Ella was paddling students, did she ever ask any student to do anything...inappropriate? To remove any clothing, for instance?"

At this question Jean and Chuck leaned in slightly and held their breath. Even the hanging puppets seemed to go still, their swaying arrested for a moment. Kayla told us later that it seemed as if they wanted her to say yes, as if yes would help them win a bet they had placed.

"No," she said.

"Think carefully," Officer Kelly urged.

"No," Kayla repeated impatiently. "That's nasty."

"Okay!" the officer said, her voice forced and breezy. She leaned back in her folding chair. "I think that's all my questions, Kayla. Do you have anything else you want to tell us?"

"When are Amber and Jamal and the twins coming back?"

The officer and Jean shook their heads and smiled tightly, but Chuck leaned forward and said in his gentle, public-radio voice that Amber couldn't talk on the phone, but if Kayla had a message for her, maybe they could pass it along.

He listened to Kayla's message with a pained expression on his face.

Brandon was next. He sat on the loveseat beside his father, a television repairman who had closed down his shop on the east side of the city and come over right away. He wore a name tag and smelled faintly of dust and plastic. He patted his son's knee awkwardly.

"He was used to being called in to school, because my sisters were always getting into trouble," Brandon said afterward. "That was the first time he had to come because of me."

They were both sitting under the figure of a short king with a white beard and a red nose. The wooden-shoed jester dangled over the officer, and a cloaked pied piper hovered wide-eyed above the window that looked out over the playground. Brandon was distracted by the way the breeze from the air conditioner made the puppets kick. It took a moment before he realized the officer was asking him a question.

"Brandon, did you ever witness Ms. Ella being physically violent towards anyone in the class?"

"Violent? No."

"Hitting. Like spanking students," Officer Kelly persisted.

"Oh. You mean paddling? Sure."

"Were you paddled?"

"No. Just Dawn and Amber. You should talk to them." The king's feet danced near his ear. Brandon pushed the puppet away.

His father turned to him, bewildered. "Why didn't you come to your mother and I?" he said. "Why didn't you tell us this was happening?"

Brandon shrugged. "Amy and Suzy get spanked all the time," he said. "And you said that being strict isn't such a bad thing. You got paddled too, you said."

"This is different," his father said.

"All right, Brandon," said Officer Kelly. "Can you tell me about any of these incidents?"

"The last time was because of Cassandra."

Brandon gave another account of Amber's research project and Dawn's incomplete statue. At some point the lady officer must have radioed the officer in the basement, because he asked for a box, went up to our classroom, and took the papers off of the walls. Then he found the paddle in Ms. Ella's desk and added that to the box, and he took the Cassandra off of the windowsill and laid her on top, so that her blank face stuck out of the box when he carried it back downstairs. We watched from the basement windows as he loaded it into the back of the squad car.

"And when Ms. Ella was paddling the students," Officer Kelly said to Brandon, "did she ever do anything you would consider inappropriate?"

"Inappropriate? No."

"There was never any touching? Any physical contact, besides the paddling?"

"I don't know. They hugged, sometimes."

"Who?"

"Ms. Ella and Dawn."

"You saw them hug each other?"

"Yeah. But just for a second."

"Was it normal for Ms. Ella to hug her students?"

Brandon thought about it.

"It was more normal for students to hug her," he said.

Officer Kelly wrote this down. She asked some more questions, and Brandon answered them, and gave his message for Amber.

"It did seem really serious at the time," Brandon said later, "but I just kept getting distracted by those puppets."

One by one we went in, all of us except for Dawn, who really had refused to cooperate, who had only been in the office for five minutes when she came out again, her face streaked with tears, her father following behind. They disappeared through the front door. Dawn didn't stop in the basement to say goodbye. Tracy and Kayla were outside under the magnolia, and they watched the Brodies' minivan disappear around the corner where the cop car had turned with Ms. Ella in it, just an hour before.

Bryce went last. We found out later that they'd wanted to question him first, but his mother, a restaurant manager, was in the middle of a lunch rush at the Shoney's out in Stone Mountain, and she was the last parent to arrive. She pulled up to Stillwater in her Honda Civic and rushed to the office with her uniform askew. She was a severe-looking woman, a chain-smoker with a clogged voice.

Bryce was too tall for the loveseat, so his mother sat under the dangling puppet while he sat on a folding chair Chuck brought in from Lulu's office. It took a while to get started, because his mother interrupted several times to declare she was going to sue Jean and Stillwater School. Bryce told us that part when we called him days later, furious—when we found out what had happened next.

"Mrs. Hayes, please," Officer Kelly said. "We understand you're upset. But right now, we need to focus on your son's statement."

She turned to him.

"Bryce, when Amber's mother called your house last week, you told her something that Amber told you about Ms. Ella. Can you tell us what that was, please?"

"She said she was inappropriate," Bryce said.

"Inappropriate in what way? What did Amber tell you?"

"She told me that she stayed after school in the classroom and Ms. Ella paddled her and made her take her clothes off."

"When did Amber tell you this?"

"I don't know. October, maybe. Or November."

Officer Kelly scribbled on her clipboard. "Did Amber tell you anything else?"

"She said that, afterwards, Ms. Ella told her that if she didn't tell anyone, she would take her on a trip. Just the two of them."

This detail was straight out of the Herky Dyer case, but no one remarked on the similarity. Bryce went on, boldly summarizing the same case but with different characters. If Amber and Ms. Ella were ever discovered, they planned to flee to Mexico, just like Dyer and the sixteen-year-old girl.

"It's good that she was arrested now," Bryce said, "or she might have already crossed the border."

"Did you ever tell anyone else what Amber told you?"

"No. Amber didn't want me to."

Bryce's mom recovered from her shock and began shouting at Jean again, louder this time. We heard her all the way in the basement. A moment later, we saw the lady officer walking her down to her car, Bryce shambling after them.

All these details would come out slowly, over that summer and the fall beyond, in phone calls and during sleepovers and on long, hot Saturday afternoons at the Glenwood Public Pool. None of us has ever forgiven Bryce. Only Jamal said once that he felt a little sorry for him, but that was after Bryce came forward and admitted what he'd done, after it was too late. Maybe it was unfair, the way he came to bear the weight of our hatred, the way a lie told by a thirteen-year-old boy came spinning out of that office like a shuriken thrown in an action movie, cutting swiftly through everything.

But none of us knew that he'd told that lie at first, and when we went home and called each other that night, our biggest questions were what was due that week and whether Ms. Ella and Amber and Jamal and the twins would return to school. We discovered we'd all said the same thing, even Bryce, when Chuck asked us if we had a message for Amber. We all told him to tell her that we hoped she would come back soon, and, if not, that we'd see her in the fall, at the Renaissance Academy.

Chapter VIII

OF COURSE, there was no Renaissance Academy in the fall, and no more news of it, either.

Instead, we were sent home with work packets for the last two weeks of the term, set adrift on an uncertain summer where we all went from being invisible to being much too visible. Everyone started to tread gingerly around us. Our relatives stopped talking when we came into a room, or smiled and asked if we wanted something. Our parents took our sides when we fought with our cousins and siblings, and some of us, those whose parents hated guilt more than credit card debt, got new Super Nintendos and slap bracelets and *Terminator 2* tapes. A series of long-denied pleasures suddenly descended, unearned, upon us. Kayla's mom took her to Myrtle Beach; Wei's family visited the Jersey Shore. None of us got a straight answer about why Ms. Ella had been arrested. When we asked, our mothers and grandmothers and aunts and cousins and family friends and older siblings smiled at us in a sad sort of way and changed the subject.

Gradually, we learned that the news of Dawn's paddling had been inflamed by rumors, had taken the shape of something else, something darker and more insidious. Then Jean saw the opportunity in the rumors and seized it.

Dawn took it the hardest. Amber's mom still refused to let her see any of us, but Dawn found ways to talk to her secretly on the phone, late at night, and reported back. In this way, we learned that Ms. Ella had been charged with assault and that Amber had to testify at a hearing. Dawn told us about it at the Glenwood Public Pool, where Tracy's sister was a lifeguard. It was a muggy Saturday in July, and the pool was filled with kids shrieking and splashing and lining up to do cannonballs into the deep end. Dawn stood waist-high in the shallow side, and we stood in a little semicircle around her: Tracy in her yellow bikini, Kayla in her red one, Jamal in his swim trunks with his goggles pushed up over his forehead, Brandon sunburnt and perched on the side in a T-shirt and shorts, his legs kicking back and forth in the water.

"She told me her mom found her diary, where she wrote all the times she got paddled," Dawn said. "She found it in Amber's room and took it to give to the prosecutor. I told her she needed to find it and destroy it. But she didn't."

"Maybe she was scared of what her mom would do," Jamal said. "If it was missing, wouldn't she know that Amber stole it back?"

"Who the fuck cares?" Dawn cried. "I told her she had to destroy it, because they wouldn't understand. They would blow it all out of proportion. But she didn't because she's a pussy and now it's gone into evidence for the hearing and it's her fault."

"Isn't it Bryce's fault?" Tracy said. "He's the one who lied."

"Yes, and he admitted it," Dawn said. "Then they didn't have anything. If Amber would have destroyed the journal then we would all be getting ready to go to the new school, instead of Peachtree High."

We were all silent at this, because no one had said anything definite yet about school in the fall, and now we understood how it was going to be. Dawn slapped the water with her hands and looked back at us defiantly, her wet hair plastered back in a braid. She was the oldest of all of us, had just turned sixteen that summer. She also looked more developed than the other Stillwater girls, her breasts filling out the top of her red one-piece, her hips growing into the wideness and softness of our older sisters and cousins.

Beside her, we felt childish and unheroic. The whole drama had centered on her, after all—her and Amber. Dawn was the only one of us who had refused to answer the officer's questions, refused to talk to Chuck. Her fierceness reminded us of those fall days back at Stillwater when she was working on sketches for the Cassandra statue, captioning them with lines from *Agamemnon*. We would pass by her desk and look over her shoulder at the violent drawings, the capital lettering: AND WRATH IS THE MISTRESS RECOILING. BLOOD DRINKERS COME IN SISTERLY RIOT. Now, in her swimsuit, with her strong shoulders and her angry stare, she was the sole possessor of a martial grit we had all lost, or were never special enough to have in the first place.

That fall, we started our freshman year at Peachtree High, dissolved into the giant swarm of people, took classes where we read textbooks and studied for tests, passed each other silently in the crowded hallways.

Where Stillwater had been cozy and small and made of brick, Peachtree High was large and mazelike, made of glass and concrete, exploding with motion. Everywhere we looked, we saw strangers: groups of goth kids with black hair and lip rings, skater kids with boards in hand, B-boys in tracksuits and Adidas. The hallways and classrooms and bathrooms were crowded with bodies. Bodies holding Walkmans and Gameboys and purses and backpacks and Trapper Keepers and athletic bags full of sporting equipment. After school, more bodies congregated outside, at the drop-off circle or spread out along the sidewalks in front of the auditorium, or walking in little clusters down to the courthouse square, hollering at the people they passed.

We'd been used to having one teacher who did everything, but here we went to different teachers for every subject and then back to our first teacher of the day for homeroom, like pinballs shot around the giant buildings. It was easy to get lost between classes, to get stuck in front of our lockers fiddling with the combinations. Then we had to run, our backpacks thumping, to be in our seats before the bell rang.

At Stillwater, we had all been in the same classroom together, but here most of the students in AP and Honors classes were white or Asian, and most of the students in general education classes were black or Hispanic. It was how they kept you separated. They put Tracy in AP United States History, even though she was terrible at it, and they would have put Jamal in gen ed history if his grandmother hadn't come down and made a fuss, and probably Kayla too, if her father hadn't done the same. Finally Tracy, Wei, and Jamal all wound up in the AP class together, and when their names were called and they said "Here," a few of the other kids turned to look at them, curiosity flaring on their faces.

A redheaded girl leaned over and spoke to Wei. "Aren't you from that school with that teacher who got arrested? The one that was on the news?"

"Yes."

"I heard there were lots of you here."

"Did you," he said, staring straight ahead.

The rest of us collected similar stories. We gathered in front of the auditorium after school that first day and shared them. How the other kids knew about Stillwater. How the teachers smiled at us brightly, a bit *too* encouraging. How we'd all received textbooks that we had to give back at the end of the year, and no primary sources. How we were supposed to read the textbooks and take tests. How the other students didn't all know each other: when they were called up to the board together, or put in groups, they introduced themselves.

It was exactly like Ms. Ella said it would be, we agreed.

Crowded.

Bureaucratic.

Indifferent.

At first, no one saw Amber. She wasn't in first period AP US History with Wei and Tracy and Jamal and she wasn't in Honors English 1 with Dawn or Brandon or Kayla. Tracy wondered aloud, after school, if her mom was homeschooling her, or if they had moved into another district. But then Kayla saw Amber sitting in the glass-walled admissions office when she was in the hallway with a bathroom pass, and the next day she turned up in Tracy and Kayla's lunch period, in the cavernous, echoing cafeteria where kids crammed together in groups of ten around tables meant for six, in cliques whose shifting power alliances were impossible to understand. They waved, but Amber didn't see them in the throng.

Then, that afternoon, there was the scene with her and Dawn in the third-floor girls' bathroom.

The girls' bathrooms at Peachtree High were gray and narrow, with four stalls apiece, and just a couple of feet between the stalls and the cement walls where girls leaned, talking, waiting, peering impatiently under the doors. Lines formed quickly and wound out the door into the hallway, so that the door was always propped open by someone's body and passing students could glance in and see girls washing their hands or applying lipstick in the mirrors over the ancient, groaning sinks.

Amber was standing at one of the sinks, sallow-faced, washing her hands, when Dawn spotted her from the hallway, came in, and grabbed her arm.

"Hey!" Amber said, twisting away.

"What did you tell them?" Dawn said, pressing Amber against the sink. The loud chatter in the bathroom fell silent and all the girls in line stared, Tracy and Kayla among them.

"It's nice to see you, too," Amber said. "You didn't ask, but I'm doing great."

Dawn ignored the sarcasm. "The hearing," she said. "What happened?"

"Nothing happened!" Amber cried. "They made me talk about the paddling, and the DA showed them pictures of the bruises that my mom took, and they showed my diary to the judge. But Ms. Ella's lawyer said Ms. Ella hadn't broken any laws. The DA tried to say the punishment had been too harsh, but then her lawyer said I was anemic, which is true, so I would always have bruises over nothing. The judge said that Ms. Ella couldn't teach again, and that was it. The DA said the judge gave her a light sentence, because he liked her."

"Liked her?"

"He liked what she had to say. I think she got up on the stand and talked about her teaching philosophy, stuff like that. I didn't see that part. They took me back to the DA's office."

"That was *their* teacher?" said a pretty, popular girl in front of Kayla. "She sounds messed up in the head."

A few other girls in line agreed, loudly.

A toilet flushed and a redhead in a Kurt Cobain shirt came out and said, "Excuse me." Dawn let Amber's arm go and stormed back outside, jostling the rugby player who was standing in the doorway.

"Excuse you," the player said. "Bitch."

Amber slunk out a moment later.

We might have tried to talk to them, to get more of Amber's side of the story, to bring it back to Dawn. Or at least we could have eaten lunch with them sometimes, if separately, could have brought them both onto the misfit island we had formed for ourselves in the roiling sea of Peachtree.

But that January, a week after we returned from the winter break, news got out that Stillwater School was going to be shut down. Someone had tipped off the IRS—Hank or

Tilda, we thought, or maybe Ms. Ella herself—who launched an investigation and found that Jean had been embezzling tuition money and using it for personal expenses, like her Roadster and her antique puppet collection.

When the story came on the news, our mothers just shook their heads. "Oh, my God," they said. "How did we not see it?"

"Her husband worked at Turner Broadcasting," said our fathers and uncles and grandparents and aunts and cousins. "He was loaded. You didn't see the books. You couldn't have known."

Word got around about a class action lawsuit, and the whispers and stares from other Peachtree students began again, just weeks after they had finally stopped. That was when we started to drift apart. It was too much, having Stillwater back in the news like that. It was time to seek other things, say goodbye to our past. In this way, the size and anonymity of our new school was an advantage. It was easier to find new activities, to make ourselves lost to each other.

Tracy split away first: she had her sister's popularity to build on, and she eventually passed Kayla and Amber at lunch to go sit with a table of girls wearing chokers and eyeliner, smiling apologetically as she went by.

Jamal joined Model UN and made it into the pool of students who would go to DC to compete in the finals.

Kayla spent all of her time with the drama club kids, doing lighting and theater makeup.

Amber got a work-study position at the library, where she surrounded herself with books.

We still nodded and waved when we saw each other, and sometimes we stopped to chat, but we didn't meet up after school anymore. Whenever we saw Dawn in the square, sitting at the counter of the Cheesy Slice, talking to Ms. Ella's tall, strange son, we felt a little embarrassed for her.

By the time we graduated, everyone at Peachtree High had forgotten about Stillwater Alternative School, and the city had forgotten about it, too. The old Stillwater building had been sold to a daycare chain, then to a tutoring and test prep company.

During the boom that followed the 1996 Summer Olympics, a developer bought it, razed the playground and the magnolia to the ground, filled in the swampy field with cement, and leased the lot to a moving and storage company. A small fleet of moving trucks, their tires aligned in a perfect row, were parked in the field where we had played kickball or gossiped or strewn wood chips with our feet. Four long blocks of cement units with aluminum, garage-style doors filled the grounds where we had once given our first reports. At night, when we drove by the lot, the doors flashed silver in our headlights, like so many pairs of shut, slumbering eyes.

Chapter IX

TWENTY YEARS LATER, when we heard the news of Dawn's suicide, we came together.

Well, not *together*, exactly. We were too estranged by then, some of us in Atlanta, some of us in other states, other countries, other time zones.

But we found each other on the wall.

Tracy started it. She posted the obituary Dawn's father wrote for the *Atlanta Journal Constitution* and tagged us, and we wrote replies underneath.

"How awful," Kayla wrote. She was in LA now, doing props and makeup for slasher flicks. "She was so talented."

Brandon, a father of four, shared it and wrote, "This hurts my heart. An old classmate just two years older than me. Tell everyone that you love them today, because you never know if today will be their last day."

On we went like this, all of us except for Amber, who was in Atlanta still (Tracy explained), running an antiquarian bookstore, but didn't have any of her own social media accounts. We filled up the wall with anecdotes about Dawn, about the modest reputation she'd built for her artwork, about the mural she had done at the MARTA station, which we stopped to admire whenever we came back to visit family. Our posts grew longer, swollen with sudden lurches of memory, generating sympathetic blue thumbs from other users, Tracy's friends. We kept writing, filling in everything we never said after the arrest, after everything fell apart. We wondered if we should chip in and send flowers to Amber's bookstore.

"But were they even friends anymore?" Wei wrote. He was the farthest away of all of us, working for a financial company in Hong Kong; all of his posts came in later than ours.

We tried to remember.

"They didn't talk to each other at Peachtree," Jamal pointed out. He was in DC now, with his boyfriend from Georgetown, working in international affairs. "They didn't talk to each other for years."

After a week of the posts growing and growing, Tracy invited us to a private group. She called it "Stillwater School, Atlanta, 1992–1993." For the description, she wrote, "Stillwater was an alternative school in Atlanta, Georgia, in the eighties and early nineties. This is a place for Stillwater alumni to gather and share their memories."

She found a picture of the closed school online and posted it as the cover photo. The photograph had probably been taken by a journalist around the time of Jean's embezzlement trial. The journalist had stood across the street to capture the magnolia and the crumbling sign in front. The framing seemed designed to make the school look dowdy and suspicious, but the brick shone in the late-afternoon sunlight and the crocuses were in full bloom. A squirrel under the magnolia was standing on its hind paws, looking straight at the photographer.

Tracy's cover photo started a trend. Kayla found some pictures from the DC trip, scanned and posted them, and tagged us so we could see pictures of our younger selves standing in front of the Lincoln Memorial wearing Air Jordans and Converse and fanny packs. "Look at us!" we wrote. More puffy blue thumbs collected under the pictures.

Brandon scanned in a picture of a kickball game. It took place in the fall: the leaves were yellow and red, and we were all wearing long-sleeved shirts or windbreakers. Brandon's mother had photographed him in the instant before a kick, his leg drawn back, his brow furrowed with determination. Behind him, Jamal, Amber, Dawn, Bryce, and Wei stood in line, waiting for their turn. Everyone's eyes were on the ball, all of the force and energy of the picture directed at that one object.

Wei was the one who posted the picture with Ms. Ella in it. It was one of the few pictures any of us had of her. It was strange: as present and sharp and centered as she is in our memories of those days, she appears in very few of the surviving photographs, and then almost never as a main figure but often as a blur turning away or an arm just in the margins, like those ghostly, fading phantoms of Victorian spirit photography.

The picture had been taken on the day we left for the class trip. We were lined up in front of the board. Ms. Ella stood to the right of us, grinning.

Jamal was the one who noticed the shadowy object on

the windowsill. He enlarged it and reposted it for us. The Cassandra.

"I remember that statue!!!" Tracy wrote underneath. "It was actually really good. I wonder what happened to it??!!"

We filled up the comment space with our speculations.

"If it still exists," Jamal wrote, "it has to be in an evidence room somewhere. In a police station or a courthouse. Or in off-site storage."

We pictured the Cassandra in some dimly lit, musty basement full of metal shelves, in a box with handwriting scrawled across it: *The State of Georgia versus Eleanor Hallstrom, 1993.* Every now and then some rookie or intern would pass that box on a thankless errand, and they would pause to inspect the curious object poking out of the top, maybe even reach into the box to withdraw the statue and turn it, slowly, in the direction of the bare light bulb that would be dangling overhead. We imagined that moment, that glimpse of the Cassandra, still eyeless, now brittle with age. Bits of the papier-mâché would have crumbled off. Her arms would be outstretched still, her unfinished mouth prophesying to no one.

Part Two:

Atlanta and Madeira Beach,
June 2012

Chapter I

It was a Thursday in early June when Amber discovered the body.

She had stopped by Dawn's apartment on her way home from the bookstore to pick up some rare book catalogues she'd lent her a few weeks earlier. She found her best friend slumped over on the sofa, lips parted and arms at her sides, limp, in an easeful posture. If Amber had not noticed the pill bottle or the faint, unnatural blue pallor of the skin, which was already cool to the touch, she would have thought Dawn was napping. She looked at Dawn's horrible posture, at her limpness, and then, feeling sick, turned away.

An art book with glossy pages lay in front of the body, open to a disturbing painting Amber had never seen before. The scene took place in a shadow-filled bedroom, with an unmade twin bed extending from the left side of the painting into the middle space. A young man, maybe in his teens or early twenties, sat on the end of the bed, dressed in a suit and tie. Behind him, partly turned towards the viewer, his mother stood to the side of the bed and removed his jacket. Her arm smothered his mouth and pulled his head back against her violently, so that all Amber could see of his face was frightened eyes and the shadow of his mother's face over his brow. The gesture seemed more threatening than motherly, almost predatory, although the mother's face was placid and vacant.

The man's sister stood in front of him, helping her mother remove the jacket, her back to the viewer and her head turned a quarter to the left so that her profile was visible. Her expression was sinister, her jawbone pronounced; her pelvis thrusted aggressively, suggestively, against her brother's. Off to the right, apart from the three central figures, stood a second sister in a burst of sunlight in front of the window, watching greedily, clasping her hands in a way that reminded Amber of bullies cracking their knuckles. The whole painting had an aura of lurid inexorability, like funhouse distortions, like something lived once and remembered forever afterwards in nightmares. This was *The Family* by Paula Rego (1988), a caption informed the reader.

In that gentle, limber light, in the hushed presence of death, the figures struck Amber as blasphemous. She closed the art book and slipped it into her bag.

Yet the image lingered in her mind as she made calls, waited on the front steps, and numbly answered all the questions that followed. First the police arrived, then the medical examiner. For the police, Amber retraced her steps through the apartment, showed them the spare key Dawn had given her. She listed the surviving relatives to be notified: Winston, Dawn's husband; Cheryl, her daughter; and Elijah Brodie, her father. She responded to their other inquiries, one by one. No, she had not seen Dawn in several weeks. No, Dawn had never mentioned suicide, hadn't made any threats. No, she didn't want to see a medic herself; she just wanted to go home. All the while, the sister's violent glare and the mother's approving gaze floated before her. The medical examiner snapped photographs. Dawn's body was zipped into a bag, carefully, almost lovingly.

"What?" Amber said to the officer who stood before her as the body was carried out. This one was younger than the others, in her thirties maybe, around Amber's age. She was scribbling in a notepad.

"Are you sure you didn't notice anything else when you came in?" she repeated. "A note near the body, or anything like that? Something she might have left behind?"

"Oh," said Amber. "No. There was nothing. Just the pill bottle."

Outside, a small crowd of neighbors had gathered on the sidewalk, watching solemnly, their arms crossed, murmuring. The young officer walked Amber past the crowd to her car. Amber could feel the heavy art book in her bag, bumping against her thigh.

"Can I call anyone for you?" the officer said. "A sibling or a friend, maybe? A partner?"

"No," Amber said. "Please. I just want to rest here for a second, and then I'll go."

She sat in her car and watched the officer's figure recede into the crowd. She put her hand in her bag and touched the book's smooth cover. A sudden pain seized her abdomen and she hunched forward, sobbing.

Rush hour traffic streamed past on Piedmont, rapid, indifferent.

After she composed herself, she drove home and called Cheryl.

"I can't believe it," Cheryl said bitterly. "I was supposed to be celebrating my graduation."

"Where are you?"

"Home."

"Stay there. I'll be right over."

Cheryl opened the door. She was eighteen, short and wiry, dressed in overalls and battered Vans, with spiky, platinum hair and patches of freckles across her cheeks and chest. Thick slashes of black liner set off her wide, hazel eyes. A silver ring flashed from her lower lip. She had her father's muscly shoulders and legs but her mother's bold stare. She threw her arms around Amber, who held her close, feeling the young girl's sobs against her shoulder.

Eventually Cheryl withdrew from Amber's embrace, wiped the back of her eyes, and picked up a tea kettle.

"I'm all out of black tea. Lucy used to do the shopping." She pronounced her ex-girlfriend's name with a hint of derision.

"That's all right. Where's your dad?"

"On his way. He was on tour in Scandinavia and now he's stranded in Reykjavik. First flight he can get puts him here on Sunday morning."

Cheryl slammed the kettle down, turned on the burner,

and let the gas stream out—for too long, Amber thought, repressing a little scream as Cheryl struck the match at last and the flame leapt a full foot off of the burner.

"Why don't you let me take care of that?"

"No, I got it," Cheryl said. "I've lost my mother, right? I have to do things for myself."

She carried the tea into the living room, past rows of her own mounted and framed pictures. Cheryl had been a serious photographer since she was in middle school and had recently been experimenting with digital alterations. One photograph depicted a group of tulips with sinister faces, another an oak tree whose branches dissolved into fractals.

Amber stood for a moment and looked at the photograph over the loveseat. Cheryl had recently won a prize for this picture. It bore the Dali-esque caption "Portrait of My Mother Painting, Surrounded by the Content of a Nightmare," and it depicted Dawn standing at her easel, holding a brush and looking straight at the lens. Her dark eyebrows were drawn together, accenting the small vertical wrinkle that appeared in between them, and her lips were slightly parted, as if she were in the middle of a sentence. Her body was whole and intact except at the extremities, the top of her head and the tips of her fingers and bare toes, where it became a series of small, bright dots, a disintegrating swarm of colors. A threatening vapor gathered strength and force at those contact points where her body started to come apart.

Amber helped Cheryl move the lens caps and straps and filters off the coffee table to make room for the tea. Cheryl sat down and leaned her head on Amber's shoulder.

“I mean, when you think about it, it doesn’t make sense at all,” she said, staring at the trail of steam rising from her mug. “I mean, she’s emotional. Was. But she was happy. She was looking forward to this residency. And it just doesn’t seem like her. Sleeping pills?”

“She could be complicated sometimes,” Amber murmured.

“Right? Like the mural by the MARTA station. I went to look at it right after Winston called.”

Cheryl always referred to her mercurial stepfather as Winston, even though he referred to her as his daughter.

“I cried here for an hour and then I went to go see it. Did you ever notice how there’s that part in the lower left corner of it, that coyote mangling something?”

Amber nodded.

“No one in the world would let any artist put something like that in a touristy City Council mural, but she got away with it. She never asked. She just did whatever she wanted.”

“She was always like that,” Amber said. She pulled away from Cheryl a little to look her in the eyes. “Listen. Whatever happens, you know that this had nothing to do with you. Right?”

“I know that!” Cheryl cried. “At least, I know it wasn’t my fault or anything stupid like that. But did she even think about me when she did it? Without even leaving a note?”

Amber stayed and cooked dinner. She offered to bring Cheryl home with her afterward, but Cheryl thanked her and refused.

“I want to stay near the mural,” she said. “If I change my mind, I’ll come over later.”

The funeral took place the following Saturday, at the Catholic church Dawn's father had attended for as long as Amber could remember. The reception was at Winston's house. Amber had visited many times when Dawn and Cheryl still lived there, but she always felt a little surge of awe upon entering it.

It was a modest, single-family house, not ostentatious but designed with an architect's eye for the flow of space. An east-facing kitchen gathered and reflected the light in the morning, while a garden patio on the western side of the house opened onto a thick green lawn as gentle and continuous as a golf course. The kitchen area flowed smoothly into the dining area and from there into the living area in a series of unbroken planes, punctuated by window seats and throw cushions and handmade shelves.

Cheryl's high school friends were gathered in a little group by a set of large bay windows, all dressed in black, radiating a palpable awkwardness. Just weeks before, they had all celebrated graduation in this same house. Now they huddled silently behind Cheryl as she talked to a group of Dawn's coworkers about her remains.

"My grandpa let me take some ashes and pick out an urn," she was saying. "There are so many different kinds. Keepsake. Cold cast. Fossil stone. I went with a purple keepsake urn. It's going in my living room, for now, I guess. With her picture. But it just doesn't seem like enough."

Amber spotted Winston alone in front of a window, staring out at the front lawn, where some of the guests' children were chasing each other across the grass, shrieking. He had changed from his funeral suit into a black button-down that revealed his tan forearms. His graying brown hair was gathered in a ponytail that hung down his back. He was holding a plastic cup of red wine.

Amber touched his arm gently. "Do you want me to go outside? Ask the kids to be quiet?"

"No. It's nice to watch them." They stood together silently. After a moment, Winston said, "I just can't believe her father's not here for this."

"He's coming as fast as he can. He's on the other side of the world."

"It's no excuse. We all should have been watching out for her. Everything was too much. Our divorce, and losing the new mural commission." Winston's jaw tightened. He drained his wine and set the empty glass on the windowsill, too hard. "We never should have let her go to Alexandria alone, to that residency. It was just too much, with the paperwork from the attorneys and Cheryl graduating and everything."

"This isn't your fault, Winston."

He gave her a long, haunted look, turned, and headed towards the drinks table.

That night, as Amber sat up in bed, restless from too much alcohol and coffee and dessert, with the art book open to *The Family* on her lap, she went over Winston's theory again and again.

It didn't seem right.

Dawn had been unhappily married to her second husband and hadn't loved him for years when they finally separated. She had told Amber this just months before her death, over a couple of pints at the Railside Tavern, although Amber had kept the information to herself. And Dawn had been excited about her new apartment, about Cheryl's graduation, about the next phase of her life.

"I was a teenage mom," she'd yelled over the girls in a nearby booth singing Journey at top volume. "You know? I love Cheryl, but I was just a baby when I had her. I'm ready to live on my own, for the first time. Spread out. Start some new projects."

She hadn't cared about the retracted second commission from the arts council, either. "A touristy Old South pornotopia," she'd called it. She had, in essence, gotten herself taken off the project when she refused to include Stone Mountain, with its grandiose etchings of Robert E. Lee, Stonewall Jackson, and Jefferson Davis on the side.

"If the arts commission really wants to beautify the city, they can take down some of these slave-society monuments," she'd said as they walked together through a leafy Decatur square, pointing at the flame-topped obelisk that rose out of a small garden. "Who dedicated that one? The fucking United Daughters of the Confederacy."

So it hadn't been her divorce or the lost commission. Amber was sure of it. And Dawn had acted the same as always in the months leading up to her death: fiercely companionable, spending evenings with Cheryl at Amber's house, turning up at the store to run the register and look through old order catalogues when Amber needed a break. Calling at strange hours, bursting into Amber's kitchen on weekend afternoons, her hair disarranged, to complain about some customer at the art store or some fight with Cheryl or Winston.

Then, just as suddenly, Dawn had disappeared off to the residency in Virginia, but that was typical of her too: periods of intense friendship and togetherness always alternated with intervals of fretful, panicked distance.

Amber had learned to leave her alone during these phases. Dawn would come back when she was ready, and interfering would only drive her into a fury, make her absences more vengeful and protracted.

Often, she produced her best work during these retreats, returning after weeks of isolation with sketchbooks full of terrifying illustrations: women with gaping mouths and wide, terrified expressions; women placed on the table as dishes, like elaborate, prepared fish; women dangling from the ends of fishing poles, grinning fiendishly as they hung from their feet, upside down. No gallery would ever show these, but drawing them seemed to give Dawn the release she needed in order to create the paintings that would sell and bide her time at the barista jobs she strung along beside her Easel shifts. So Amber and Cheryl and Winston had all come to expect good things from these little excursions; indeed, Amber would have been less surprised by everything if Dawn had been at home for the weeks leading up to her death, working at the art store and slowly filling with rage.

Cheryl was right, Amber reflected. It made no sense for a woman like Dawn, a woman bursting with morbidity, not to leave a note, a clue, a reason.

The figures in *The Family* stared at each other, frozen in their ghastly struggle: the affirming downward gaze of the mother, the wide, terrified eyes of the son, the sister's combative, threatening posture. Slowly, they began to resolve themselves into familiar figures, figures Amber knew.

She looked at the clock. It was five in the morning, just two hours before the flight was due to come in from Reykjavik. If she wanted answers, she couldn't get them from Winston. She had to go to the only person who knew Dawn the way Amber knew Dawn. To her first husband. To Cheryl's father. To Monty.

And through him, to his mother, their old teacher, the woman who had taught Dawn to finish what she started.

To Ms. Ella.

Chapter II

MONTY, MS. ELLA'S son, had lived in the same duplex off Freedom Parkway ever since he sold his mother's house. It was a two-story bungalow split in two, each half a mirror image of the other: two white doors, two front windows, two driveway spaces. A large Japanese maple on Monty's side threw the symmetry off balance, raining purple leaves onto the front lawn.

He was already in the doorway when Amber walked up the lawn. Still tall, still loping, still tattooed Monty. Still an anarchist, still bashful, still wearing his favorite gray Ramones shirt. Unlike Dawn, he had never remarried, although Amber suspected he'd had affairs in the cities where he toured, casual lovers in Montreal or Philly or LA. He and Amber were not especially close, but years of seeing each other at Cheryl's birthday parties and sports games had made them familiar and direct with each other. Amber imagined he felt the same way she'd always felt around Dawn: entranced, invisible.

They embraced.

"I'm so sorry, Monty."

"I'm sorry, too."

"Where's Cheryl?"

"Upstairs, napping." He gestured up at her old bedroom window, a pane of stained glass that overlooked the street. "She picked me up from the airport at six this morning."

"How was the trip?"

"Exhausting."

He told her about Sweden and Norway while he fixed coffee in the little kitchen that faced the small backyard, about the midnight sun and the phone call from Winston to his hotel, and the sudden journey, and the long, strange stopover in Reykjavik where, still in shock from the news, he had taken a late-night walk along the Old Harbor.

"Only drunk people were still out. All the stores were closed and there were boats tied up all along the harbor, hundreds of them. You could see the mountains. I just stood there and watched this group of teenagers charging drunken tourists ten *króna* apiece for rides in a shopping cart. Everyone around me was wasted. All I could think about was that drawing she did of Lake Lanier, when Cheryl was five. The one of her standing at the campfire. Our last family vacation."

He stopped abruptly and placed a mug in front of Amber. "I'm rambling," he said. "Sorry."

"Don't be." Amber took a sip of coffee, her copper bracelets jangling. "Have you talked to Winston since you got back?"

"Twice," he said, wincing a little. "He called once when I was at the airport this morning and again about an hour ago."

"He thinks she was overstressed," Amber said. "Because of the lost commission. And the divorce on top of it."

"He told me that, too."

"Do you believe him?"

"What do I know?" He stared into his coffee. "The last time I saw her was at Cheryl's graduation party. She seemed fine, and she was talking about a new thing she was working on. The usual."

"Same here. I saw her last at the bookstore, like always. Nothing strange."

She tried to describe that last time to Monty. Although she had gone over it again and again in her mind as she lay awake the night before, its ordinariness made it hard to recall.

It had been about a week after the graduation party, maybe more. Dawn burst into the store late one morning in a short green sundress, her hair freshly cut into an angled bob that accentuated her neck. At thirty-five, she had lines that radiated from her eyes and mouth, giving her face a mature depth and dimension that made people think she was wiser than she sometimes was. Her cheeks announced her moods, flushing red whenever she was angry. They were only light pink on that day, when she strode up to Amber, who was stocking inventory, and said, "Come on. Put that down. Let's go to lunch."

"I can't. I'm the only one here today."

"Then I'll bring it back. Sushi?"

Without waiting for an answer, Dawn strode out of the store and returned fifteen minutes later with a take-out bag. They sat on stools behind the register and ate. Dawn talked about the show they were watching together at Amber's house on Sunday nights, a favorite topic among Cheryl and her friends.

"People send hate mail to the woman character because they think she's real, but if you ask people why they like the guy character when he's a narcissistic, power-hungry asshole, they say he's just a made-up character and to calm down about it," she said. "Women aren't even allowed to be make-believe!"

"It's a double standard," Amber agreed. "I read that people yell at her in public for ruining his game."

"At least the show avoids the tired plot where he has an affair with a younger woman," Dawn said, painting wasabi delicately onto her dragon roll with one chopstick, as if she were wielding a fine brush. "But he still founded a meth empire, which I think is pretty patriarchal."

As usual, Dawn had been brash, Amber quiet and acquiescing. It was an unremarkable conversation, the kind she and Dawn had every time they got together, in the store, at art galleries and showings, or on weekend mornings when they went on slow jogs down the winding trails at Fernbank, cyclists whizzing past in their neon Spandex. They had discussed Amber's upcoming convention in DC. Dawn had agreed to rotate the unstaffed shifts at the store with Cheryl while Amber was away.

Before leaving that day, she had taken a few more of Amber's rare book catalogues, to work on her series. Three of her still lifes, in the *memento mori* tradition, hung on the far wall of the bookstore. The first depicted an octavo, the second a quarto, the third a folio, all modeled on volumes from the store. Each book was surrounded by relics of death. Skulls. Wilting flowers. Snuffed candles. Bitten fruit. The objects grew progressively larger, along with the books, so that the first skull was tiny, a squirrel's skull, the middle a dog's, and the last a human's, its discolored teeth biting down on the top of the book's worn spine.

"We need a painting of a miniature here," she said, peering at her own work with a dreamy, proprietary satisfaction. "The pattern gets bigger. I want to disrupt it. Show the death of tiny things. They matter, too. Barren seeds. Moths. A bumblebee."

The bell above the door jangled violently as she went out.

That was it. There had been no mention of the lost commission, and no mention of the divorce.

"That's what I remember too," Monty said. "Just that she was sick of the commission and that she couldn't wait to get to the gallery in Alexandria. And that she was happy to get out of the city for a while."

"What gallery was it?"

"Potomac something. Potomac Haven, maybe. Or Potomac Gallery. Experimental place."

They were silent again, sipping their coffees. Amber turned her question over and over in her mind, hesitating over tone, phrasing, timing. Overhead, she could hear Cheryl moving around upstairs, socked feet on creaking floorboards, the sound of water rushing through pipes.

Monty read the silence and said, "I haven't been able to reach my mother."

"You have a number for her, then."

"She doesn't have a phone. She's down in Florida still. Some motel in Madeira Beach. She used a pay phone to call Cheryl on her graduation. I got the number from Cheryl and tried to call about an hour ago. No answer."

"So she doesn't know."

Monty shook his head.

"She and Cheryl were talking again for a moment, this spring, but Cheryl hasn't mentioned it since. Dawn and I were against it. I haven't spoken to her in years. This isn't how I envisioned us talking again."

Amber thought a moment and said, "Why don't you let me tell her?"

"That's kind. But you don't have to do that."

"Just let me. It'll be one less thing you have to worry about. You can focus on Cheryl."

Monty hesitated, then picked up his phone and read off the number to Amber. She entered it into her phone and went upstairs.

Cheryl was propped up in bed, staring out at the Japanese maple, her freshly washed hair leaving damp marks on the pillow. Her earbuds were in and she was dressed simply, in a gray baseball shirt and cutoffs, her face bare of decoration except for the silver stud that gleamed from her lower lip. Without makeup, her resemblance to her mother was startling.

"How are you holding up?" Amber said, sitting on the bed.

Cheryl removed an earbud.

"I'm okay," she said. "*Most* of the time I'm okay. Then all of the sudden I see something, a paintbrush or something, or I'll drive by one of the restaurants she liked, and all of a sudden I'm not okay. I went past Sushi Paradise yesterday and I pulled over and started bawling. Then I had a dream last night that she came into my room and I had to tell her that she'd died, that she wasn't supposed to be there. It just seems like she's not *finished* yet. Like we cremated her, and we remembered her, but she's not really gone. I feel like I should do something else for her. It just all seems incomplete."

"It might feel that way for a while," Amber said softly.

"Lee got all my shifts covered at the coffee shop this week. I didn't ask him to, he just did it. He's a good boss. But the thing is, I didn't want him to. I would rather work. What else am I supposed to do with myself? I'm so tired of *crying*."

Amber covered the girl's hand with her own.

"At least I have the shifts at the store." Cheryl wiped her eyes. "Right? You're still going to DC?"

Amber hesitated. The rare books conference at the Library of Congress was the furthest thing from her mind. But Cheryl had grown up around the store and it was like another home for her. Amber knew, too, how much of Dawn was in the store, how many of the dusty volumes and reading nooks and patterns of shifting sunlight had made their way into her sketchbooks. Dawn used to sit in the corner of the store and draw, and customers would look curiously at the small woman in the corner, whose pencil moved with such intensity that it seemed to charge the air around her.

"Of course. If you want the shifts, they're still yours."

"Good. Maybe I'll think of something while I'm there, where she used to be. A better way to remember her."

"Don't try to force anything," Amber said.

They embraced. When Amber walked back outside, she stopped for a moment to admire the maple strewing its leaves on the ground and the white dandelion seeds drifting past on the breeze: the world remaking itself, blithely, indifferently, around her inward currents of grief.

That evening, Amber cancelled her hotel reservation in DC and looked up the address of the Potomac Gallery in Alexandria instead. Winston's account of the disappearance wasn't right, and talking to Monty had only further convinced her of this.

She would do her own research; she would find the answers that Cheryl wanted. She could never be Dawn. She could never be as bold or expressive and probably not as brilliant, either, but she could do this for Cheryl.

Before she went to bed, she called the number of the pay phone that Monty had given her, bracing herself to hear that voice, Ms. Ella's voice. It rang and rang. No one answered.

Chapter III

SHE SET OFF on the nine-hour drive after breakfast the next morning, arriving at her Alexandria hotel around six.

The Old Town still looked the same as when Amber had first seen it, on the Stillwater school trip with Dawn and Ms. Ella, years and years ago. Moneyed. Majestic. Historical. Grand, pillared Colonial Revival mansions loomed on either side of the street. Trees tossed their heads above the cobblestones and burst the sidewalks with their bulky trunks. Pedestrians strolled to cafés and bars and shops, all of them well-groomed and beautiful, with the indifferent elegance that comes with years of wearing designer clothes. Amber felt like a misfit in her black dress and nineties-era Docs, a discount store apparition surrounded by Old Virginia money.

Back in middle school, she and Dawn had been misfits together. Dawn drew her startling pictures and stirred up trouble and ran into the woods and argued with her teachers;

Amber shambled after her, loyal but shy. Ms. Ella came along and mentored them both, and they felt understood.

But then there was the class trip to DC and Alexandria, and the scandal, and the arrest, which Dawn had blamed on Amber with all the fury she put into her drawings, refusing to speak to her again. They transferred to Peachtree High, Ms. Ella's entire class, where the other kids whispered and stared and asked them about their weird alternative school that had been on the news.

In those years when Amber was estranged from Dawn, she threw herself into books. It was a way of keeping the feeling of Stillwater School close, all those afterschool days, the long stimulating conversations with Ms. Ella and Dawn that she missed.

It had taken years for Dawn to forgive her. When she showed up on Amber's doorstep, Amber was eighteen, graduated, and had started working in bookstores. Dawn had dropped out and had a four-year-old daughter.

"Just until I get back on my feet," Dawn said, looking not at Amber but down, and whatever resentful triumph Amber felt in that moment went flat at the sight of the deep misery in Dawn's face.

"Come inside," she said.

By some unspoken rule, they never talked about Stillwater School or Ms. Ella. Maybe they both sensed that even the mention of it would tear the whole fragile thing apart. They picked up where they'd left off. Dawn might stop by the bookstore for lunch, or Amber would watch Cheryl when Dawn had to work, or whenever Dawn had one of her long, depressive, absent spells. Sometimes Cheryl would come to Amber and confide in her when she was upset with her mother, and Amber comforted her, feeling a little surge of validation.

And now, Dawn had abandoned her, had left her scrambling after answers for Cheryl on her own. Amber felt a rush of grief and resentment that propelled her the rest of the way to the Potomac Gallery.

It stood at the end of a leafy street lined with pubs and gift shops. Inside, a giant, hulking structure assembled from old circuit boards occupied the middle of the space. There was a neon pink refrigerator with its door propped open, fully stocked with replicas of grenades; an old rabbit-eared television with its screen and insides removed to reveal a miniature Nativity scene. With difficulty, Amber made her way through the crowd, searching for someone with a name tag or a clipboard.

At the back of the gallery, she saw a young woman about Cheryl's age with micro braids and a nose ring, clad in paint-spattered fatigues and a black halter top. She was working, shaping something out of clay on a small table. Every few minutes a visitor would stop to watch, sip wine, grow bored, wander off.

The woman took no notice of the spectators. Her hands kneaded the clay, stopping from time to time to work with a modelling knife. Amber watched the beginning of a bird taking shape in the brown lump, a small beak emerging, the clay slowly transforming into aerodynamic, avian lines and curves.

"I like the bird," Amber yelled over the music.

The woman cupped the hand with the knife to her ear.

"The bird," Amber yelled again, louder. "I like it."

"Thanks," the woman said. She glanced at Amber's shabby clothing. "You sculpt, too?"

"No, but I had a friend who did. Here, in residency, actually. Dawn Hallstom. You know her?"

"Dawn? Nope. It's just me and Ricky in residence this summer."

"She's not here now. She would have been here in May. Short woman, about my age. Her hair was dyed blonde."

"Wait, I do remember her." She stopped molding the clay and looked at Amber. "She had an installation she was going to do, a kitchen, but with carnivorous plants and stuff growing up out of the drains and coming out of the cabinets. I saw the plans for it. It was pretty sick, actually."

"Yes, yes, that was her," Amber said. "How long did she stay?"

"She didn't stay. She was here for like a week and then she fucked off somewhere else. Left all of her stuff. It was a waste, actually. Pretty disrespectful."

"Did she say why?"

"She didn't say anything. She kept to herself. She wasn't feeling it, I guess." The woman went back to her clay. "She wasn't all that friendly, to be honest."

"Can I see her stuff? The stuff she left?

"I mean—it was just supplies, and Ricky and I divided it all between us, since we had to clean up." She peered at Amber, suspicious now. "Why do you want to know? You her ex or something?"

"Just an old friend," Amber said. "Thank you for your time."

She checked out of her hotel early the next morning and walked around the Old Town, trying to imagine Dawn's final days in the city. She passed shops and boutiques, their window boxes spilling over with flowers and American flags. She sat in a café and watched the King Street Trolleys go by, sleek tourist buses with jaunty red siding.

She tried to match Dawn's tempo as a walker: hasty and impatient, then stopping abruptly to admire something, to grope for her digital camera or her sketchbook. She would have stopped here, Amber thought, admiring a tree that had ruptured the sidewalk around it into ruins: a symbol of irrepressible nature, a nightmare for wheelchairs and crutches and strollers. But would she have stopped here? she thought, watching tourists snap pictures in front of the Spite House. America's narrowest house was only seven feet wide, cobalt blue and cowering between its magnificent, grandly shuttered neighbors.

After lunch, she found an unoccupied bench in a shady corner of Market Square and called the pay phone number again. This time, a hoarse woman's voice answered.

"Tanya?" said the voice.

"Hi, I'm calling for a guest," Amber said. "Eleanor Hallstrom is her name."

"Who?"

"Eleanor. Ms. Ella."

"Don't know her."

"Which hotel is this?"

"Fuck off."

The woman hung up. Amber stayed on the bench for a moment, a little startled by the sound of vulgarity in this genteel cobblestone square with planters of bursting azaleas. Then she left Alexandria, as clueless as when she had entered it.

She stopped by an ATM and did a few brief calculations. She filled the gas tank and checked her maps program. Thirteen hours. It was six o'clock. She went inside the gas station and bought a coffee.

Twenty minutes later she was on I-95, heading south towards Madeira Beach.

Chapter IV

AMBER ARRIVED in Madeira Beach around eleven in the morning, after a nap and a vending machine breakfast in a rest stop outside Jacksonville.

It was a small town sandwiched in a long line of competing beach towns, each fading imperceptibly into the next like a series of dissolves in a film. A two-lane boulevard with palm trees along either side ran parallel to the water, which was visible, in glimpses, between pastel oceanfront resorts and tiki bars.

Amber stopped for lunch and coffee in a fishing village called St. John's Pass, built around a series of boardwalks that looked out over the Gulf of Mexico on one side and Boca Ciega Bay on the other. Afterward, she walked past lobster restaurants and bars filled with tourists in colorful sundresses and Hawaiian shirts. Cover bands played classic rock on outdoor stages. Flocks of seagulls flew over a horizon dotted with gaudy parasails. Amber, who had not seen Ms. Ella since she'd testified at the hearing, had a hard time picturing her scholastic, bookish middle school teacher in this noisy, neon, tropical town.

She drove up and down the boulevard on the evening of that first day, looking for pay phones to match the number Monty had given her. There were only a few remaining, their silver surfaces beaten and scratched by wind and rain, the half-booths that sheltered them covered in graffiti and stickers. Sometimes their receivers were missing, or trails of red and blue wires hung from the vandalized insides of the booth. Amber stopped at each one to study the numbers, squinting through vulgarities scrawled in Sharpie.

In this way, she learned a good deal about the rest of Madeira Beach, about the parts not pictured in the rack of snorkeling brochures and restaurant coupons at her nondescript budget hotel. She learned about the dock a few blocks from St. John's Pass where smugglers moved pot and heroin off large boats filled with netted fish, about the alley behind a convenience store where young men went to shoot up, about the short promenade on the far side of the bay where sex workers met their clients. A few people stared or asked her for money. No one seemed concerned about her presence. Her plainness was a kind of cloak that enveloped her, made her an unthreatening bystander.

After a quick dinner back at St. John's Pass, she called Cheryl.

"The store is great," Cheryl said. "I sold that copy of *Shirley* from the case. A hundred bucks. How's DC?"

"It's great." Amber cringed at the lie. "Listen, how are you hanging in there? I was thinking of staying a few extra days, doing some sightseeing."

“Sightsee away. There’s nothing happening here. I like to be in the store. I’ve been looking at that series of still lifes she was doing. The three on the wall.”

“She was going to do a miniature next,” Amber said, remembering. “She was looking for examples in the catalogues.”

“Miniatures. I like to think of that.”

“Me too,” said Amber.

She found the right phone around nine that night, in the parking lot of a cheap motel. The number on the front matched the number Monty had given her. She returned early the next morning to investigate.

Madeira Beach Motel, the sign read. *Extended Stay Rates.* Below it was a blinking neon sign: *Free Ca le T* . The *b* and the *V* were dark, leaving the sign like a mouth with missing teeth. Just under it was a parked Honda coupe with its engine idling. Two gaunt, sleepy-looking women in cutoffs and scuffed heels leaned in the driver’s side window, talking to a man in sunglasses. The motel itself was a grey, two-story building that faced away from the street, as if turning its back on the world.

Amber parked and walked around the pool to the checkout office.

She rapped twice on the Dutch door with the sign that read OWNER HAS NO ACCESS TO SAFE. The top half swung open and a disheveled, copper-haired woman about Amber’s age, in bare feet and a bathrobe, leaned out. Behind her Amber saw an overstuffed filing cabinet and, on top of it, a monitor flashing black-and-white security footage of the dismal parking lot. Beyond this makeshift office was a messy room with an unmade bed and a television playing loud cartoons. Two little girls sat on the bed, still in their pajamas, staring at Amber with wide, silent eyes.

"No room right now," the woman said. "Come back at noon."

"Oh," Amber said. "I'm not checking in."

"You checking out?"

"No, no. I'm looking for a guest."

The woman's eyes narrowed.

"You a Jesuit?"

"What?"

"You the police?"

"What? No. I'm an old friend—"

The top half of the door slammed shut. Amber waited a moment, knocked one more time, and gave up. She walked around the motel's perimeter, past railings covered in drying swimsuits, past doors and curtains closed sullenly against the day. The pool area was kind of pretty, even inviting: a flat, blue plane of water sparkling in the late morning sun; a deck paved with orange and green and blue Talavera tiles. But there were no children's toys, only empty bottles and cigarette butts on the low tables around the pool. Staticky FM radio played from an old boom box plugged into an extension cord that stretched across the walkway and disappeared into the check-in office.

On the other side of the pool, she noticed a curtainless room with yellow caution tape stretched across the open doorway. The bed and walls were bare. A tattooed man in a white T-shirt, long basketball shorts, and yellow latex gloves was spraying air freshener on a sooty carpet. He noticed her watching.

"Fire," he said. "Some asshole fell asleep smoking. Burned down the bed."

Amber clutched the doorframe.

"Is she okay?"

"He's fine. Minor burns. Got out of the hospital and fucked off somewhere else. Didn't pay his bill, either. Left all his shit here. Now because of this asshole we have to start a non-smoking policy in the rooms."

Amber relaxed. She detected an accent. Eastern European, maybe. He jerked his head toward the pool. She noticed a small golden cross dangling around his neck, catching and reflecting the light.

"You wanna smoke, you got to go over there. You smoke in your room, you get kicked out."

If Ms. Ella was still a smoker—and Amber felt somehow certain that she was—then she would have to come outside. Amber found a tattered paperback under the passenger seat of her car, settled herself into a filthy chaise lounge, and devoted herself to a morning of waiting.

For the first hour, nothing stirred except for a few darting geckos.

Around ten, there were signs of life in some of the rooms. She heard televisions switch on, toilets flush. A few guests trickled out to sit by the pool and smoke. Amber was surprised at their deference to the motel's new rule.

The first and earliest smoker was a skinny man in his twenties with a mullet and sunglasses. Then there was a trio of women in hot pants, loudly complaining about another woman named Rose, and after them a lone man in a black suit and gold chain whose red eyes glanced at Amber so sorrowfully that she had to look away.

As morning changed to afternoon, the sun high and bright, she worried that she wouldn't recognize Ms. Ella, that the years had changed them both too much. But when she came through the rusting pool gate, Amber knew her immediately. She wore a blue sweatshirt that read TAMPA BAY across the front, cargo shorts with a maze of pockets, and cheap flip flops. Her hair was loose and bore the shades of many fading dyes. Dark roots mixed with patches of red and blonde, framing a face that had that distinctive tan of beach residents: deep and permanent, making her skin look tough and impenetrable. From a crumpled soft pack of Camels she selected one, put it between her lips, and lit it, with some difficulty, against the light breeze that swept across the lot.

Amber studied her, trying to identify the feeling that rose up in her chest. The last time she'd seen Ms. Ella, she was fourteen and had just testified against her to the district attorney. Afterwards, she followed her mother to the parking lot next to the courthouse. Ms. Ella came out onto the courthouse steps and lit a cigarette. She was talking to her lawyer, a tall guy in a suit, laughing at something he'd said and gesturing energetically. None of what had happened, either at Stillwater School or in the courtroom, seemed to have changed her. She just stood there, vibrant and indomitable. Amber stared.

"Come on," her mother had snapped, grabbing her hand.

The woman who sat in front of her now in a beach chair, puffing distractedly, seemed small and vulnerable: her posture hunched and defensive, her body hidden in bulky clothing. Amber approached her.

"Ms. Ella."

The woman squinted at Amber. The dark brown of her eyes, the startling black irises, jolted Amber with their familiarity. She sat down on a deck chair.

"Do you remember me?"

Ms. Ella looked at her for a long time, not moving, not smoking, so that a gray cylinder of ash formed at the tip of her cigarette. Her fingernails were too long and the nailbeds were discolored.

"You a Jesuit?"

"Excuse me?"

"You here to serve? Mission work?

"What? No." Amber leaned forward. "I was one of your students, at Stillwater. In the nineties. In Atlanta. I was a friend of Dawn's. Your daughter-in-law."

Ms. Ella closed her eyes. Under her breath, she hummed a little.

"Ms. Ella." Amber reached out and touched her shoulder. Those eyes opened and looked back at her.

"Did my son send you?"

"No. I offered to come."

"I do have a son."

Amber thought she saw a tear in the crease of the left eyelid. "It's okay. It's been a long time. I—"

"I just don't know you," Ms. Ella said louder. The man

with the cross was moving around the parking lot, sweeping trash into a dustpan. He looked up.

"Then maybe we could start over," Amber said.

Ms. Ella gazed blankly while Amber talked. She explained who she was again, and what Stillwater was. She watched Ms. Ella steadily, testing which of her words or memories might call forth a flicker of recognition, an answering signal of remembrance.

None came. Instead, something strange was happening to the eyes. They were fixed on Amber, brown and focused, but as she continued talking their expression seemed to retreat inward. Then, as Amber transitioned to talking about Dawn's marriage and art career, even this expression vanished and left just a pair of uncomprehending pupils. Amber thought of a cold bird, ruffling its feathers as it sat on a branch, its ruff growing bigger, its neck and shoulders disappearing.

When Amber finished abruptly, too wary to mention Dawn's death, Ms. Ella looked back with an expression so open, so fearful, that it made her feel an invigorating and sharp sense of cruelty.

"Okay," Amber said at last. "I've bothered you enough today. Thanks for your time. I'll come back tomorrow. Would that be okay?"

"Do whatever you want," Ms. Ella said, standing up. "Everyone here does. Why shouldn't you?"

That evening, back in her hotel room, she allowed herself to feel her disappointment for a brief, foolish moment. She felt the old jealousy. Some part of her had wanted to see that Ms. Ella remembered her, just as much as she remembered Dawn. But she had forgotten them both. She had forgotten everything.

Amber started to call Monty but changed her mind. Instead, she spent an hour googling terms like "memory loss" and "disorientation" and came up with a list of symptoms for dementia. A caregiver's website gave a list of suggestions:

1. *Talk to your loved one in a quiet environment.*
2. *If possible, talk to your loved one in the morning. Early mornings are better for many people who suffer from dementia.*
3. *Don't try to do too much at once.*
4. *If your loved one gets upset, or defensive, change the subject and move on to something more positive.*
5. *Ask simple questions with yes/no answers.*
6. *Show visuals if you can.*

Visuals. Amber wasn't on social media herself, but she ran accounts for the bookstore. A quick search of a few Stillwater names turned up pages with privacy settings. Then Amber remembered a chance encounter at a Waffle House with her old classmate Tracy, who had become—what was it?—an influencer, Tracy had said over a plate of hash browns, narrowing her pencil-darkened eyebrows. She had looked officiously at Amber's bare face, suggested fuller brows and a smoky eye.

Amber clicked on Tracy's page. True to form, she had no privacy settings. Her feed was a jumble of makeup brands, product reviews, and inspirational quotes. A collage of strained vitality.

Amber clicked on "Photos." Tracy had scanned school pictures of herself from every grade, ascending from innocent kindergartener to louche marketing graduate of an online university. Amber kept clicking, found a group photo from Stillwater, and saved it.

She went back to the motel on the following morning, a bright day where the heat made everything shimmer and the blue water of the pool was still. The air conditioners in the rooms rattled and dripped warm puddles onto the scorched concrete.

Ms. Ella sat in a chair under a faded green umbrella, in the same sweatshirt, with the same crumpled pack of Camels and a tattered notebook in her lap. She seemed to remember Amber's visit the day before and did not object when Amber sat beside her at the table and opened her laptop.

"I thought we could look at a picture together."

The picture showed their entire Stillwater class on the end-of-the-year trip, standing in front of the Washington Monument, squinting into the sun. There was Jamal, in one of his horizontally striped shirts, a fanny pack around his waist; Tracy, wearing wrist bangles and lip gloss; Dawn, down in the front, on one jeaned knee. Amber was with the tall kids in the back, between Kayla and Ms. Ella, who was grinning and rambunctious in a gray blazer and white Nike high tops. Everyone wore the expressions of concentration and focused happiness typical of a pre-digital world, when you only had one or two tries to get the picture right.

"I want to show you some people." Amber enlarged the photograph and moved over the faces, one by one. "These are your former students. This is me, when I was thirteen. I was bookish and liked to read. You used to encourage me, give me different books to read and write about on my own. I still do it. This is you. You took us on a trip up the eastern seaboard, at the end of the school year."

Ms. Ella peered at the screen and nodded, the self contemplating the self. The morning did seem to be a better time. Amber moved on.

"This is Jamal. He was the smartest one of all of us. He studied international relations in college and became a diplomat, I heard. This is Tracy. She was always into fashion. She's starting her own makeup brand now, I think. Cruelty-free. And this is Dawn. She and I were best friends. Dawn was an artist. Her first big art project was for your class. Cassandra, the priestess from *Agamemnon*. It used to sit on the windowsill. She never finished it."

Amber stopped. Ms. Ella was nodding.

"You remember her?"

"I remember her. It's finished."

"What's finished?" Amber said, startled.

"The Cassandra. I have her now." Ms. Ella was still nodding, vigorously. "It's all done. She came down here to finish it."

Chapter V

"MS. ELLA didn't have many visitors after Dawn left," said the man who cleaned the motel. "She just kind of holed herself up. Stopped coming out."

His name was Yuri, and he had emigrated to Tampa from Moscow twenty years before with his family, when he was still a boy. Now he did maintenance and repairs for two Madeira Beach motels, in exchange for wages and free rooms, and he was in recovery.

He told Amber all this as they walked together in the residential neighborhood behind the motel. After Amber showed Ms. Ella the picture, Ms. Ella grew frustrated and went inside. Amber looked up to see Yuri with his broom, openly eavesdropping because of the names he had heard, the names they kept repeating, Dawn and Cassandra. Amber, at a loss, had explained her grim mission. Yuri took the news of Dawn's death with the philosophical equilibrium of someone who had lost many people—three to overdoses alone, he said, including one woman who was a close friend, but then he looked away and changed the subject back to the art object. The Cassandra.

"The only people who came to see Ms. Ella were the Jesuits, Maria and Caleb. They do mission work here sometimes. They're radical Jesuits, not what you would expect. Haven't been around much lately. But they take people to run errands, to chapel, to recovery meetings, stuff like that. Most people don't socialize around here. Not with each other, anyway. So it was kind of cool when Dawn came down to work on it. Made it feel like people really lived here. Like a community."

He described it: the art station Dawn had set up with wooden boards and tarps in the clearing behind the motel, the statue base she had formed out of wire. She started working in the morning, before the sun was too high, when the little clearing looked cool and pure in the shade.

"At first, she worked on it alone. I stopped by every morning to look at it while I was doing the rounds."

"She just left it out there? No one messed with it?"

Yuri shook his head.

"No one messed with it. She put it in the shed, at night. But we wouldn't have done anything to it. We liked that she was there, working on it. In a mask and stuff. Looking like a scientist. It was interesting."

"Why?"

He looked off across the shallow lake to the right of the road. The shoreline wound alongside the pavement as if the two were in an elaborate dance, road and lake, lake and road, stepping in tandem past inlets filled with torpedo grass and over small hills that rose and fell, weaving in and out of the rhythm. Geckos clutched the sides of boat docks, forming momentary friezes. On the far shore of the lake was a busy gas station, its lot filled with scorching, glittering cars. A lone heron picked its way along a guard rail. Just behind it, a man pumped gas into a large red Chevy.

"There's nothing good here," Yuri said finally. "Nothing grows here. Look at this lake. Half the fish are dead. Look where the gas and oil runs off, over there, under that guard rail. Look at this whole state. Erosion and drought. Storms. The ocean's getting higher. All these shorelines will be gone, one day. Soon. But while she was working on it, it was like something good was happening, like something was making progress here. I know that probably seems stupid to you."

"It doesn't."

"You live in a big city, right? You have arty shit you can go see all the time. We don't have that here. While she was working on the Cassandra, it was right at our doorstep. I liked talking to her about it. And she *talked* like a normal person. She wasn't stuffy. I could relate to her."

He described the project's stages: the application of the foil, the mixing of the clay, the slow beginnings of Cassandra's face and limbs. Amber pictured it, translating his description into what she herself knew of Dawn's work. The Cassandra would have grown feverishly, ever thicker and more substantial.

"She finished it in the morning, a few weeks ago," Yuri said. "Once she finished it, it was like she didn't care about it. She put it in Ms. Ella's room and fucked off. Never said goodbye to anyone."

"She could be like that," Amber said. "Temperamental."

Yuri shook his head.

"It wasn't that. Temperamental is fine. Lots of people here are temperamental. But it seemed like she just hated it. She said if anything ever happened to Ms. Ella she wanted me to throw it away. All of a sudden it was just for her and Ms. Ella. It had been something for all of us, but then it wasn't. She didn't want anyone getting near it."

They had reached the dead end where the road stopped and the lake began. They stood on the grassy slope and looked across the water at the gas station, at the heron. Its feathers were pale gray, its beak long and yellow, its head plume black and sporty, like a racing stripe. It perched on the far end of the guard rail and stared down into the water, searching for fish.

"So then what?"

"That's it." Yuri shrugged. "Ms. Ella has it. She won't let anybody see it. Not me, not the Jesuits, nobody. When Maria and Caleb come now, she makes them wait outside. She's very jealous about it. I guess she knows it'll be worth something. Especially now. When you tell her that Dawn's dead."

Amber thought of the Cassandra, locked away. Across the lake, the Chevy pulled away and a battered Ford took its place at the pump. The heron had stopped looking into the water and was looking directly across the lake. It took a small step forward and raised its wings, as if daring them to jump.

Chapter VI

After her walk with Yuri, Amber knocked on Ms. Ella's door and asked to see the Cassandra statue. But Yuri was right: Ms. Ella was strangely protective of the statue, and of the other sketches Dawn had done during her brief stay in Madeira Beach, when the rest of her family thought she was in Alexandria.

"No," she said curtly and shut the door in Amber's face. Amber waited and knocked again. No answer.

She returned to the pool to wait. Half an hour later, Ms. Ella came out with a folder of papers and sat down at a dirty table. She began to shuffle through them with her back to Amber.

"What's all this?" Amber said, moving to a seat across from her.

"It's something else," Ms. Ella said. "A new project." She gave Amber a furtive glance and slid the folder across the table. "You can look at it, if you want."

Amber opened the folder and sifted through the contents: page after page of Ms. Ella's cramped, left-handed cursive, the same handwriting that Amber remembered from Stillwater but messier now, smudged with coffee stains, redolent of ash. All the pages were loose and only some of them were numbered at the top. Many of them were scratched out entirely, giant Xs drawn across whole paragraphs, with arrows connecting some sentences to others, farther down on the page.

"What is this?"

"It's a relic," Ms. Ella said with a strange laugh.

"A relic of what?"

"It's my book. My new book. I want to put the pages in order. They were in order."

Her gaze wandered to the potted palm in the corner of the pool area. It was so tall that it seemed to rocket out of its dirty pot, defying the cigarette butts that littered its soil, the chemical vapors of the pool.

"But they got out of order." Ms. Ella lit a cigarette. "You can help me put it back together again."

"I don't know, Ms. Ella." Amber picked up the first page and squinted at the writing, trying to make out the words. It seemed to be a paragraph about history, about the Tocobaga chiefdom of Old Tampa Bay, but then it veered into an anecdote from Ms. Ella's own school days, something about teacher training. "I can't tell what it's about."

"You're smart, I remember. You'll figure it out."

Amber saw that there would be no Cassandra without the book and so, for an hour, she tried. She sorted through five pages of what seemed to be an introduction. It began, "The hurricane of 1848 was the fiercest to hit Tampa Bay. It tore Pinellas in half and ripped the area we call St. John's Pass out of the coastline."

Amber read further. The next few paragraphs continued to describe the destruction of the hurricane, but on page three the writing shifted into an account of the Spanish-American War, fifty years later.

"The Cuban cigar workers in Ybor City wanted a free Cuba," Ms. Ella had written. Then she seemed to become aware that the sentence had come too soon, that there was more to tell before it, but she was unable to find her way back to the original idea. The prose continued with its account of the Cuban independence movement, growing more strident as if to beat the confusion back into a corner, to badger it with noise. As she sat by the pool Amber felt hot, stifled. The air around her grew thick with incomprehensible language. She had a sense that Ms. Ella's words were floating off of the page and circling confusedly in the late afternoon light. All the while Ms. Ella was muttering and going through the rest of the papers in the folder, sometimes interrupting Amber to show her another part of the work, a page she seemed to think would solve everything, as she thrust it into her lap.

At six Ms. Ella stood up, gathered up the folders, and said she was going to bed. "You'll come back," she told Amber. Except she called Amber *Amy*, and looked confused. Amber nodded.

She drove down to St. John's Pass and ate a slice of pizza on a patio filled with plastic furniture, watching the seagulls dive at the trash cans. Afterwards, she found a quiet corner of the boardwalk near a closed parasail rental shop and called Cheryl.

"How's DC?" Cheryl asked.

"It's fine. I saw some historical artifacts today." Strictly speaking, Amber thought, this was true. "How's the store?"

"The store's fine. Slow. But I had an idea for something. I was talking to my friend Edie."

Amber tried to pick Edie's face and name out of the dozen friends Cheryl had introduced her to at the graduation party.

"From the Peachtree Collaborative art space. The owner knows Mom's work from the mural and said we could do an art show to commemorate her. I asked if we could do it the seventh of September. Her birthday."

"That's fantastic, Cheryl."

"I think so too. It just feels like I'm actually doing something, you know? Something she would have liked. I've got commitments from three different local artists who know her work and are going to do homage-type pieces—real, imaginative ones, nothing sappy. I want to include some of her more recent work too, though. Something new."

"Maybe I can find something," Amber said. She thought of the hidden statue, suddenly invigorated.

"I'd like that. Newer stuff would be great."

Armed with a new energy, Amber drove back to the motel. The rooms were alive now, glowing with lamplight, as the noise of laughter and music and television drifted into the parking lot. Ms. Ella was waiting by the pool, her face obscured in the twilight. Amber could just make out her shadowy figure in the dark by the glow of her cigarette. She set down Ms. Ella's takeout order, a plastic container of lobster bisque.

Ms. Ella passed her another batch of papers, this one held together by a blackened rubber band. Amber's heart sank.

"What is this?"

"The next packet."

"The next packet?" She caught Ms. Ella's wrist. "How many more packets like this do you have?"

"Twelve. Maybe ten."

"Listen, Ms. Ella," she said firmly, leaning close to her in the darkness so that she could meet her eye. "I will help you with this. I will. But I want you to let me take the statue of Cassandra that Dawn made while she was here."

"I can't let you do that. She didn't want anyone to have it, except for me."

"I know. But Cheryl is really interested in it. You and Cheryl get along, I know. Monty told me you had reconnected. She'd like to include the statue in the memorial."

"What memorial?"

A chill ran through Amber's chest. She had spoken quickly, without thinking. She took a deep breath.

"Ms. Ella," she said. "It's a memorial for Dawn. That's what I came down here to tell you. She's passed away."

"Why don't you just ask her for permission first?" Ms. Ella said.

"Ms. Ella." Amber set the papers down and moved her chair closer. "I can't do that. She's passed away. I'm so sorry, Ella."

This time, she understood. She was quiet for a long time, staring into the pool while Amber talked, unnerved, into the silence. She told her about Winston's phone call, and the pills, and the funeral, and the last conversation she'd had with Dawn. When Ms. Ella looked up at last, her eyes were wet, teary.

"But why?" she said.

Amber stayed by the pool for an hour, talking, as the sun set and more guests began to gather around the water. She told Ms. Ella about the life Dawn had had in those years after Stillwater, after showing up on Amber's doorstep. She told her about Winston, and the mural by the MARTA station, and the job at Easel, and the series of still lifes Dawn had painted for the bookstore.

In turn, Ms. Ella shared some of her memories of Dawn in the time of Dawn and Amber's estrangement. She told a story about a walk she and Dawn had taken in Centennial Olympic Park that ended at the Etowah Mounds, about forty miles northwest of Atlanta. Amber suspected that these had been different events, but she listened anyway and filled in whatever details Ms. Ella couldn't.

"It wasn't a bad life, and she wasn't unhappy," Amber said, for the third time. Ms. Ella was holding an unlit cigarette in her palm like a lucky charm.

"And Cheryl?" she asked.

"Devastated," Amber said. "But she wants to put on a benefit show in her mom's honor. And it would mean a lot to her if she could include the statue. And anything else Dawn worked on while she was here."

Ms. Ella shook her head. "I can't just give it away. Especially not now. She wanted me to keep it. I can't go back on someone's last wishes."

Amber sighed. "Let me take a picture, then. For Cheryl."

"Yes," Ms. Ella said, after a moment. "A picture. For Cheryl."

Chapter VII

AMBER WENT to get her camera. When she returned, Yuri was standing on the walkway, pulling an overstuffed trash bag out of a can. He called out to Ms. Ella, who was standing in front of her door, fiddling with her key card.

"You okay, Ms. Ella?" he called out.

"Fine, Yuri," she muttered, whacking the card against the sensor a few more times. Amber took it from her, turned it around, and tried again. The door opened with a click and a beep.

"Don't forget to run your air conditioning, okay, Ms. Ella?" Yuri called after them. "It keeps the other rooms cool, too."

Ms. Ella ignored him.

Amber followed her into the room. It was hot and close. An unmade bed, half-covered in books and papers, dominated the right side of the room. Empty cans and cups were littered across the dresser and the nightstand. Sheets of paper, covered in a tight, illegible scrawl, hung from the walls.

Amber remembered the Stillwater classroom, those many long afternoons after school with Dawn and Ms. Ella, surrounded by that writing.

She went to the air conditioning unit in the kitchenette window and switched it on. A blast of cold, belabored air filled the room and set the dust dancing in little eddies.

"Don't listen to him. It's my goddamn room," Ms. Ella said, coughing. She switched off the unit. "I don't like that cold air. It hurts my lungs. And it blows my papers everywhere."

Ms. Ella's room did indeed seem to be in motion: the paper sheets lifting themselves gently from the walls, the loose notebook pages on the kitchen table rising and drifting down to rest on the worn linoleum.

"It's back here," Ms. Ella said.

She led Amber to a small corner behind a jutting wall where a dresser or large cupboard must have once stood. Now it was empty save for a small table.

On this small table, elevated by a stack of ancient Florida phone books, stood Dawn's statue of Cassandra.

She was about two feet tall, grey-bodied, with muscled arms and long tresses sculpted down her back. Her arms were outstretched and her lips drawn back in prophecy. Her eyes flared and rolled back in her head.

It was an arresting statue, made with skill; Amber, thinking back to the first Cassandra, admired the confidence of the mature sculptor's hand, the hand that had lovingly shaped those little details: the slight dimples in the back of her elbows, the curls along her brow, the rippling folds of her tunic.

Amber's eyes wandered along the draping of the tunic. In places, through the white clay, she glimpsed faint patterns in the paper: hints of pinecones and roses, suggestions of hexagons. She bent forward to look more closely. The images, whatever they were, were faint, like the reflection of the stained glass windows on the faces of Dawn's funeral guests.

Then Amber saw a hint of a bright green blossom on a trailing, emerald cluster of vines and felt a stab of panicked recognition in her stomach. She stared. The Cassandra stared back, her gaze blazing, her mouth passionate and grotesque. Amber was still and silent for so long that Ms. Ella grew impatient.

"Well? Aren't you going to take the picture?"

She raised the camera to her eye, aimed, and snapped. She moved to the side of the statue for a profile shot and knelt down to get a low-angle one.

She realized that her hands were trembling.

"I'm done," she said. She had only taken five pictures. She wanted, right then, to be as far away from the room as possible.

Ms. Ella seemed to share her wish. "All right, you got what you came for," she said. "Come back tomorrow. Send me pictures of the show. I wish I could talk to Cheryl," she added, her eyes misting over, "but my health is not good."

It was dark outside, and riotous. Guests stood around the pool talking loudly, some of them arguing, some of them clinking bottles together; no one was swimming. Beyond their noise frogs croaked amid the trees, a low, grunting bass line under the high shrieking of crickets.

Yuri was standing a few feet away from her parking space, pushing a cart of towels and cleaners into the shed. He stopped when he saw her.

"What did you think?"

"It's good." Amber groped for her keys, frantic.

He looked at her closely. "Well it might not be a masterpiece," he said, "but could you do better?"

She started the engine.

"All right," he said through her open window, as she pulled away. "See you tomorrow. Text me one of those pictures when you get a chance. Don't forget."

"I won't," she said.

She drove to St. John's Pass. The bars were full of music and light; the air smelled of salt and pizza and fish. Tourists in sandals and T-shirts strolled the boardwalks. Children screamed, ran in and out of arcades. Two police cars idled in the parking lot, their drivers leaning out of the windows to talk. Amber drove by slowly, her heart thumping.

She grabbed her camera and made her way down to the bike path that stretched across the black water. The water was choppy: tomorrow, a storm would come. Already she could see the currents throwing spray against the piers; already, she could sense the deadly, hateful rush of the bay.

She released the memory card from the camera. It felt flimsy and light in her palm.

She raised her arm and hurled it overhand into the water.

A flock of gulls flew screaming overhead, denouncing her crime.

Back in the car, she dialed Cheryl's number.

"Hey." Cheryl's voice was puzzled. "Everything okay?"

"Everything's fine. I just wanted to tell you I can open the store tomorrow."

"Already? Did you come back early?"

"I'm on my way now," Amber said. Only then did she realize she had stopped shaking. "I'm on my way home."

Part Three:

Atlanta and Madeira Beach,
1993–2012

Chapter I

Atlanta, 2012

THE TROUBLE had begun on the morning of Cheryl's high school graduation.

Like much trouble, in Dawn's experience, it began with a call. Cheryl's phone on the kitchen counter, buzzing. Cheryl herself in the bathroom, getting ready. Dawn saw the 813 area code and grabbed the phone on instinct. That voice. Dawn, already dressed tastefully in snug black trousers and a low-necked white blouse, a thin strand of silver beads around her throat, felt herself slide through the device and back to age sixteen when she heard it. She stood up taller, gripped the counter for support. She was thirty-five.

"Dawn?" the voice was saying. "I didn't call for you. I called to wish Cheryl a happy graduation."

"How did you get this number? Did Monty give it to you?"

"I just called to say happy graduation." The voice was flat, unresponsive to the ire in Dawn's own. "She's my granddaughter."

"Don't ever call here again," Dawn said. "Stay away from her."

Dawn hung up. Cheryl was standing in the kitchen doorway, in the sleeveless blue dress she and Dawn had bought together, her skin red from heat and temper.

"How dare you answer MY PHONE!" she said. She marched across the kitchen in her bare feet, the force of her stride making her heels thunk and toes slap against the tiles, and snatched the phone out of her mother's hand. She squinted at the screen.

"813? Who *was* that?"

Dawn and Cheryl had long ago made a pact to never lie to one another. The pact began when Cheryl was in middle school. Dawn had found a week's worth of detention slips in her backpack, all of them with forged signatures. There had been a screaming match, a reconciliation, and a long talk. The mother and daughter had agreed that they would keep no secrets and make no judgments.

Ever since, Cheryl had told Dawn about all of her friends, her coming out, her girlfriends and hookups, the parties she went to. Dawn, in turn, had been honest when she and Winston had started growing apart, and about her tense relationship with her own father. All throughout high school, these exchanges had fostered an openness and equality between the two that was the envy of Cheryl's friends.

Dawn regretted it now.

"It was your grandmother. Monty's mother. She was calling to wish you a happy graduation."

"And you wouldn't let her talk to me? What the fuck? I'm calling her back right now." Cheryl hit redial.

"No you aren't," Dawn said, moving to grab the phone. Cheryl stepped quickly through the small living area, flung the door open, and went out onto the stoop, frowning.

"Hi, can I speak to Grandma?" she said. "Ella. Eleanor. What do you mean? Can you go get her? Oh. Okay. Fine."

She hung up, came back inside, and threw her phone on the couch. "That number is for a *pay phone* and now I'll never get to talk to her unless she calls back, which she won't, because of you. My own grandmother!"

Wisely, Dawn kept silent, recognizing the peak of her daughter's anger in the way she opened and slammed the closet door when she got her shoes out, the outbursts that followed in the car on the way to the auditorium. But as Cheryl's phone buzzed with text messages and she typed rapidly in response, her fury subsided. By the time she was in line, waiting to receive her robe and cap and surrounded by friends, she seemed to have forgotten about the fight.

Dawn had not. Distracted, she took her seat in the upper part of the auditorium, alone, only seeing Amber, Monty, and Winston sitting farther below when it was too late. The throng of parents and relatives was too dense for her to make her way down to them. She was pensive throughout the ceremony as each blue-robed figure crossed the stage, perking up only when Cheryl's name was called.

She had not heard Ms. Ella's voice in thirteen years.

Monty, to her knowledge, had kept his grudge. He'd sent his mother a check after the sale of the house and redirected her mail. In recent years there had been something of a détente, by post: a birthday card, once; a brief letter exchange about the sale of the orange grove and the part of the proceeds Ms. Ella wanted to contribute to Cheryl's college savings.

But never a call.

After the ceremony, she searched for Monty but lost track of him in the chaos of hooting, happy graduates lining themselves up for pictures and sorting themselves into cars. It wasn't until she was standing in the familiar kitchen of her old house with Winston, in a circle that included Monty, Cheryl, and Lucy, that Dawn heard the dreaded reference. They had all just toasted and drunk an inch of champagne from their plastic cups. Cheryl said, looking straight at Monty: "Guess who called today? *Grandma.*"

"Who?" Monty's shock was genuine.

"But Mom answered it and I didn't get to talk to her. Can you imagine?" She rolled her eyes theatrically—for Lucy's benefit, Dawn thought. "My own mother! Keeping me from my aging grandmother who loves me. All because of some old feud that nobody remembers."

"Fireworks!" Winston's voice called from the front porch. "Everyone outside!"

When the girls were out of earshot, Dawn turned on Monty.

"Did you give her Cheryl's number?"

"Of course not. What the fuck? I don't want that woman anywhere near my daughter."

"If you didn't give her Cheryl's number, then who did?"

"She probably looked online or asked someone and they found it for her." He rubbed his eyes. "I need to think."

"We could take her phone away. You could call your mom and tell her to stay away from her."

Monty thought about this for a while, slouching against the counter. "No," he said at last. "Cheryl's like you. Stubborn. If we let it go, if we pretend we don't care, she might drop it."

The following weekend, when Dawn and Winston were helping Cheryl and Lucy move into their studio apartment, Cheryl's phone rang. She went out onto the back stoop to answer it. Dawn was left to steer half of the sofa through the narrow front door, backwards. Winston held up the other end, while Lucy, frail and already exhausted in a sweaty white shirt and cutoffs, gave a series of incoherent instructions from inside the living room.

"Left. But catty-corner," she was yelling as Dawn concentrated, trying to hear Cheryl's conversation. "Like, tilted. Not to the left, to the right. Can you tilt it but also lift? Like a lift-tilt?"

Now Winston took over, issuing booming, solicitous instructions from the other side of the doorway, his shoulders pressed against the sofa arms. Dawn gave up on eavesdropping. When Cheryl came in, twenty minutes later, she said, "Well? And how is she?"

"She's fine." Cheryl went into the kitchen, opened the refrigerator, and took out a plastic bottle of water. Drank. Said, "She's over that bronchitis or whatever she had."

"Still smoking," Dawn said. "You've talked to her before."

"Last Saturday. We're going to talk again next Saturday. The Jesuits remind her."

Winston came into the kitchen, breathing heavily, sweat blotching his gray shirt.

"What Jesuits?" he said, to his stepdaughter.

"The radical Jesuits who do good deeds," Cheryl said mysteriously, not wanting to get Winston involved.

Dawn thought about it for two weeks. She thought about it during one of her "spells," as Amber called them, when she withdrew from everyone and everything and stayed at home. She thought about what she would tolerate.

A visit would be one thing. Dawn could take Cheryl down to Madeira Beach for that, could meet her ex-mother-in-law in a lobster restaurant that overlooked the water. They would sit in the restaurant, she and her daughter and Ms. Ella, who was now in her sixties and emphysemic from decades of smoking. They would all be holding silver lobster crackers in their hands and their fingers would gleam with butter. Cheryl would gush, eager to discover shared memories, searching for traces of her origins in this woman she had not seen since she was a toddler.

And Dawn already knew how that conversation would end. With Ms. Ella, still brilliant and commanding somehow, even in poor health, regaling Cheryl with tales of triumph and persecution. Cheryl would be swept up in the drama of it, and Dawn would have to talk her down, afterwards, in the car.

A supervised visit would be one thing, Dawn thought.

The bigger problem was that Cheryl was eighteen and could go see her grandmother anytime she wanted to. Dawn had no legal right to stop her. And now everyone had a phone, all the time, everywhere. Ms. Ella didn't, Dawn was sure of this, but

Cheryl did, and Ms. Ella had the number. They could email. And all this contact would bring about what Dawn feared the most. Ms. Ella's voice would get into Cheryl's head, poison her thinking, poison her art.

And what could she do? Go to the police? The charges against Ms. Ella were twenty years old now, and she had never raised a hand to Cheryl, never even threatened her.

Dawn wandered through Piedmont Park one morning with unbrushed teeth and hair, past groups of joggers and skateboarders, past squirrels scrambling for acorns and chimney swifts pecking and flitting in the magnolia bushes. She imagined the scenario.

Officer, I have a problem, she would begin. My mother-in-law wants to talk to my daughter.

The officer's slow gaze would move over Monty first, over tattoos that could never quite be hidden under long sleeves and collars, then over Dawn, with her GED and psychiatric history and bouts of unemployment.

Officer, you don't understand, she would say. She's a threat.

How many times has she contacted your daughter?

Three times. That we know of. So far.

The officer's eyes would drop, the hand with the pen coming to rest on top of the clipboard. The phones would be trilling. Real cases: gun violence, domestic assaults.

If you would just take a seat back out in the waiting room, the officer would begin.

Dawn would not let her daughter be chained to that voice, all of her beautiful independence lost. Her self-esteem. Her future.

She thought about calling Amber, took out her phone and put it away again. That was not a truth she had told, would ever tell, even though she knew Amber had her suspicions.

There was nothing to be done. Dawn bided her time, took Monty's advice, and dropped it, at least around Cheryl. It was the beginning of the summer. The days stretched out long and warm, the outdoor concerts and festivals were beginning, and the streets were bursting with dogwoods. Cheryl was living on her own for the first time, no longer at Winston's or Dawn's, still working at the coffee shop, getting her portfolio together, exploring the city without curfews or classes to stand in her way.

In this, at least, Monty was right: when Dawn dropped it, Cheryl dropped it too. She had her mother's zest for confrontation and vengeance; obscure, smothered hostilities were not her style.

One Sunday afternoon, the week before Dawn started her residency at the Alexandria gallery, Cheryl left her phone sitting on the kitchen table at the new apartment to go help Lucy hang a painting. Dawn grabbed it, entered Ms. Ella's number in her own phone, and replaced it.

Over the next week, from her hotel room in Alexandria, Dawn called the pay phone in Madeira Beach five times, to no avail. On the sixth time, she finally got a hold of someone who went and knocked on Ms. Ella's door.

"It's you! You know I was going to call on Saturday," came Ms. Ella's voice on the line, a little anxious. Dawn had given Cheryl's name instead of her own. "Is everything okay?"

"It's me, Ms. Ella."

There was a long silence. Then Dawn heard the flick of a lighter, a deep inhale.

"I want you to listen to me," Dawn said.

"I thought you might call."

"I'm her mother. I want you to stay away from her."

"Listen. My son has forgiven me." Privately, Dawn doubted this. "It's been thirteen years. I'm not going to keep shaming myself. You and I can have our differences. But you can't cut me out of my granddaughter's life. She has nothing to do with any of that."

"And that's how it's going to stay. You're going to stop contacting her."

"You can't make me."

"I'm going to come to Florida," Dawn said, "and we are going to discuss this until you understand."

"There's nothing to discuss. I'm her grandmother."

"I'm coming to Florida," Dawn said again.

There was another long silence. Then: "Fine. It's the Madeira Beach Motel. Room 126. You'll have to get your own room." She hung up.

Chapter II

Atlanta, 1993

DAWN'S OWN CONSPIRACY with Ms. Ella had begun after the hearing, in the fall of her first year at Peachtree High.

Hot mornings stretched, catlike, into humid afternoons. The scarlet oaks in the square blazed and dropped plump brown acorns on the sidewalks. People walked slowly in the shade underneath, holding soft drinks and iced coffees in sweating plastic cups. The buses in the station sat wheezing, releasing gusts of air conditioning each time the doors folded back to admit a passenger.

It was four o'clock, and Dawn was sitting alone at the counter of the Cheesy Slice, staring at her English textbook. She'd been coming here almost every day, alone, and after a while Monty came to expect her, clearing off the place where she sat, refilling her soda glass, even lingering at the counter sometimes to talk to her, although he said little when he did. Unlike his mother, he was quiet, withholding even, but some of his mother's passion leapt out when he talked about the music he liked or asked about Dawn's drawing. He was nineteen and tall, the tallest boy she had ever seen, with hair that spiked along his scalp in neat green triangles. He had brown eyes like Ms. Ella's. Sometimes, when she leaned over the counter to show him her sketchbook, she felt her skin very close to his, and his eyes dropped down to her neck or her breasts and then away. It was hard to shake the uncanny feeling his eyes gave her, Ms. Ella's brown eyes in Monty's face.

On the day the conspiracy started, Monty came over, wiped his hand on his apron, and picked up her empty tray. Without looking at her, he said, "You know out back? Where I park the van?"

"Yeah."

"Meet me there tomorrow. I get off at three."

"Tomorrow? Are you sure?"

He shrugged. "My mom said I should bring you. She says it's okay now."

Dawn barely slept that night, bristling with anticipation. The next afternoon, she pushed her way through the throng of boisterous, chattering students outside Peachtree High and met Monty in the alley behind the Cheesy Slice. He was slouching against the front bumper of his van, one booted leg crossed over the other, but he straightened up self-consciously when he saw her.

Dawn stopped a few feet away to admire his van up close. It was an eighties work van, a Chevy with a black-and-white checkerboard pattern stretching along the bottom from wheel to wheel. The rest of the van, from hood to sides to tires, was completely covered in spray-painted graffiti. A grinning skull adorned the passenger door. Blood-red circle-A symbols danced across the side, and lacy, painted spiderwebs covered the back doors. She stepped forward to help Monty move an amp and a bunch of electric cords off the front seat and into the back.

"You play music?" she said.

"Bass and drums." A bit bashfully, he showed her his calloused fingers. "See that? My hands are fucked."

"You live in here or something?" She pointed at the blanket and pillows in the back.

"Sometimes, when I play a show. My band has a show coming up. In Athens."

He rooted around for a cassette in the rubble of the glove compartment and slipped it into the tape deck. Dawn had only heard Dead Kennedys once before, on one of the mixtapes Bryce had given Amber, and she was grateful for the loud, driving guitars that blasted away the need for conversation.

She felt too giddy to speak. All summer there had been the empty house with her father, empty the way it had felt in those initial months after her mother left. The separation from Ms. Ella had happened just when it seemed like Dawn was on the brink of something new, poised at the edge of a chasm, confident of her strength to bound across and land gracefully on the other side. And then there had been the arrest, and the chasm had reappeared, yawning and indomitable.

It was just a short delay, she thought now; she would see Ms. Ella and she would get back on track again.

Monty drove, adding the motion of the van to the mayhem of the guitars, his long legs folded into the seat, his knees almost touching the wheel.

They glided down Ponce de Leon and onto the parkway, past the golden dome of the capitol building and the sleek windowed skyscraper where Dawn's now-absent mother had once worked, then continued into the northern suburbs, where the sidewalks disappeared and the houses grew larger, lawns swelling out between them, the grass parched and dry in the late summer heat. They pulled up in front of a yellow two-story house with cracked vinyl siding and a porch that coiled anaconda-like around the entire structure. A dogwood tree spread green branches over the driveway.

"This way," Monty said.

She followed him through a garage filled with musical equipment into a bright, tidy kitchen with books stacked in an alcove by the doorway. Dawn glimpsed a few titles: Castiglione's *The Book of the Courtier*; Erasmus's *On Copia*. There were more books in the dining room—Dawn caught sight of bulky teacher-training textbooks called *Creating Lifelong Learners and Effective Curricular Design*—and even more in the living room, which had shelves full of American history volumes: Dee Brown's *Bury My Heart at Wounded Knee*; *A People's History of the United States* by Howard Zinn. Overstuffed binders and notebooks were crammed in alongside them. Sun poured down from three skylights in a vaulted ceiling.

Ms. Ella rose from an armchair in her Philly Eagles T-shirt. Dawn ran to her.

"Ms. Ella!" She wrapped her arms around her teacher's waist and took a deep inhale, smelled the familiar smell of cigarettes and peppermint. Ms. Ella embraced her back and Dawn, against her will, began to cry.

"Um," Monty said, from somewhere behind her. "If you need me..."

“That’s all right, Mon,” Ms. Ella said.

Dawn heard his footsteps treading back through the house, the opening of the garage door. There was a screech of static and the low, electric hum of an amplifier. A moment later, he began a series of tuning exercises on a bass guitar, winding scales in different keys, accompanied by the steady tock of a metronome. Dawn buried her face in Ms. Ella’s shoulder and sobbed more violently.

“Hey.” Ms. Ella pulled away and studied Dawn’s face. “What’s all this? What’s going on?”

“I hate it,” Dawn cried. “It’s like you said. Big and crowded and boring. I miss our class and our projects. I miss you.”

Ms. Ella led her over to the sofa, guiding her around an old television on the floor that played *Jeopardy!* on mute, and handed her a tissue. She listened while Dawn poured it all out: the scattered, anonymous classrooms, the teachers who lectured straight from the book. Passing old Stillwater students in the hallways. The mind-numbing tests, the rote memorization of names and dates. The overpraise and A grades for papers Dawn had barely spent any time on.

“And the worst thing is that no one understands,” Dawn said. “I try to explain the accelerated program, the after-school projects, how everything should be harder, and people tell me I sound crazy or something. Crazy for wanting something different.”

“That’s how people are, when they don’t think,” Ms. Ella said. “They just don’t know how they’re being cheated. They’re brainwashed by the system. Blind.”

“I can’t do it for four whole years,” Dawn said. “I just can’t.”

Ms. Ella handed her another tissue. "I'm sorry that I can't open the Renaissance Academy," she said. "Jean was against me, you know. And then Amber betrayed me."

"I know."

"But I might be able to help in a different way. A bigger way. In a position where I would have more power. Where I could change the system."

Dawn dried her eyes. "What do you mean?"

Ms. Ella picked up a notepad off the coffee table and handed it to her. Dawn read, in Ms. Ella's angular, impatient handwriting:

> *In Defense of Discipline*
>
> *Our schools are in crisis. For too long, we have neglected our nation's children. A system of public education, haphazardly funded and everywhere uneven, has failed them. Look inside the classrooms of our state. You will find overcrowded rooms, missing books and supplies, overburdened teachers. You will find students who are bored, rebellious, under-challenged, and disengaged. No doubt about it, our students have been robbed: of meaningful exchange, of individualized attention, and of life skills. But what have they been robbed of the most? Discipline.*

Dawn looked up from the notepad.

"What is this? A speech?"

"An editorial. To launch my campaign."

She stood up and started pacing across the room. Dawn remembered how she used to pace in front of the board in the same way, back at Stillwater, when she was excited by a shift in the class discussion or a provocative student remark.

"My campaign for Georgia school superintendent," Ms. Ella said over the noise of Monty's bass. "For the November 1994 race. The incumbent, Simmons—what has she done? Gone along with budget cuts, instituted more standardized testing, consolidated more rural schools. But nobody challenges her because her whole family is in politics. Her dad's the mayor of Macon. She has two cousins in the Georgia House. It's basically a sinecure, her position. It's time to vote her out. Get some fresh blood in there. Someone with new ideas. Someone with vision."

She was pacing more quickly now. Dawn felt a little surge of energy in the heavy air as Ms. Ella moved back and forth, in and out of the sunbeams.

"That's where you come in." Ms. Ella stopped and pointed at Dawn. "Amber, she was a good researcher. But she couldn't think on her feet. She didn't have the drive, the passion. You do. You showed initiative. You went and introduced yourself to Monty, you can see through all the bullshit at Peachtree High. You know that students deserve better, and you're ready to fight for it. I want you to help with my campaign."

"Me?" Dawn said. For a moment she was back with Amber in the Stillwater classroom, working feverishly, waiting for Ms. Ella to choose—but there was no Amber here, only Ms. Ella, thrilling and private, and hers, only hers.

"I'll do it," she said. "Where do I start?"

Ms. Ella pointed at some file folders under the coffee table. "Those are the first things to sort. I need to finish drafting this editorial, then we can go over that material and pull anything we need for policy statements."

Dawn knelt down and began sorting the files into categories: teaching philosophy notes, accreditation paperwork, donor correspondence. The bass line of The Breeders' "Cannonball" rumbled at a plodding, dirgelike pace through the house.

Together they watched a contestant solve for the clue *The period when the dinosaurs went extinct.*

"Think fast. What is it?"

"Cretaceous!" Dawn said.

Monty gave up on "Cannonball" and started playing the intro to "Sweet Child O' Mine." The bass notes boomed and made the walls vibrate slightly. Dawn bent back over the files with a sudden, keen surge of purpose, which she realized she had not felt since the day Ms. Ella walked out of Stillwater and their little community scattered. They were over now: those listless days of staring at textbooks, of shuffling from class to class, of being unable to sketch. Now, for the first time in months, she worked.

At five Monty turned his amplifier off and drove Dawn back to the alley behind the law offices across from Peachtree High. A group of kids were leaving soccer practice, carrying duffel bags and cleats. They stared at the gaudily painted exterior of Monty's van.

"See you tomorrow?" Dawn said.

"Tomorrow but not Wednesday or Thursday. I have to work both evenings."

"Okay," Dawn said. "See you."

She sat on the auditorium steps and waited. Inside, the drama club was rehearsing *Antigone*, and their voices drifted outside whenever a student came barreling through the wide double doors. One of the actresses was strolling up and down the hallway, running her lines, each time with a different emphasis.

"I do them no *dishonor*; but to defy the State,—I have no *strength* for that," she read. "I do them no dishonor; but to *defy* the *State*,—I have no strength for that."

At five thirty, Dawn's father pulled into the driveway in front of the main doors. He still had on his work slacks and tie, and he looked tired, hands stiff and arthritic on the steering wheel. But he smiled when he saw her.

"Well?" he said. "How was today, kiddo?"

"It was good," Dawn said. "The school is doing a production of *Antigone*. The first meeting of the drama club was in there." She jerked her thumb at the auditorium. "I'm going to rehearse with them and try out for it."

"That's wonderful! When do you start?"

"After school tomorrow," Dawn said. "But not Wednesday or Thursday."

"That reminds me," he said. "I got tickets for us to go to a painting class the last Thursday in October. At that new studio place in the square. It's a 'Paint Your Furry Friend' class. You'll paint the cats! Doesn't that sound like fun?"

"Yeah," Dawn said, half-listening. "That sounds great."

He glanced at her. "I've been worried about you, with all the changes," he said, a little reproachfully. "I thought it would be something nice we could do together."

Dawn shifted in her seat. He had been like this, attentive and solicitous, for months, since the arrest and the rumors, which had come to him later than the other parents. He'd tried, unsuccessfully, to take her to family therapy. All the therapist wanted to do was talk about her mom, and how Dawn felt about her leaving. It was exhausting.

"I know, Dad," she said. "I'll write it down. I'll be there."

He sniffed the air. "Have you been smoking?"

"Some of the other kids do at lunch, over there, off the school property." Dawn pointed at the bus stop. "But they have to be at least sixteen and they have to have their parents' permission."

"Imagine that. Giving your kids permission," her father said, sighing.

They drove home, the sun dropping lower, the light fading from a humid orange to a warm twilight glow. The poplars along the road darkened into shadows, their branches reaching upward like arms raised in worship. Dawn pulled her knees up to her chest, rested her head on the window, and slept.

Chapter III

Madeira Beach, 2012

DAWN LEFT the residency in Alexandria and arrived in Madeira Beach around ten in the morning. As she drove past the welcome sign, she caught glimpses of the Gulf of Mexico between oceanfront chain hotels and tiki bars and souvenir shops. It was the beginning of tourist season. Families in bathing suits trooped down to the shoreline, holding neon boogie boards and foam noodles. At the sight of the water, Dawn's heart grew light. She had not been to the beach in years.

But then her maps program instructed her to turn left, away from the shoreline, and to take a two-lane inland highway lined with fast food restaurants and liquor stores and pawnshops and payday loan services.

"Your destination is on the right," said the robotic voice, with a sternness that felt like a reprimand.

Dawn pulled into the lot, parked, and looked at the motel. Three gray buildings surrounded a faded tile courtyard and a pool with sullen chlorinated water that looked still and toxic in the growing heat of the day. Bits of trash had amassed along the pool gate, takeout cups and dime bags and candy wrappers. She took a deep breath. It was as still and somber as a mausoleum, all of the curtains drawn, the only sign of human activity the flicker of a television behind the curtains of the check-in office.

She pulled her suitcase out of her trunk and walked around the pool. The sun shone overhead, but even though a light, teasing ocean breeze blew away the worst of its heat, there were only two figures sitting on battered mesh chairs by the water.

One of them was a young white woman in a thin sundress and bare feet, her skin red and flushed, nodding off with her neck tilted back unnaturally against the chair.

Next to her was a guy about Monty's age, tanner than the woman, in a pair of carpenter jeans and a Ministry T-shirt, his jaw covered in stubble. Sunglasses and a baseball hat hid the rest of his face, but Dawn could tell from the angle of his gaze that he was staring at her as she dragged her suitcase along.

Room 126 was just beyond the pool gate. Dawn knocked, hard. There was no answer. Inside, the sound of the television filled the room and leaked out into the crisp air; she could see its flashing light behind the threadbare curtains, which must have been orange once but were now faded by sunlight and smoke.

The man at the pool laughed, a sound that was shrill and predatory in the morning stillness.

Dawn knocked, harder.

No answer. She walked back past the pool to the main office. The door was locked and the blinds were drawn. A handwritten sign in the window read *Open at Noon.* Dawn could hear the noise of cartoons drifting through the flimsy door and the faint ding of a microwave.

She walked back into the pool area and stood in front of the sleeping woman and the man in the sunglasses. Neither of them had moved from the position they'd been in when she arrived. Up close, she saw that the man wore a small gold cross and had winding tattoos of wings and roses and crosses on one arm, partially obscuring the pinkish scars on his veins. He looked up at her, grinning.

"Do you know the woman who lives in that room?" Dawn said.

"Ms. Ella? Sure, we know her." He said "we" to include the girl, who was still sleeping. Dawn detected an accent. Eastern European. Ukrainian? Russian? "Smart lady. History freak. She knows everything about Florida."

"Right. Do you know where she is?"

"No. Who are you? You a Jesuit?" He sounded doubtful.

"No. Jesuit?"

"Radical ministry. They do community outreach. They help out the people. Why, you got something against them, or something? You an atheist?"

"Is that any of your business?"

He ignored this. "You a relative of hers?"

"I'm a friend."

"Didn't think she had many of those."

The dozing girl rolled her head back and forth without

opening her eyes and scratched irritably at her arm. Dawn turned and left the pool area.

"It was nice to meet you too!" he called after her, sarcastically.

She slammed the gate and walked back to Room 126. This time she stood on her tiptoes, reached over the unused window air conditioner, and knocked hard on the glass window while thumping the door with her foot.

The door opened just a crack, to the length of the chain lock. Ms. Ella's brown eyes appeared above the chain, squinting out into the sunshine and settling on Dawn, who was bleary-eyed and disheveled from a night of driving.

"Can you let me in?" Dawn said, conscious of the man's eyes still watching them. "I've been knocking for ten minutes."

"Hold up."

The door shut again and Dawn heard fumbling with the chain. At last, the door opened completely and Ms. Ella stood in the doorway amid a stale billow of hot air. Despite the heat, she was wearing a snug beige turtleneck, blue slacks, and loafers. She was makeupless and fully grey now, but still wiry-looking and upright and muscular, still invincible. There was irrepressible vitality in the arm that held the door open.

"You knew I was coming," Dawn said petulantly.

"TV was too loud." Ms. Ella moved to one side. "Come in. I'll make coffee."

She turned and Dawn followed her inside. The television seemed to be taking up all the space in the room: it was a small one that sat atop a shabby dresser, but it was playing at top volume. A local historian was talking about the First Seminole War as the camera cut away to a nineteenth-century map of Tampa Bay. A cheap mirror above the bed reflected the map, pouring it into the room's dark corners and crevices.

Looking around the room, Dawn had the impression that the rest of the place was crawling away from the noise. The bedspread spilled onto the floor, away from the screen; a folding chair turned its back. On the opposite side of the room, in the kitchenette, a small, yellowing refrigerator hummed to itself. The table by the fridge was covered with books and journals. The room was warm, too warm, and the air was sharp and pungent with cigarette smoke.

Dawn found a remote control buried in the bedspread and discreetly lowered the volume a few decibels. Ms. Ella seemed not to notice. She was sniffing the insides of two styrofoam cups. Dawn saw her rinse them out before she filled them, carried them over to the table, and set them on top of the books. The liquid was lukewarm and bitter. Looking into her cup, Dawn saw coffee grounds clinging to the sides.

"I don't have any milk or water. Tomorrow's my grocery run."

Dawn remembered the Philly accent: *wooder.* "That's okay. I don't mind it black."

"Wasn't an apology," Ms. Ella remarked.

They sat.

"How's my son?"

"He's fine. Going on tour again. Syracuse, then Toronto. And Montreal."

"He tell you to come see me?"

"Actually," Dawn said, "he doesn't know I'm here."

"Is that right?" Ms. Ella raised her eyebrows. "So it's just you and me, then."

"Were you expecting someone else?"

"No, but I don't know why you needed to come all the way down to Florida to have a conversation we could have had on the phone."

"First of all," Dawn snapped, "no one can reach you." She looked pointedly at the nightstand, at the beige telephone, the list of printed instructions glued above the keypad.

"That phone is broken," Ms. Ella said. "No frills here! But that's what you wanted too, right? To come see some squalor? To see some squalor and feel avenged?"

Dawn felt her face grow hot. "If you want to live in squalor, it's your choice. I came to talk about my daughter."

"Of course you did. But you also came to avenge yourself. I know you. And I knew it when you called. It's like I told you. Years ago. Too much vengeance. You still can't let anything go. It's okay." Ms. Ella lit a cigarette. "You can have your last word. But I'm going to talk to my granddaughter. You can't make a pariah of me."

"No one's making a pariah of you," Dawn shot back, furious.

Ms. Ella doubled over and began to cough, a long, loud, hacking cough that convulsed her body and made her bend her chest forward over her thighs again and again, as if she were caught in a mechanical loop, a character in a jammed film endlessly repeating a movement. Dawn grabbed the cigarette out of her hand and threw it in the sink.

"Jesus Christ. Is this why you have the TV so loud? So no one will hear you hacking all the time? What the hell is the matter with you? You know better than to smoke like that. It's like a furnace in here."

"Fuck you," Ms. Ella managed to say. She took a sip of her coffee and recovered, a few quakes still racking her chest at intervals.

Dawn turned, flung open the door, and went back out to the pool area. The man and the woman were gone. She walked through the clearing across from the pool and entered a modest residential neighborhood wrapped around a lake. Boats bumped gently against the docks. Lizards darted away from her pounding feet.

It wasn't going to work, she thought. The fatigue and anticipation of the journey surged over her at once, her sense of resolve receding like a shallow tide, replaced by something else, something churning and maddening and familiar.

I'm only tired, she said to herself. I am only tired and I wasn't prepared and I let my guard slip. Of course she would attack first, but I know what she's doing and I know why I'm here and what I'm going to do. I know it. She repeated this to herself, walking around and around the lake and breathing deeply, which took nearly thirty minutes.

Armed with a new resolve, Dawn strode back to the motel. She stopped in Ms. Ella's doorway, surprised.

The door was propped open and the air and sunshine spilled in, making the red paisley carpet look almost cheerful. The television had been switched off, the bed made. The clock radio on the nightstand played jaunty, staticky jazz. Ms. Ella was going back and forth to the closet, dragging out papers and files and dumping them on the small kitchenette table. Dawn walked in and picked up a page of handwritten scrawl.

"What are you doing?"

Ms. Ella's voice was muffled as she crouched in the closet, rooting through a file box. "I realize it now," she said, without looking up. "What we can do with you here. Strange that I didn't think of it before."

"Think of what?"

Ms. Ella withdrew herself from the closet, one last folder in her hand. Dawn saw that she had brushed her hair and there were small gold hoops in her ears. The vampish dark red lipstick was back, and her mouth formed into a resolute pout. She threw the folder on the table, triumphant, and turned to Dawn.

"My book!" she said. "You're here to help me write it."

Chapter IV

Atlanta, 1993

IN THE WEEKS following her reunion with Ms. Ella, Dawn's afternoons began to fall into a pattern.

On the days that Monty worked at the Cheesy Slice, she sat on the auditorium steps and worked furiously on her school assignments, reading ahead, sometimes completing a week's worth of homework at once, while the drama club practiced *Antigone* and the sound of the coach's whistle drifted up from the soccer field.

On the days that Monty picked her up, the good days, she went back to the house and worked on Ms. Ella's campaign in the den, watching news reports on the Somali Civil War and the North American Free Trade Agreement. Ms. Ella added points along the way, observations about historical or political contexts. Dawn often had a hard time keeping up with these developments, none of which was discussed in her Peachtree High classes, so Ms. Ella encouraged her to seek out information from different sources on her own and to read a proper newspaper every day.

“We have to keep you sharp,” she said. “Exercise your mind. We can’t let you get bored in that dismal school.”

Dawn felt that she learned more in those afternoon sessions than in all of her US history classes combined. Her teachers at Peachtree spoke a gentle, hesitant language; Ms. Ella spoke a language of absolutes, one that spoke to Dawn’s own passionate stubbornness. Peachtree High was incidental, a detour; what mattered were these afternoons of discussion and closeness, a closeness that was big and affirming and real. Ms. Ella’s house was as lively as her own was silent and dead. She sat among the piles on the floor or with her sketchbook in the armchair, absorbing it all.

Sometimes Monty made homemade hummus or salsa—he was the only one with the patience for cooking—and joined them in the den. He was mostly quiet, but he would listen to Dawn as she described donor pitches and fundraising strategies, or to his mother’s latest draft of the editorial. Every now and then Ms. Ella would stop pacing, look over Dawn’s shoulder, and point to a detail in something she was drawing: the shading under the dogwood tree in the yard, the motes in the wash of beams that poured down from the skylights.

“See this?” Ms. Ella would say to Monty. “You’d better pay attention to this girl. Get her signature. She’s got big things ahead of her. Art school in New York City. International exhibits. You just wait.”

Monty made the requisite little noises of admiration, but Dawn could tell he was genuinely impressed. On days like these, Dawn felt herself grow bright and polished and keen, like a rare gem. The noise and movement and bodies at Peachtree High grew dim and indistinct, faded into background noise, until the school felt like what Ms. Ella said it was: a temporary stopping place, a layover.

On other days, Ms. Ella was snappish and suddenly withdrawn, for no clear reason that Dawn could see. She and Monty would enter the house, and Ms. Ella would be upstairs in her room with the door shut and the lights off. In these moods, Monty was the only person she would tolerate, and he moved between his garage space and her bedroom, playing bass for a while, then going up to knock gently on her door, offering water or coffee or company.

The first time this happened, Dawn was in the middle of some donor paperwork that needed Ms. Ella's signature. She started up the stairs, folder in hand, but Monty called out to her.

"Don't go up there. Leave it here."

"But it's time-sensitive."

"Trust me, let it go. It's no use talking to her when she's like that."

"Is she mad at me? Did I do something?"

"No. It's just how she is."

"So what do I do with this?" Dawn looked down at the envelope.

Monty shrugged. "Wait until one of the good days."

Dawn waited. Ms. Ella didn't come out of her room the next day, either, and then Monty had evening shifts and Dawn had to wait anxiously for the following week. By then, Ms. Ella was her usual self again, back at work, and when Dawn came in, she waved and pointed at the table.

"Hey," she said, "I signed the paperwork. You can drop it in the mail."

Dawn went to ask Monty to take her to the post office, and when she returned, she started in on the next batch of forms.

Such was the rhythm of her afternoons.

Until the editorial came out.

It was published in the *Atlanta Journal-Constitution* in mid-October, and its final title was “I’m a Former Teacher. Here’s Everything That’s Wrong with Our Schools.” On the day it appeared, Dawn took the money she usually spent on lunch and bought a copy of the paper to read on the auditorium steps. It was a short piece, and powerful. Ms. Ella blasted the withdrawal of federal money for schools that had accelerated with the Reagan presidency and the inequitable practice of funding schools through property taxes.

“And what is the result of this callous and unfair system? Georgia’s schools are low-performing. Our curricula are behind the times. Our teachers are overworked and our schools understaffed. Dropout rates are rising. We blame our students for failing: failing state tests, failing to meet standards, failing to stay enrolled. But if we give our students the resources and opportunities and tools for self-discipline and self-cultivation that they need, then they will succeed. It’s time to face the facts. It’s our schools that are failing them.

“This is why I’m running for State School Superintendent in the November 1994 election. I’m a dedicated middle school teacher with twenty years of experience in the classroom, and I have seen firsthand how students thrive when they are properly challenged through a well-rounded, robust curriculum that prioritizes active learning. If elected, I will fight to channel more state and federal resources into the school system and revise the state curriculum to reflect a new teaching philosophy, one that blends traditional ideals of discipline and accountability with dynamic, student-centered education."

Dawn had read and heard the editorial many times, but she felt her brain tingle as she saw those sharp, pithy sentences in print.

The outrage was swift. Two Atlanta principals and a member of the school board for Peachtree High wrote searing defenses of Georgia's schools, pointing to the success of their musical and athletic programs.

The incumbent superintendent, a former teacher who advocated for Creationism, criticized Ms. Ella's outsider background and experience.

"She may have taught for years, but she's only spent one year in a Georgia school, with *our* students," she wrote.

All of them harped on her arrest, the year before.

"Is this who we want overseeing our precious children's education?" one of the principals opined. "A criminal?"

But Ms. Ella had just as many supporters too, and they wrote in her defense. Frustrated teachers filled the Letters to the Editor page with stories of low salaries, little support, buying supplies with their own paychecks. They wrote about the racial and economic disparities between the different districts. Proponents of private education went on the local news to talk about school choice and freedom from the state's outdated curricular standards. Some of these interviewees even went further, casting Ms. Ella as a kind of martyr who was being attacked for speaking a bold and necessary truth.

In these moments, Dawn glimpsed the brilliance of Ms. Ella's strategy. Without saying so herself, she had managed to recast her arrest as an unfair persecution, a triumph of small and petty minds. Donations started pouring in. Ms. Ella's phone rang with callers making suggestions and requesting interviews. The support came from all ends of the political spectrum, from traditionalists who applauded Ms. Ella's comments on discipline and personal responsibility to progressives who rejected those comments but embraced her philosophy of student-centered learning.

Dawn worked frantically now, updating donor lists, fielding calls and letters, listening to Ms. Ella prepare her rebuttals. There were no more long conversations about NAFTA or Somalia or breaks to watch *Jeopardy!* Dawn felt her blood grow light with the lack of dinner and sleep, her thoughts dance wildly at the fresh riot of activity.

One afternoon, two weeks after the editorial came out, the phone rang and a woman's brisk voice asked to speak to Eleanor Hallstrom. Dawn passed her the cordless and she disappeared onto the front porch, away from the noise of Monty's guitar. When she came back in, she said, "You have a nice dress? Something formal?"

"I have my Easter dress. Why?"

"Wear it on Thursday. We're going out to dinner. To meet my new campaign manager. Susan."

That Thursday afternoon, Dawn met Monty in front of the auditorium steps, pulling at the hem of her red tie-front dress. She had grown since she'd worn it to Easter services with her father, and when she tugged at the bottom of the dress it exposed more of her neckline. Monty glanced down the front and looked quickly away. He wore black slacks and a black button-down shirt. Ms. Ella must have told him to wear his mohawk down, because it rested around the sides of his head, the strands drooping over his shaved skull like the stems of an underwatered plant. To Dawn, he looked even more withdrawn this way. Vulnerable.

"You ready?" he said.

Without waiting for an answer, he turned up the volume on his Rancid tape and slid into traffic.

Dinner was at the Sunview, a rotating restaurant on the top floor of the Westin Peachtree Plaza Hotel. The glass elevator sailed up the side of the building and released them into a circular dining room with floor-to-ceiling windows all around. Dawn stopped to admire the view of the downtown skyscrapers, the buildings of flushed granite, the Georgia-Pacific Tower with its stair design, a giant stepstool into the clouds. Below these, she saw twelve lanes of stalled I-85 traffic and, farther off, patches of forest in all directions, bursts of autumn oranges and yellows and reds, a bowl-rim of fire dancing around the edges of the grey city.

A hostess in a tuxedo led them to a table right next to a window where Ms. Ella sat in a black pantsuit and a beaded silver necklace, her shag freshly trimmed and blow-dried.

A slim Black woman rose to greet them. She wore a dark navy dress and a white cardigan, a combination that gave her a vaguely maritime air of authority.

"Susan, this is Monty, my son," Ms. Ella said, as Susan and Monty shook hands. "And this is my assistant, Dawn. Susan is the Chair of the Atlanta Committee on Children's Education."

Susan's handshake was quick and energetic. "It's nice to meet you both."

"Likewise," Monty mumbled.

They sat. Ms. Ella had said it would be a dinner, but the table held only cocktails and an ashtray. Dawn looked around for a menu and, seeing none, reached for a glass of water. Monty did the same, loudly crunching his ice. They listened to Ms. Ella and Susan debate the Clinton administration's educational policies.

"There's one side that wants to throw resources at it, and another side—the old Reaganites—who want to cut the budget," Susan said. "What you have going for you is that there are local people from both sides who are interested in your candidacy. It's something we need to cultivate."

"I'm in agreement with the Clinton resource allocations," Ms. Ella said. "He's doing something about teacher training. He's doing something about overcrowding. What I can't abide is the emphasis on testing."

"Well, that's just it. It turns every student into a unit or a number. And it takes agency away from the teachers who live in these communities and know these students. They know what's best. We can't disenfranchise them."

"Exactly. What are we trying to produce? Robots who can tick some boxes? No. We're trying to create ethical people, decision-makers. *Disciplined* people." Ms. Ella took a long sip of her whiskey and soda.

Monty stirred, moving his long legs under the table. His knee knocked clumsily against Dawn's.

"What if a kid already has discipline?" he said. "I mean, what if a kid doesn't need more of it?"

Ms. Ella barely glanced at her son. "Kids don't need discipline?" she said. "You mean, the kind that keeps them from dropping out of school?"

"That's not what I mean." Monty fumbled for words. "Like if a kid already has discipline. They play sports or have hobbies, just not related to school. Maybe they need something else. From the student's perspective, I mean. I'm just saying."

Susan cut in gracefully. "I'm so glad the campaign has two such bright young people to advise us." She smiled at Dawn. "Ella's told me a lot about you and your art. I'm looking forward to working together."

The unexpected compliment warmed the space beneath Dawn's ribs, and she smiled back. Monty stared, defeated, into his empty glass.

"You two must be starving." Susan leaned out of her chair to look for a waiter. "Let's get some menus."

Back in the van, Monty drove without speaking, visibly uncomfortable in his dress clothes.

Dawn lowered the volume on the Rancid tape and said, "What did you mean back there? About discipline?"

He glanced over. "I don't know. I just mean, her approach with tough kids, or whatever, is to be even tougher on them. Maybe it's the wrong way."

"Why didn't you say so? It sounds like a fair point to me."

"I don't know. Arguing about stuff isn't really my thing. I've never been good at it. Not with her, not in school. That's why I left."

"You didn't like school?"

He concentrated on the road, silent so long that Dawn thought he hadn't heard her. But then he said: "It's not that

I don't like it. I just have trouble understanding things in school. I have a reading thing. Reading comprehension deficit, it's called."

"Oh," Dawn said.

"I can *read*," he said, a bit defensively. "It's just that when I read, I can't really understand the words. I can pronounce them, but I don't know what they all mean together. It takes me a while to understand a sentence. Too long."

He signaled right, switched lanes.

"It doesn't happen with music, for some reason. We figured it out when I got my first guitar, in middle school—a little used Fender. Anyway, it's probably why she likes you so much. She likes people who think quickly."

"I'm sorry," Dawn said.

"What for? It's just how it is."

He pulled up beside the auditorium.

"All right, then," he said, without looking at her. "See you next week."

Dawn looked out at the auditorium steps where the drama kids sat in a circle, then down to the field where the soccer coach squatted, hands on his knees, watching his players dribble.

A gust of panic, flat and cold, seized her chest.

"Oh, fuck," she said. "What time is it?"

"Five thirty."

"Fuck. Take me to the square. Hurry."

Five minutes later, he pulled up alongside Paint ATL, a cheerful, glass-windowed studio where about ten people were already gathered in front of a row of easels. In her haste, Dawn had not thought to tell him to drop her off in the back, and her father locked eyes with her the moment she stepped out of Monty's van.

He was standing in the little garden in front of the studio with his hands on his hips, his glasses misty with sweat. Dawn could see footprints in the dirt where he had paced back and forth, leaving the trail of his anger in the ground. Dawn froze, too surprised to be mad. Her father lunged for her.

Chapter V

Madeira Beach, 2012

THE JESUITS came the morning after Dawn's arrival. She got up around seven, made coffee in the dirty machine in her room, and went to Ms. Ella's. The Jesuits sat on the bed, at ease, familiar, while Ms. Ella moved from the closet to the table, collecting her checkbook and shopping bags.

They were not what Dawn was expecting. She had imagined young white men, do-gooders from some expensive private college, but one of them was a white woman in her forties with a septum piercing wearing a burnt orange dress and sandals. The other was a Mexican-American man in his early thirties with thick, close-cropped hair, dressed in chinos and a polo shirt. Tattoos of roses covered his arms. They introduced themselves as Maria and Caleb.

"How do you know Ms. Ella?" Caleb asked.

Dawn registered the way they called her *Ms. Ella* too. "I'm her daughter-in-law. Was."

"Cheryl's mother. Congrats on her graduation."

"You helped Ms. Ella get in touch with her?" Dawn asked. "The day she graduated?"

"We try to help family members reconnect, when we can," Maria said. "But it was Ms. Ella's idea. We just helped her find the number."

"I see," Dawn said.

Maria lit a tiny roach with some difficulty, sucking her cheeks in like a fish, and offered it around.

"No thanks," said Dawn. "It makes me paranoid."

"Me too."

"You like to draw?" Caleb pointed at the sketchbook under Dawn's arm.

"I do."

"We have some lovely pieces of art in the chapel," he said. "You should come join us sometime. Every week on Sunday."

"Thanks a lot, but I don't go to church."

Ms. Ella came over with her linen bags and pocketbook. "Dawn's here to help me with my book."

"Your history book?" Maria asked.

"My history book! Dawn's going to help me get all my pages in order and send them to a publisher."

"Oh, that's great," Maria said. Dawn was silent. She watched as Maria finished the roach with Caleb and whisked Ms. Ella away in a white van. Dawn had a brief glimpse of her former mentor sitting alone in one of the long van seats, talking excitedly about her manuscript, handbag in her lap.

Dawn opened the trunk of her car and began to remove her supplies: floral wire, hanger wire, aluminum foil, electric drill, a short board, clippers. She made her way to the clearing. She had discovered it on her walk the day before, in the middle of a copse of trees that divided the motel from the street with the lake. An old fire pit stood in the middle, its copper bowl still filled with half-burnt logs. Weathered green plastic chairs surrounded it, along with a few cinderblocks and a rusting grill. Overhead, the palm trees filtered the sunlight into shifting patterns of shade. Elephant ears grazed Dawn's shins, their veiny, heart-shaped leaves almost as big as the fire pit itself, as if they would absorb the steel and copper, smother it in greenery. Dragonflies with spotted wings flitted through the clearing, landing briefly on the leaves.

Dawn took an old door that was leaning against the wall of a nearby maintenance shed, propped it up on cinderblocks, and began assembling the armature. She had drawn some preliminary sketches the night before, and now, with the sketchbook propped before her, she worked quickly and easily, cutting pizeces from the hanger wire, checking the proportions, using floral wire to wrap the shoulders and spine together.

It was a fine morning; even the drab motel looked pretty in the soft light. The blue surface of the pool was clean and inviting from a distance, and the litter in the parking lot was less visible through the shady overgrowth of the clearing. The doors were all shut and the blinds drawn. The motel guests seemed to keep late hours.

During her first hour of work there was no one in the lot or pool, but as the sun grew higher, she became aware of an intermittent dragging sound on the concrete. She looked up and recognized the man from the day before, still in the same Ministry T-shirt. He was making his way through the parking lot, sweeping cigarette butts into a dustpan. As he approached the clearing, she saw that he was freshly shaven, the cross still glinting beneath his Adam's apple. He wasn't wearing his sunglasses. His eyes were a deep brown.

He leaned his broom and dustpan against a palm tree and jerked his head towards Dawn's armature, which was vertical now, a wildly gesturing figure of wire, its silhouette urgent, hysterical, against the cool backdrop of green.

"What's that going to be?"

"Sculpture."

"Of what?"

"Cassandra. From the old Greek plays."

He shook rainwater off a chair, sat down, and watched her work for a while.

"What for?" he asked.

"It's for my friend."

"Where's she at?"

"Out with the Jesuits. Grocery shopping. Where's your friend?

"What friend?"

"That woman. Yesterday. From the pool."

"Dee?" He stretched his legs out. "She's with her son today. They went to play Skee-Ball up at St. John's Pass."

"She has a son?"

"Three years old. He lives with his grandma. In Tampa."

"I have a daughter."

"No shit. How old?"

"Eighteen."

He laughed: a low, long laugh of disbelief. "No offense," he said. "It's just that you don't look like you fuck."

"And what would I look like? If I fucked?"

"I don't know," he said. "Calmer."

"Is that true of all the calm people you know?" she said. "Are you calm because you're fucking someone?"

Dawn said this to throw him off, to match his bluntness with her own, but he took her question seriously and grew quiet and reflective.

"I'm calm because of recovery," he said. "And chapel. And I'm calm because I have my art, too. Look."

He pulled out his phone and showed her a series of photos, all of them taken in one of the motel units. Each one featured a junk object or set of objects that he had repurposed and decorated. There were two large frying pans transformed into mirrors, a coffee table made from a tree trunk and a bicycle wheel, and a task lamp with a long, movable neck, to which he had added a yellow duck bill, felt eyes, a pair of webbed yellow feet. The playfulness of the objects reminded her a little of Cheryl's photography.

"Those are really good," Dawn said, meaning it.

He shrugged, accepting the compliment as his due, and put the phone back into his pocket. "You can go on my Flicker if you wanna see more. My handle is @madeitmyself. My name's Yuri."

"Dawn."

"All right," he said, turning back to his broom. "Good luck with your statue. You can use the shed if you want."

"Isn't it locked?"

"Only when I say so."

He showed her the keychain on his waist and moved off through the parking lot without a farewell.

As she began packing aluminum foil onto the figure,

filling out the wire with silver muscles and tendons, she thought about his tone and sneer when he said the word *fuck*, in that pornographic, violent tone the boys at Cheryl's high school used. The last time had been in the old house, in the late morning. What made it *fucking* exactly? The quickness and furtiveness of it. It was angry and compressed. There had been something heartless about the aggression of it. The feckless affair over, and still pointless, shortly after it had begun. Of course, there had been many other times after that day, a few times with Monty at the lake, and with Winston later on, times that were gentle and forgiving and ferocious in their own way, but those hadn't been *fucking*, somehow. Maybe Yuri was right.

The Jesuits dropped Ms. Ella off at noon, just as Dawn was getting ready to break for lunch. Dawn went to help her carry in the bags. There were reasonable choices: milk, cans of ravioli, apples. Dawn understood that Maria and Caleb must have insisted on the produce.

Ms. Ella divided the groceries between the small cupboard and the mini-fridge. Then she produced a giant roll of paper, the kind Dawn remembered from Stillwater, and told Dawn to hang it on the walls.

"I want to get my outline up," she said. "Take some notes while I talk through the plan."

Dawn hung the paper on the walls in between bites of microwaved ravioli while Ms. Ella sifted through her handwritten notes again, sorting some of them into piles on the bed.

“There is no rigorous history of St. John’s Pass that begins with the indigenous people who lived in this area before the Europeans arrived,” Ms. Ella said. “My book needs to start with the Tocobaga people in the Tampa Bay area. Then, after that, with the Seminoles who planned to fight against the slaveholding Southern planters. Pre-1848 first. Write that down. Then, we can move on to the 1848 hurricane that created the Pass.”

As she sorted, she told Dawn different chapter numbers to write down with a Sharpie on the giant paper. Dawn listened and scribbled, feeling herself quietly react to something: not the subject matter, which she found genuinely fascinating, but something in Ms. Ella’s tone, some confidence that the book was the best way to put Dawn off of whatever she had come to say. She would not tell the story Dawn was looking for. She would tell the story of the Pass instead.

But I can last as long as you can, Dawn thought calmly. I can last until you have no more of this to pretend about.

At sundown Dawn set the pen down at last and left Ms. Ella brooding over the notes that covered her walls. She walked back out to the parking lot. Yuri was nowhere in sight. On the upper level, beside the railing, guests stood smoking or scrolling through their phones. Televisions burbled and pulsed behind the curtains. Here and there a salamander clung to the wall or to the side of a potted plant; here and there a car started, throwing bright spots of light over the smooth water of the pool. Blue twilight settled around the motel, thick and irrepressibly beautiful.

Chapter VI

Atlanta, 1993–1996

After Dawn recovered, she and her father fought on the sidewalk in front of the studio. Inside, the painters looked up from their easels. Passing commuters gave them a wide berth, hastened their strides.

"I can't believe you were *following* me and *spying* on me!" Dawn cried. "What are you, a fascist? I'm sixteen! I can't take a break from the play? I can't take one day off?"

"Like hell you took a day off," her father said, his voice low and menacing, "because I know you aren't in a play, and that you haven't even been to drama club at all this semester, because Mr. Morton told me."

"Then Mr. Morton is a liar!"

"But he did say he sees you leave campus after school and go meet that boy in that grimy van. So now it's out, what a liar you are. How did you meet him? How long have you been seeing him?"

Dawn was silent, digesting this idea. A white Dodge Stealth pulled up to the stoplight, its radio thumping Shaggy so loudly it made the sidewalk tremble, and drove away. She thought of Monty's eyes on her chest in the red dress and the way he looked away, too quickly.

"I don't care," she said at last. "I don't care that you found out." And then she said, "I'm going to keep seeing Monty," only realizing as she said it that Monty was her ticket to Ms. Ella, or only then fully understanding that it was so.

"No, you're not. You know why? Because if he's eighteen, and he looks like he is, then he'll be in jail for statutory rape. You know why else? Because you're never going to leave the house again."

Dawn laughed viciously.

They drove home in livid silence. Dawn ran upstairs, slammed the door, and locked herself in her room. She stayed there throughout dinner, drinking from half-empty cans of soda that sat on her windowsill, then relieving herself in a houseplant Amber's mother had given her in better days.

She fell asleep on a pillow damp with sweat and rage and missed school the next morning. Her father banged on her door, threatening to take it down. After half an hour of this she heard his footsteps retreat and approach again, this time with the drag of chair legs, and she fell asleep again, more peacefully.

Around one that afternoon hunger overcame her and she slunk out at last, prodded by the smell of herself, the acrid taste in her mouth. Her father jerked his head up, suddenly; he had been dozing.

"I'm sorry, honey," he said, opening his arms.

"Dad." She pressed her face into his chest. "Dad. I'm hungry."

"Okay," he said. "Let's make you something."

He tried not to show his relief, but Dawn felt a little surge of triumph. She knew they had both been afraid of what she might do, knew it because her father had stayed home from work just to wait with her, to pace the stairway outside her door like a reluctant, frightened jailer.

Thus the war began.

On one side were her father and a family counselor named Dr. Emmy; on the other side were Dawn and Monty, although he didn't know it yet. Dawn plotted her moves carefully. She was young; she was fighting a war of attrition; she had stamina.

Over the course of three weeks, she wore her father down with all the obsessive artfulness of a painter. She followed him around the house every evening as he made dinner and drank his Budweiser in front of the TV, asking questions, picking fights. When he cried out, exasperated, for Dawn to go away, Dawn said, "But where can I go? I'm grounded, remember?" or she went into her room, moved her stereo speakers in front of the door, and blasted Metallica or N.W.A. at top volume.

When her father came to the door fuming and ordered her to turn it down, she burst into hysterics, crying and pummeling her bedclothes, hurling things from her dresser or closet. After these tantrums, her room looked like a junkyard. Shards of broken pottery littered the carpet. Disemboweled stuffed animals leaked their cotton insides, and souvenirs from her father's business trips lay smashed and scattered in different directions, the small, headless figure of a hula dancer abandoned in one corner, her severed ukulele in another.

He took Dawn to see Dr. Emmy every week, and when Dawn refused to cooperate the counselor said things like, "Give her time. She'll talk when she's ready." She suggested they try to keep an atmosphere of peace and love and patience in the home and reintroduce small freedoms to avoid traumatizing Dawn further.

Dawn laughed at this, contemptuously, but she also gleaned infinite mileage from these sessions. If her father spoke sharply to her, she went red and silent, waiting for him to apologize and correct his behavior, or she screamed, "Why are you keeping me here?" until he spoke softly to her, held her on the sofa, stroked her back.

At night she talked loudly to herself or went into the hallway bathroom and flushed the toilet again and again, until he came out in his pajamas. Dawn wailed, "All the stress is making my stomach hurt," and made him rummage through the cabinets for Pepto Bismol or go downstairs to fix soup and crackers. After three more sleepless nights, he took off work and brought Dawn to a doctor who examined her and found nothing physically wrong. He referred Dawn to an adolescent psychologist, who talked to her for an hour about her mother and prescribed Depakote, which she slipped under her tongue at breakfast and spat out when she was in the bathroom brushing her teeth.

She eavesdropped from the church steps as her father talked to Ms. Davis, a woman in their congregation.

"I don't know what to do," he said. "If I keep her home all the time, then I'm 'traumatizing her further.' If I don't, then she'll run off to that boy. I just can't do this on my own."

"It might take time," Ms. Davis said. "You just have to stay strong and pray on it."

"I can't do this alone," her father said. "I just want it to be over."

Dawn listened, unmoved. The next afternoon, after school, she grinned to herself when she saw her father waiting outside the school at three, the first car in line at the pick-up spot. He was standing in front of his minivan and scanning the crowd intently, as if getting there first would somehow keep her in his sights.

At lunch one afternoon, during the third week of her punishment, she waited in the girls' room in the back hallway by the athletic center, and when all the monitors were directing the students towards the cafeteria she opened the window and went out of the building and around the athletic complex to the back of the school. She ran behind the football field, her figure hidden by the large banners that covered the fence, and took a long, circuitous route to the Cheesy Slice. The restaurant was in the middle of the lunch rush, the line of customers winding out the door and around the small patio, and Dawn had to wait in the alley by the dumpster for almost an hour, missing her next class, before Monty came out at last, carrying a bag of trash. He wore a red apron, jeans, and a black mesh hairnet fitted over his combed-down hair. He had a new tattoo on his right shoulder, just above his elbow: a skull nestled in in a bed of roses. Dawn left her backpack on the ground, stepped forward, and reached for him.

"Dawn!" He looked down at her, wincing a little. She'd grabbed him too close to the still-healing tattoo. "Where have you been?"

"I can't come in the afternoons any more. I miss you." She pressed her mouth to his in a quick motion she had mentally rehearsed during the long, dull days at school. She had to stand on her toes to reach him and felt him brace with surprise, then relax and kiss her back. After a moment his hand slid tentatively to rest on her hip. Dawn stayed on her tiptoes and kept her neck tilted to the side, unsure, at first, what to do. Then she remembered how he had looked at her breasts in the car and pressed her chest against him. He responded by kissing her harder, but that made it uncomfortable to hold her head in the right spot, and a cramp seized her neck. She broke loose.

"I'm sorry," he said, looking concerned. "Did I…was that too far? I thought…"

"No, no," she said, rubbing her neck. "I liked it, it's just… is there maybe somewhere else we can go?"

Together, they looked down the empty alley at the row of dumpsters and the reeking grease trap.

"There's the van?" he said.

They had to move boxes of band merchandise and hang a blanket over the clear divider between the back of the van and the front. He tried to be gentle with her, to keep going with just the kissing, but she unbuckled his pants. He froze.

"Dawn. I don't have any...protection."

"It's okay," she said.

She lowered herself onto him, burying her head in his shoulder so he wouldn't see her wince when he entered her.

Afterwards she buttoned her jeans—neither of them had gotten completely undressed—and kissed him on the mouth, longer this time.

"I'll come see you tomorrow," she said.

He nodded, bewildered. His hairnet had come off and his hair was spread behind him like wilted violet fronds. Dawn touched the shaved side of his head lightly and let herself out of the van.

She came to see him five times after that, enough that it began to feel like a ritual. She learned to call the Cheesy Slice first from the pay phone outside the courthouse, to take the key from the top of the front tire, let herself into the van, and wait.

She learned what his calloused fingertips felt like against her bare skin and how his work clothes smelled like garlic and marinara. She learned how he was silent for a moment when there was something he wanted to say, and how to wait for the silence to be over. She discovered a new erotic thrill that shot through her as she lay naked in the cold van, wrapped in blankets, the heat of Monty's body against her, while outside the office workers left the restaurants and cafés, calling out goodbyes, their heels clacking on the pavement.

She pictured Amber and the other students who would be at lunch or in their third period classes, learning about imaginary numbers and the Monroe Doctrine and practicing typing drills, and she felt infinitely wilder.

Sometimes, afterwards, she asked about the campaign. She'd been following the stories in the local news.

"It's good," he told her. Polls showed Ms. Ella's numbers edging up on the incumbent's. "Mothers for Better Schools just endorsed her. She misses you, though. Says she can't find anything without your help."

Dawn pressed her mouth to his.

A month later, in December, she came downstairs and into the kitchen on a chilly morning. Her father was outside, tossing a string of Christmas lights along the hedge, moving slowly and deliberately, like a cowboy practicing the lasso.

She waited for him to come inside, and when he did, she threw the wet white stick down beside his coffee mug. She said, "You have to let me see him now, because I'm pregnant."

He looked at the twin pink lines. He started to say something, then bit his lip and said instead, coolly, "Congratulations. You've done it now, haven't you?"

"I told you not to try and stop me."

"Yes, you did." He went upstairs, visibly shaken.

It was anticlimactic, this tactical refusal to react, but Dawn had what she wanted. After another week of fighting, her father suggested they discuss adoption with the family counselor.

"But I want to keep it," Dawn said. "I want to give my kid a home, with two parents."

As a Catholic, and a single father himself, he could not legitimately object. He started working longer hours, leaving Dawn to go sit at the Cheesy Slice again, to give Monty the news during a slow shift at the counter.

"Oh, shit," he kept saying, over and over.

"I can't stay with my dad," she said. "It's not a good place. I have to come stay with you."

"Okay," he said. "It's just—is *that* a good place?"

Dawn was silent; she hadn't thought this part out.

Then he said, "I guess we make it a good place? Figure it out. That's what couples do, right?"

It was the first time either of them had used that word. Dawn reached out and took his hand. He promised to tell Ms. Ella that evening and to start asking for the afternoons off from work so he could drive Dawn to her doctor's appointments.

By the time Dawn moved into Ms. Ella's house, the subject had been settled. It had been settled over a long series of phone conversations, some of which involved Monty, most of which didn't. The problem, as Ms. Ella saw it, was how to spin it for the campaign.

"Simmons's campaign will blame me," Ms. Ella said. "Susan says the public is hard on teen moms. Unless."

"Unless we get married."

"Unless you get married. It's legal if the girl is at least sixteen and pregnant. You don't need your parents' permission for that, actually." Her voice trailed off. Dawn waited. When Ms. Ella spoke again, she sounded bold, like her old self. "It's just this thing we have to do, because this is Georgia, and it's how people think, and we have to play their game. But it doesn't have to be a big thing. Just think of it as a strategy."

In January, Dawn and Monty were married at the courthouse in the square, across from the Cheesy Slice. Ms. Ella watched from the gallery. Monty carried the cheap, simple wedding bands. He wore his hawk up for the occasion, and Dawn wore a flowered dress, the same one she had worn to the Skyview dinner. Dawn's father had not been invited.

The woman who helped them with the marriage license said they could only marry without her father's permission if Dawn brought a letter from the doctor that confirmed her pregnancy, and when Dawn returned to the office, letter in hand, the woman looked at it without blinking and said she was legally required to send a notification of the marriage to her dad. Dawn knew he had received the note when he showed up at school on a cold Friday and waited for her at the drop-off point. He had not been to work that day, she saw, and maybe not in many days: He wore his weekend jeans and a wrinkled gray T-shirt, and his beard had grown out. When she walked over and hugged him in a surge of sorry gladness, he silently handed her an envelope with bills sticking out of it, climbed back into the car, and drove away.

So they became a family, her and Monty and Ms. Ella and the little girl who grew in her body, small now, only three inches, the doctor had said—only a finger's pressure in her pelvis but slowly rearranging her organs.

Ms. Ella watched these developments from a pragmatic distance. There had just been the one time, on the phone, when she sounded strange; now that Dawn was moved in, she said, they had to step up the work on the campaign, take advantage of the time before the baby was born. When she was finished helping Ms. Ella, Dawn worked with Monty to get the house ready, installing baby gates across the stairways, boxing all the breakables. They converted one corner of Monty's room into a nursery. Dawn taped up photos of tigers and fish from old issues of *National Geographic* and fashioned a planet ceiling mobile from coat hangers and construction paper.

Monty quit his job at Cheesy Slice and got a new one barbacking at a club downtown, to earn more money. He started interning two afternoons a week at Peachtree Punk Records, an indie label run out of a garage on Spring Street near the old 688 Club, where oldtimers still lingered to reminisce about the Atlanta shows they had seen, the Butthole Surfers and the Circle Jerks. Ms. Ella had been critical of Monty before, but now she sometimes remarked to Dawn that he was starting to show initiative. Monty's take was a bit different.

"We have to show our daughter that we do things we love," he told her. Dawn felt a cruel pity rot through her gut, where the baby was.

At school, the other students whispered about her in the hallways and in the cafeteria. Dawn noticed it whenever she passed a lunch table of girls, or when she saw Tracy standing at her locker with a group of boys, whispering and pointing. She grew tired and defensive and asked her algebra teacher for permission to sit and work in his classroom during lunch. He looked a little bewildered but said yes. She sat surrounded by empty desks while he graded and worked. She sketched or did homework, her stomach churning.

In her second trimester, she went to the main office and told the secretary she wanted to drop out.

"Do you have your parents' permission?"

"I'm sixteen," Dawn said. "I don't need it."

"Wait here."

She disappeared into a back office. A moment later, she came back and explained that all students who completed the withdrawal paperwork had to go to a mandatory exit appointment with Mr. Berman, the college counselor, and Ms. Yang, the social worker.

Dawn met Mr. Berman the following afternoon in his small office behind the trophy cases on the first floor. He was a stocky white man in his fifties. Pennants from UGA and Georgia Tech and Morehouse and Spelman and Kennesaw State hung from the ceiling, their flags and shapes and bright colors reminding Dawn of a used car dealership. He sat across from her at a cluttered desk, looked down at her file, and cleared his throat.

"So you're Dawn Brodie," he said. "From that little school—what was its name?"

"Stillwater," Dawn said.

"Right! Stillwater." He looked at her expectantly, but Dawn said nothing. "I read that woman's editorial."

"Did you."

"Some of it is nonsense. But she can write. I'll give her that."

Dawn glanced at the clock. Twelve thirty.

Mr. Berman folded his hands on top of her file and smiled politely. "So you've indicated that you want to withdraw. Why is that?"

"I've learned what I needed to learn here," she said. "I'm going to get my GED and work on my portfolio and apply to art schools in New York City. New York Academy of Art is my first choice."

"New York is expensive. Most kids go to UGA. Or Georgia Tech." He squinted, remembering. "There was a kid from here who went to art school, though. Class of '90. He went to Savannah College of Art and Design. About four hours away."

"Did he."

"He was interested in graphic design. Wound up making quite a lot of money, I think. Has his own firm and everything now, downtown. He gets big accounts. CNN. Coca-Cola."

"I'm more interested in drawing and painting. And sculpture."

"My advice? Think about graphic design or arts management," he said. "That's where the money is."

Dawn stood up. "Thank you for your advice," she said. "I need to be going. Another appointment."

"All right," he said.

She passed him the paperwork, watched him sign it, and left.

Ms. Yang's office was even smaller and harder to find, tucked at the end of a long hallway of storage and cleaning offices. A white noise machine hummed in the waiting room, and a framed diploma from the women's college Agnes Scott hung on the wall over a rack of brochures.

Ms. Yang rose from the desk when Dawn knocked on the open door. She was young, a stylish Korean-American woman with a pink Chelsea haircut. She wore a black vest and black trousers over a pair of black All-Star high tops. Dawn had seen her many times before, from a distance, while other girls in the hallway grew quiet and whispered, awed by her youth and unconventionality. Once, Dawn had seen her at the mall with a hoop in her septum and a wide-necked shirt that revealed twin star tattoos on either side of her collarbone.

Dawn sat across from her and told her about art school, New York, the baby. When she was finished, Ms. Yang said, "And?"

"And what?"

"That's your prepared answer," Ms. Yang said. "The one you tell everybody. But not me. Why are you doing this?"

"Because—because I want to be with Monty. When I'm living with him and Ms. Ella, I can help with her campaign. I'll be *gainfully employed*."

"Campaign?"

"Her campaign to be superintendent. I've been working with her for months. We have a plan to change education for the whole state. Get funding for the schools and make it so the kids have better opportunities. I know what it's like to go to a program like that and it changed me and made it so I could do good art. If something like that existed here, to be honest, I wouldn't be dropping out."

"Let me get this straight," Ms. Yang said. "You're dropping out in order to promote better education?"

"I don't expect you to understand," Dawn said.

Ms. Yang got up, went into the waiting room, and came back with a handful of brochures. Dawn glanced through them. One advertised a depression hotline and the other was a leaflet from Planned Parenthood that listed fees for prenatal services. The one Ms. Yang wanted her to see, the one the other brochures were an excuse for, was simple. It had graphic art of a pastel clipboard and a heart on the front, as if to minimalize the sensationalism of the word printed at the top. The print merely asked if you were considering an abortion, as you might consider a dress choice or an invitation.

"I don't want that," Dawn said. "I decided to do this. My baby needs me."

"Yes," Ms. Yang said, a little impatiently, "but what do *you* need?"

Her next student arrived and knocked on the door. Ms. Yang reached for the paperwork, signed it, and handed it back to Dawn.

Dawn took the forms to the main office, received her copies, and lingered for a moment in the hall. It was almost two. Everyone was in their fourth period class. And here she was.

She caught a glimpse of something: an alternative path, one where she'd stayed in the classroom, swallowed the Depakote, acted with the students in the play. Maybe even made things up with Amber. It felt strange to be leaving school in the middle of the day, to be the only one in the empty hallways. She pulled two sketchbooks out of her locker, left the rest of her supplies behind, and walked out of Peachtree High for the last time.

In front of the doors, she waited briefly for someone to come out and stop her. No one did.

Cheryl was born on the sixth of August, at four in the morning. Dawn gripped Monty's calloused hand throughout the delivery and blew out her breath in long, slow puffs like the nurse showed her. When the baby was placed in her arms, she held her and stared as the morning approached, fingers of light slipping tentatively into the hospital room. The baby had Monty's long fingers, his and Ms. Ella's brown eyes, and Dawn's bold stare.

"Wow," Monty kept saying, when Dawn transferred their little girl into his arms. "She's beautiful."

Cheryl squirmed and began to scream. Dawn reached for her again, her protective instinct overcoming her longing to lie back and rest. Monty beamed down at them.

Dawn understood, from this moment on, that Cheryl was to be hers and hers only. Monty got up at night, fed her, changed her diapers, took her to doctor's appointments, and washed her little bibs and pastel onesies, but it was Dawn who Cheryl always wanted, Dawn who Cheryl always screamed for whenever she entered or exited a room. She was the only one who could soothe the baby when her stomach was upset or when she could not go back to sleep. Whenever Dawn sat down for a few moments to try and draw, she would hear Cheryl cry, and the cry seemed to be coming at her from all directions, from inside her own body, from inside the empty paper before her.

"Dawn," Ms. Ella would call out. "Can you get her? I'm on the phone."

She could not say that no one had told her. Her father had warned her, and Ms. Yang had warned her, and the family counselor had talked to her seriously too, tried to help her understand how much work it would be. Because of all this, she refused to complain, even when she was going on three hours of sleep, even when nursing made her chapped and sore, even when her father called, unbeknownst to Ms. Ella, and begged her to come home.

Dawn had a full-on breakdown, finally, one exhausting evening after Monty left for work. Cheryl had been fussy all day. Ms. Ella was downstairs preparing for a meeting with Susan. Dawn flung herself on the sofa and started weeping.

"You could help me, you know," she said bitterly. "Just go take her for me. Just for an hour, so I can take a shower and brush my teeth."

"Uh-uh," Ms. Ella said over the sound of Cheryl wailing upstairs in her crib. "I've got work to do. The election is coming up. You know that."

"But I've been helping you with the campaign," Dawn said. "Almost every day, for months. I'm just asking you to help me back for an hour." Ms. Ella ignored her and kept working, so Dawn got louder. "I did all that election stuff for you. I married your son. I gave birth to your granddaughter."

"I did not make you do any of that."

"What do you mean?" Dawn cried.

"I mean that you decided to do those things. You made choices. You're not helpless. I asked you to help me with the election; I never forced you. I did not force you to marry my son. I did not force you to have a child."

"*You* asked him to bring me here. Then *you* told me all that stuff about the Georgia laws and teen mothers."

"You decided how you would act," Ms. Ella said again. "You made choices."

Dawn sprang off the sofa. In her fury, she grabbed the nearest breakable thing, Monty's CD player, and hurled it to the ground. It grazed the coffee table, upsetting one of Ms. Ella's crystal ashtrays, which broke into glass shards. A gray mushroom cloud of ash rose up in its wake.

Ms. Ella froze and stared, her brown eyes completely

vacant, and Dawn cried louder, rending her clothes, clutching fistfuls of her own hair. Upstairs, Cheryl had stopped her wailing, so that the only noise in the house came from Dawn herself, a prolonged, feral rage that she barely recognized as coming from her own worn and collapsing body.

Ms. Ella stood up slowly, deliberately. She gathered her folders from the floor, stepped carefully over the shards of glass, and left the room. A moment later she appeared again in the foyer between the living room and the front door, wearing her blazer and carrying her briefcase.

"Where the fuck do you think you're going," Dawn demanded, following her to the doorway.

"To my meeting with Susan," Ms. Ella said. She looked back at Dawn with something like fear but also blank incomprehension, as if Dawn were speaking in a different language. "I'm sorry for you, Dawn. I really am. But I can't let you interfere with my work."

Dawn wept for an hour after she left, at first from anger, then from betrayal, and then with sudden guilt at how long she had left Cheryl upstairs on her own.

She went up and comforted her, played with her, finally got her down for a late nap, and then stood humiliated in front of the mess in the living room. It took her another hour to pick and vacuum and wash all the glass shards and ashes from the carpet and carry the broken CD player out to the curb, at which point she became obsessed with the problem of what she would tell Monty. When Ms. Ella's car pulled up in the driveway, Dawn went out to greet her, almost falling into her embrace.

"I'm sorry," she kept saying. "I'm so sorry. I'm so sorry."

Ms. Ella held her for a long time under the porch light, the milkweed tickling their waists. "It's nothing," she said. "It's over now. Forget about it."

"I thought you wouldn't come back."

"Of course I came back. This is my house."

"What am I going to tell Monty? About the CD player?"

"Just tell him it fell," Ms. Ella said.

Monty looked at her strangely when she told him this, but then she added, "I was just so tired from taking care of Cheryl, I whacked it down when I was cleaning," and he nodded as if he understood. He wrapped his arms around her, and Dawn had the strange experience of being forgiven twice, for different versions of the same mistake. Ms. Ella was back at her paperwork in the living room; she didn't look up once.

After this episode, Dawn swallowed her fatigue. She nursed and soothed and fed and bathed Cheryl and grabbed minutes of sleep, half-naps, while Ms. Ella picked up the threads that Dawn had dropped: the endorsement requests to members of the Atlanta Board of Education, the phone calls to prospective voters, the meetings with Susan to discuss final strategies. Dawn looked into the alert, watchful eyes of her daughter and felt a tremendous love and a terrible claustrophobia. By the time election day came, in November, she had not left the house in weeks.

Chapter VII

Madeira Beach, 2012

DAWN'S NEXT WEEK in Madeira Beach fell into a routine. In the mornings she went out and worked on her statue, mixing the clay in her room and transporting it in plastic ice buckets out to the clearing, where she dabbed a scratch coat over the tinfoil, shaped the gray mixture over limbs and muscles, and knifed eyes, eyebrows, and an open mouth into the soft head.

At lunch, she moved the statue into the shed, let herself into Ms. Ella's room with her second key card, ate canned pasta or soup, sketched a little, and helped with a couple of hours' work on the book project. If Ms. Ella was having chest pains or coughing, they skipped the book, and Dawn made her go for walks down to St. John's Pass, walks Ms. Ella only agreed to if she could take cigarettes and stop at the different historical plaques to lecture Dawn on the history of the fishing village. They spent the most time in front of the plaque about the 1848 hurricane that had created the pass. Dawn stared out at the water as Ms. Ella spoke, imagining the vortex that had gathered over the sea, torn into the land, rearranged the face of the island.

They strolled along the pier past the arcades and boat rental shacks topped with faux red lighthouses, past the solitary fishermen at the railings. They watched tourist families eating crab and shrimp on patios under giant umbrellas, gambling cruises disappearing slowly into the horizon, and groups of teenagers laughing, and Dawn thought of Cheryl back in Atlanta, longing to call her yet fearing what Cheryl might ask. In the evenings, they watched history shows or the news or sat by the motel pool, eating sandwiches or takeout from one of the restaurants on the Pass. Dawn's credit card debt soared higher and higher.

Once, in the late morning, Yuri and Dee joined Ms. Ella and Dawn in the clearing. Ms. Ella was scribbling in one of her notebooks. Dawn was molding the Cassandra's fingertips. She looked up and noticed that Yuri was holding a copy of *Paradise Lost*.

"Book club," he said to Dawn. "At the chapel."

"Did you finish it?" Ms. Ella asked.

"Not all of it," he said. "I read the parts you mentioned. Satan's speeches, and all of that."

"And what did you think?"

"You're right. His speeches are more interesting than God's."

"And why is that?"

"I don't know." Yuri watched Dawn work, thinking. "Because he's a failure. He failed and got kicked out. Alienated from his loved ones. A lot of people can relate to that. Addicts can relate to that."

Ms. Ella put her notebook down and nodded. "Did you notice he isn't a beast, either? Milton's Lucifer isn't a reptile. He's human, like you and me. And he understands the nature of psychological torment. 'The mind is its own place, and in itself / Can make a heav'n of hell, a hell of heav'n.'"

"He's the devil on earth," Yuri said.

"Like her." Dee pointed at Dawn's statue. She'd been sitting back in the plastic chair; now she leaned forward, her eyes glittering. Dawn wondered if she was high.

"Dawn is talented," Ms. Ella said. "Dawn is the real thing. Always has been. There's only one person more talented than her, and that's her daughter, Cheryl."

"Oh yeah?" Yuri said.

"She's going to come down here and visit, show us her photographs. Late summer, maybe. You'll see."

Like hell she will, Dawn thought calmly. But she herself felt the tug of Ms. Ella's intellect, saw the way it worked on Yuri.

After the sun set, the motel parking lot became a hub of idling engines. Guests, both familiar ones and ones Dawn did not recognize, strolled across the lot, speaking to drivers, congregating on balconies, going in and out of rooms. Dawn could hear English and Spanish through the curtain, sometimes the splash of something being thrown in the pool. Other times she could hear Yuri's voice talking loudly and excitedly in Russian.

Around ten at night, Dawn left Ms. Ella's room and went to her own. A couple of divorcees. A mother-in-law and her daughter-in-law. A couple of spinsters, Dawn thought, who didn't fuck. No one cared; no one in the main office or in the parking lot gave them a second look. Dawn was just another temporary resident, a person who'd dropped in and would vanish just as suddenly, like the dragonflies who perched on her Cassandra statue, fluttered for an instant, and departed.

Chapter VIII

Atlanta, 1994–1996

SUSAN HOSTED a watch party on the night of the election returns. She lived in a majestic house on Piedmont Park, with white furniture and chandeliers and photographs of relatives in the military, and a front garden bursting with azaleas. Dawn and Monty had childcare for the night, and they sat in the living room with Susan and her two well-dressed, crew-cut teenaged sons, eating kettle corn and stuffed mushrooms from a snack tray. Ms. Ella and Susan both paced anxiously. Ms. Ella wore her black pantsuit and Susan wore a red sheath dress and heels that clacked across the parquet floor.

The up-ballot races were announced first, then the race for school superintendent. Simmons won easily, with sixty-one percent of the vote. Dawn stared at the two campaign photographs on the screen: Ms. Ella, with her brassy, direct gaze, and Superintendent Simmons, with her polished smile and professionally whitened teeth.

"Certainly a decisive defeat for Eleanor Hallstrom, the insurgent candidate from Philadelphia," the male newscaster intoned. The way he said it made Ms. Ella's expression in the photo look somehow tortured, broken down.

"That's a fucking joke," Ms. Ella said.

Susan touched her shoulder and disappeared in the direction of the ringing phone. When she came back, she handed Ms. Ella the cordless and a short congratulatory script to read to Superintendent Simmons. When that was done, she gripped both Ms. Ella's hands in her own.

"Remember, this isn't over," she said. "Go home and get some sleep. Be with your family. Tomorrow, we'll talk. We'll plan our next moves."

Back at home, Ms. Ella said, "I'm going to my room," and disappeared. An hour later Dawn and Monty peeked inside. She was lying on the bed, on her side, in the dark, facing away from the door. They waited another hour and cautiously opened the door again; she was still in the same position.

"Mom," Monty said.

"Go away."

Monty made soup and brought it to her in silence; it stayed on the dresser, untouched. The next morning, she was still in the same position. It took all of Monty's powers, and all of Dawn's help, to convince her to get up and shower.

"I'm not working today," she said.

"Mom. It'll make you feel better. Come on."

"This was your fault." Ms. Ella moved her son's hand off her shoulder. "You and Dawn. You got busy and you sabotaged the campaign. You sabotaged me."

Dawn stood in the doorway, speechless.

"Just give her some time," Monty said.

"Is she crazy? We didn't sabotage her campaign!"

"Forget about it. She doesn't mean it."

He called his older cousin in Florida, Louise, who had grown up with Ella and had helped her through her divorce, years before.

"Don't bother," Ms. Ella said, when he brought her the phone. "I'm not talking to anyone."

"She's family."

"Don't bother," she said again.

Monty grabbed the phone, swore. Cheryl was in Dawn's arms. She took one look at her father's face, at this new and unfamiliar rage, and began to wail.

It would be two years before Ms. Ella could begin campaigning again.

In the interim, she began working as an educational consultant, driving all around the sweeping suburbs of northern Atlanta to meet with administrators at private and charter schools. Monty graduated from barbacking to bartending and picked up extra shifts, while Dawn took a part-time barista job in the afternoons. The two of them became expert schedulers, sitting down with calendars after Cheryl fell asleep, calling out instructions and updates as they passed each other in the doorway. Dawn began speaking to her father regularly again: a lunch here, a phone call there. She brought Cheryl to see him sometimes, and he bought little treats for his granddaughter and folded money into the pocket of her knapsack when Dawn wasn't looking.

On days when Ms. Ella had a full schedule of meetings, she was her old, invigorating self: animated, forceful, bursting with plans for the schools and for her future campaign. Her energy transferred to all the objects in the house, transferred to Cheryl even, now walking and speaking, who would clap her hands excitedly at her grandmother's restless pacing.

But then there were days, sometimes entire weeks, where the work cooled off—teacher workdays, school holidays, summer breaks when administrators were out of town—and Ms. Ella became listless, deflated with boredom. On these days she was sullen and withdrawn and sometimes began drinking early in the day. Nothing cheered her up, not a phone call with Susan nor a game with Cheryl, although she sometimes pulled herself together, just a little bit, to take Cheryl on a walk or give her a bath.

"I wish you wouldn't leave them alone together," Monty said one night, in bed.

"Why not? She's home more now and it keeps her busy. Besides, I can't watch Cheryl every second of the day."

"So ask your dad to watch her. I'm serious. I just don't like her to watch Cheryl without you or me there."

They argued about it in low voices but deep down Dawn knew he was right, and after that whenever Ms. Ella watched Cheryl she stuck around or, if her dad wasn't at work, asked him to babysit while she went to her shift at the coffee shop.

Ms. Ella's depression worsened. She stopped doing housework, and the living room grew cluttered with empty bottles and take-out containers. She fell behind on her bills. Monty took over the mortgage, moving money from his mother's account into one in his own name. Dawn learned, for the first time, how much debt Ms. Ella was in from her legal fees and the costs of the campaign.

"It's one thing for the three of us to get thrown out on our asses," Monty said to his mother as she signed the mortgage over. "But your granddaughter needs to have a roof over her head."

As the initial shock of losing wore off and the days and months slipped by, Dawn felt herself harden towards Ms. Ella, felt all of her pity evaporate at the sight of her mother-in-law lying in bed like that, blasted and indifferent and vacant. She could get up and go to work if she really tried, couldn't she? Why would Ms. Ella, who left her husband in the dead of night, outracing a Kansas tornado, be so broken by this loss? Why would a woman who had nearly raised an entire school in revolt give up on her life because someone else beat her? Dawn felt all of her respect drain away whenever she looked at Ms. Ella's grief-blanched face, whenever she removed another empty bottle from her room.

"Any kind of activity is good for her," Monty told Dawn as he was leaving for work one evening. "Try and make her do some work."

"I can't force her to work."

"Just sit with her. She'll work a little if someone is in the room with her."

Dawn tried. She brought her sketchpad and pencils into Ms. Ella's bedroom while Cheryl was napping and sat by the window to draw.

Ms. Ella was lying on her back, staring at the ceiling. "It's my fault," she moaned.

Dawn ignored her. She concentrated on the scene outside the window, sketching the brown-headed nuthatches who were twittering at the backyard feeder. Her ears grew accustomed to the rhythmic scratching of the pencil in her sketchbook. Ms. Ella's voice broke that rhythm again, suddenly and strangely.

"It's my fault," she repeated loudly. "I was too wrapped up in myself, in the campaign, in trying to get my career back. I didn't see that you were suffering."

Dawn looked into her face. She looked fragile and contrite; Dawn found it unappealing. She went back to her drawing. She was silent for the next ten minutes, finishing her sketch. Then she set it aside and said, "Are you saying that because you want to apologize, or because you want me to tell you you're wrong?"

Ms. Ella's eyes grew cloudy, but she said nothing.

"You need something to keep you busy," Dawn said, a strange power welling up in her at this odd pantomime, this reversal of power. "You get back to work and I'll draw. Go on. You do some work. I'll draw."

Ms. Ella got up and left the room. A moment later, she appeared with a file box filled with papers from the North Atlanta Charter School.

"Good. Work on that," Dawn said. "Don't talk to me about guilt, or whatever. In fact, don't talk to me at all. Focus on you."

Later that night, Dawn heard Monty's van in the driveway and went to meet him in the kitchen. They shared a late dinner at the counter: microwaved lasagna and one of Cheryl's half-eaten bananas. His clothes smelled like beer and cigarettes and when he ate he slumped over, the fork moving mechanically from the plastic dish to his mouth.

"Thank you," he said, covering Dawn's hand with his own. "I don't know what I would do without you."

"Don't thank me," Dawn said. She swivelled his stool away from the counter to face her. Their lips met. She did all the work, climbing onto the foot rung to match her body to his, one eye looking over his shoulder in case Ms. Ella came down to the kitchen, feeling a strange, exalted new thrill.

The next morning, Dawn went to Ms. Ella and dropped a folder in her lap.

"Work," she ordered.

Ms. Ella looked up, eyes puffy and red-rimmed.

"Work. I have to go to the coffee shop. I'm taking Cheryl to my dad's. When I come back, I want these plans to be done."

Ms. Ella's hand moved over the folder, a bit absently. Still, she was paying attention.

"I need for you to get up and work. Move. Wash your face. Get yourself together. I'll see you when I get home."

Dawn worked her shift in an abstracted fury, clanging the dishes together as she washed them, steaming milk unnecessarily so that customers wouldn't make small talk with her. She pictured Ms. Ella puttering around the house in jogging pants and sneakers, ignoring Dawn and Cheryl's breakfast dishes, percolating in her messy, tragic bedroom. On the drive home, Dawn felt stern and buoyant with anticipation.

When she walked into the kitchen, Ms. Ella was sitting at the table, freshly showered. Like a child, she held out her work for Dawn to see.

"I did most of the forms," she said.

"That's good," Dawn said. "When is the deadline with the school?"

"Was. Last week."

"Okay. Then you need to call their administrative assistant and tell them you'll finish everything and drop it off tomorrow."

Monty was getting ready for his night shift at the bar, sifting through the mess on the counter in search of some utility bill. He gave Dawn a questioning look, but she ignored him.

"Eat," she told Ms. Ella.

Ms. Ella ate.

"Now go work," she told her, when the plates were cleared.

She worked.

That night, Dawn sat beside her and drew until Ms. Ella fell asleep over the files. Dawn's drawings from that month were filled with distortions: houses with chimneys spiking deep into the ground, human subjects with their features in all the wrong places, highways that arched up, cat-spined, and twisted themselves around and upside down like roller coasters.

She found, to her fury, that she still heard Ms. Ella's voice in her head when she drew, that voice that told her to stop drawing cartoons and fantasies. Her pencil strokes grew darker, more violent, as if to scratch out the memory of her mentor's complaints.

In April of 1996, the year of the Summer Olympics, one of the bands on the Peachtree Punk label invited Monty to go on tour with them through Savannah, Athens, and Asheville. Their bass player had a family emergency at the last minute and Monty already knew all the songs. He told Dawn he had turned them down, but she told him to go.

"And leave you here to take care of everything?" he said. "No way. I won't do that to you."

"It's just for a few weeks," she said. "You've been working really hard for all of us. You deserve this. I can handle things here. You'll regret it one day if you don't go."

He still looked unsure, so she kissed him and spoke into his ear. "You remember what you said about Cheryl?" she said. "You said it's important to show her that you can do things you love. Do it. I'm okay here."

He left early in the morning on a Thursday. Dawn, Cheryl, and Ms. Ella came down to the driveway to see him off. He moved back and forth from the house to the van, loading up clothes, equipment, tapes.

Dawn held Cheryl and watched him. At age twenty-one, her husband had settled into his long, loping frame. He had never been handsome exactly, but fatherhood and family responsibilities had made him more present and less self-conscious, and had given him a sense of goodness that other women seemed to notice, in supermarkets and gas stations. Watching him load and arrange the amplifiers and mic stands in the back of the van where they had conceived

Cheryl, Dawn thought of how much he had changed. The audience members would glimpse it too, in small moments, in the way he held his bass close against his body and played as if the notes were entering his body through his fingers and circulating back outward onto the strings in a private loop: throbbing, sacred, transformed, like a transducer changing light into electrical signals.

They stood in the driveway, waving, as he pulled out onto the street. Dawn noticed that he allowed himself a brief expression of relief as he backed the car out, when he thought no one was looking.

"Well," Ms. Ella said bitterly. "I guess he gets a vacation."

"He deserves it. He's been working really hard."

Ms. Ella disappeared into the house.

He was gone for four weeks, leaving Dawn with Ms. Ella's debit card and pin number, a check for the next mortgage payment, and a long list of phone numbers.

During his absence, Dawn fell into an eager, compulsive schedule of drawing, her pencil moving with a new fluency. She had stopped sketching regularly when her daughter was born; now, she found herself eager to get back into a routine. Ms. Ella did her consulting reports, and some of her old vigor returned.

In the evenings, after work, Dawn cooked simple dinners of chicken or rice and they ate it off trays in front of *Jeopardy!* After Cheryl fell asleep, Dawn and Ms. Ella sat on the porch and watched the shadows of shaggy milkweed and the blooming dogwood tree lengthen across the yard. If it was raining, they went into the kitchen to drink nightcaps and play Scrabble, listening to the sound of droplets plunking into the gutters.

On the first warm Saturday in May, two weeks after Monty's departure, Dawn walked into Ms. Ella's room at eight in the morning and said, "Get up. We're going out."

"You shopping today?" Ms. Ella said, sleepy.

"Get up. It's a beautiful day out. Let's go see that new Olympic park."

Like most Atlanta residents, they had avoided downtown since construction for the Olympics began. Traffic had been rerouted, and big sections of Baker and Marietta Street had been closed off to the public. It was a hassle to get anywhere. They'd followed the debates and controversies that came with Atlanta winning the bid for the summer games: complaints about the city's Confederate past, countercharges by the mayor and his supporters that pointed to the city's civil rights history; millions of dollars of private investment, the mushrooming airport. The new housing developments and redevelopments, the expansion of the stadium, the mass arrests of the homeless who slept in the city parks.

Now Dawn drove Ms. Ella's car right into the heart of it all, through traffic jams, past street vendors and giant throngs of pedestrians. She parked and led them into the new Centennial Olympic Park, a wide, grassy expanse ringed by skyscrapers. The walkways were made of thousands of personalized, engraved bricks that had sold for thirty-five dollars in the months leading up to the park's construction. Dawn counted the different languages around her as they walked the paths: Japanese, French, Hindi, Spanish, Russian.

The main attraction of the park was the Fountain of Rings, a series of water jets arranged in five circles like the Olympic symbol. Children in bathing suits ran in and out of the water, shrieking, and Cheryl ran to join them. Dawn followed, holding a beach towel and straining to keep her daughter in sight amid the crowd of running, splashing bodies.

Five minutes later, Cheryl had a tantrum about a boy who was hogging a water jet. Dawn soothed her, dried her tears, and sent her back into the fountain.

She and Ms. Ella walked along the outer perimeter of the water jets, over another row of engraved bricks. *The Schulmans. The Wanzos. Denise and Jim.* Some of the single-name bricks said where people were from, too, as if to compensate for spouselessness with place. *Cole Bond, Marietta. Bill Grice, Kennesaw.*

"All she ever does is throw tantrums," Dawn said.

"It will get better," Ms. Ella said. "It was the same thing with Monty. When he got a little older and learned more about the world, I started to like him more. Before that, I just felt like a care source. A food source. When he started school, he got more interesting to talk to. You'll see. Just give it time."

Dawn watched Cheryl, the composite of the people Dawn loved the most, splashing and screaming with delight, her unbrushed curls dripping with water, one pink water wing crooked on her dimply upper arm. She admitted to herself, silently and for the first time, that her first two years of motherhood had been a long tedium, punctuated by flaring, picturesque moments: Cheryl's first smile, Cheryl's first word, Cheryl's first step.

Dawn took Ms. Ella on a series of outings in the city. She

worked mornings at the coffee shop and then picked up Ms. Ella and Cheryl and drove them down Freedom Parkway, the buildings shooting up before them, seeming to wobble slightly in the humid, late-afternoon haze. They drove past teenagers milling in Freedom Park, their skateboards scraping along the winding paths. Joggers moved in steady, bouncing rhythms. The grass was ripe and green with the spring. They went to The King Center, to Oakland Cemetery, to the Jimmy Carter museum, to the Margaret Mitchell House, to the World of Coca-Cola where fountains of soda made graceful arcs in the air while tourists clapped and took pictures, past the Krog Street Tunnel with its bright, ever-changing graffiti shifting like the contents of a kaleidoscope. Afterwards, they went to fast-food restaurants or family-friendly chains where Dawn ordered fries or tater tots for Cheryl and watched Ms. Ella nurse a cup of coffee.

"We used to go on day trips at Stillwater," Ms. Ella said. "You remember? Get out of the classroom and go look at everything up close. You liked the Oakland Cemetery. You used to draw pictures of the tombstones. You'd spend all afternoon sketching them."

"Yeah," Dawn said. "I had a lot of time to sketch. That was before Monty and Cheryl and everything."

"It was just you and me, back then," Ms. Ella said.

Dawn remembered how much she had enjoyed the history classes at Stillwater. She had not thought about those history classes much since Cheryl's birth. When Ms. Ella fell silent at last, Dawn paid the check and drove the three of them home along the dark highway, strangely stimulated by the crowds and chatter and lights and traffic.

At night, when Ella tossed and turned in the fitful grip of nightmares, Dawn stole into her bed with Cheryl and read to both of them, quietly, until they all fell asleep: Ms. Ella snoring gently on one side of the bed, Dawn in the middle, and Cheryl on the other side, kicking her legs restlessly into her mother's lower back.

Monty came home in the afternoon of the last weekend in May. Dawn was at the kitchen table, working on a sketch of the water jets Cheryl had played in at the park, trying to capture the way they flung bits of water in all directions, like sparklers crackling with white fire. She heard the van in the driveway and went out to greet him. He was wearing a white Cramps T-shirt and his beard had grown in, making him look a bit older and more dignified. They embraced.

"Where's Cheryl?"

"Upstairs, napping. Your mom, too."

"Can we talk? On the porch maybe?"

"Is something wrong?"

"No, not at all." He kissed her forehead.

They sat on the creaking porch swing, her short legs next to his long ones, the dogwood tree by the driveway shedding its white petals on the lawn. He told her about the last stop in Asheville, about a morning he spent hiking in the Blue Ridge Mountains, about the long weekend the band spent in Savannah.

A pair of monarch butterflies, dancing in the milkweed, caught Dawn's attention. She had heard Monty's stories from the road already, during the phone calls he'd made from pay phones in cheap hotel rooms. The morning alone in the mountains, where he saw a grouse and two red foxes; the bar in Savannah where, post-show, he bonded with the owner over his record collection.

She'd had few stories to offer in return. Mostly, she'd given statistics about Cheryl's schedule. How long she had slept, and when. What she'd eaten, or not.

"I've been leaning on you too hard. I realize that now. I feel so guilty about it. I thought it would be better for us to stay here, less disruptive. But it's not fair that you've been stuck at home all the time, caring for my mother and Cheryl at the same time. I know that's not what you wanted for yourself. What we wanted for ourselves. So I was talking to Rus. In Savannah. At the Far Bar."

Dawn thought about the sketch she had left on the kitchen table. After she was done with the water jets, she wanted to do a study of the Olympic tribute sculpture she'd seen in the park. She had taken a picture of it, and now she studied it every night before she went to bed. It was made of greenish bronze plates in a fan shape. Three-dimensional figures of athletes moved through the bronze, their bodies split by the plates, so that each side showed their bodies in profile. The sun hit their backs and cast shadows before them. The first figure was a woman, her hair flying behind her, followed by two men. They were naked, or so Dawn remembered them, their genitals cleverly hidden by the bifurcating placement of the bronze plates, their bare thighs and torsos striated with muscle, their arms and legs frozen in eternal leaps forward.

Monty looked at her, waiting.

"What did you just say?" she asked.

"I want for us to move there."

"Move where?"

"To Savannah. Rus said he could use the help starting in the fall because his main bartender is moving at the end of the summer. You could get your portfolio together, get your GED, and apply to SCAD. Cheryl could grow up near the beach."

"What about your mom?"

He took her hand. "Like I was saying. We'll help her sell the house, if she wants to. We'll just be a short drive away, four hours. We'll still see her. But we'll have our own space. Our own lives. It's what's best for us and for Cheryl. She'll be in kindergarten soon and you're ready to go back to school, don't you think? It's time."

"I don't know," Dawn said. Suddenly there was a future, and it was wide and beautiful and enticing and almost too stimulating, like an aria played at high volume.

"Take some time. Think about it," Monty said.

It only took the afternoon and evening for Dawn to recover. It had not seemed right at first, it had not been what she wanted back at Peachtree High, in Mr. Berman's office, but wasn't it what she wanted now? Dawn was in the early stages of what she would later understand was a profoundly adult realization: the realization that she could revise herself. That night, she rolled towards her husband in bed and said, "Yes. I'll go. We'll go."

He was almost asleep. He opened his eyes and drew her in, close. "Really? Are you sure?"

"I'm sure. You're right. It's time. But how do we tell her?"

"Let me handle that," Monty said.

"In September?" Ms. Ella said. "*This* September?"

"That's when the job opens up," Monty said. "We don't have to get the house sold before then, but we do need to move out there."

"But that's in four months."

"Right."

They were sitting in a Chili's by the side of a sweeping four-lane highway that cut through their suburb. Rows of red booths, separated by plants, snaked through the dining room. Neon chili peppers and beer signs glowed on the walls. Impatient families lingered outside, holding table pagers. Monty had thought it would be better to give his mother the news in public, but it was a Friday night and crowded, and by the time they got a table and ordered they only had half an hour before he had to leave for work.

Ms. Ella had come straight from a school district meeting and looked sharp in a blue blazer with a red scarf around her neck. Monty wore his bar shirt and looked defeated already. Dawn wore a tie-front top that felt fuzzy and hot in the full room. Cheryl scribbled red crayon all over a paper placemat. Three margaritas stood between them, untouched, on the bright Talavera tiles.

"The campaign starts up again this fall." Ms. Ella glared at Monty. "It's a busy time for me. And you guys just want to take off, right in the middle of everything."

"No one is doing this on purpose," Monty said. "That's when the job starts, is all. We'll still be close by."

"You know I'll have no one here to help me."

"You have Susan."

"Susan is my campaign manager. I have no one to help me at home. You've known about this all along, haven't you? You've just been waiting for the right moment to go and carry out your selfish plans. Move to some podunk town on the coast. To tend bar!"

"We'll just be a few hours away," Dawn said. "We can come down on weekends and pick up the campaign stuff. We can talk on the phone every day."

Monty held up his hand as a warning. He took out his wallet and threw three twenties on the table.

"This is what's best for me and my family," he said. "I wanted to take you out, to tell you. To celebrate. Because I thought you would be happy for us. You should be happy for us. I get that you aren't. But this is happening. Whether you like it or not."

He left. Cheryl's eyes followed him in wonder. Dawn drank the rest of her margarita straight down and reached for her husband's. Ms. Ella was watching her steadily.

"So that's it," she said. "He just makes all the decisions now."

"It's my decision too. Remember? I wanted to go to art school. I wanted to travel. When will I do any of that? Now is the time. If we don't move now, then Cheryl will start kindergarten and we'll be stuck here."

"You wanted to go to art school, but on your terms. Up north. And instead you're moving to Savannah? Because that's what your husband wants? That's not the tough girl I met at Stillwater."

The food arrived, steaming and overseasoned. "Can I have a box for his? He had to leave," Dawn said to the waitress, and busied herself cutting up bits of quesadilla for Cheryl. Ms. Ella used a stack of napkins to edge her hot plate to the side and leaned forward.

"Listen," she said. "This is a classic case of a wife doing something because her husband wants her to. You need to step back, look at it from a distance. You can't see it. But I can. I've been married before. Trust me on this. My husband made me move from Philly to Kansas and I regretted it for the rest of my life. Don't make the same mistake."

"This is not the same thing," Dawn said, but her voice came out less firm than she wanted it to, less solid.

"Oh, it is," Ms. Ella said, picking up her fork. "Oh, it is."

They began packing in June. Monty brought home empty liquor boxes from the bar, and they spent a few hours a week filling them with their belongings: Monty's cassette and CD collection, Dawn's old schoolwork and GED prep folders, Cheryl's drawings and toys. When Monty was home, Ms. Ella ignored them and worked in her room with the door closed. In the evenings, when Monty was at work, she came downstairs to survey Dawn's progress. She did not mention the move again; now, the subject seemed juvenile, beneath her. Sometimes she plucked an item out of a box, examined it, and put it back quickly; other times, she sat on the sofa in the den and pored over it, more carefully.

"I remember this," she said one evening. "The drawings you did when we were at the Olympic park. These were good."

Dawn leaned over her shoulder. Ms. Ella had a sketchbook in her lap, open to a half-page drawing of herself and Cheryl in the park. Ms. Ella was carrying the toddler and showing her the fountain jets. Cheryl was clapping her little hands in delight while her grandmother leaned her gently into the spray of water. Dawn had sketched both of their upper torsos but not the lower half of Ms. Ella's body or the fountain.

"It's not bad, I guess."

"Just look at how much you've improved! Since I first met you. Those juvenile sketches."

Those juvenile sketches were packed away in her father's attic somewhere, Dawn thought. She wondered if he had thrown them out, or if he still kept them.

"You should finish this one," Ms. Ella said.

Now that she was packing to leave, Dawn began to feel a sense of nostalgia about the house. The den where they sat, working on the campaign. The shabbily wallpapered kitchen where Cheryl had taken her first steps. The garage where Monty had rehearsed for his tour. The porch swing where Dawn sat, sketching or reading, during afternoons when Cheryl was napping or playing quietly in the yard. Everything was moving so fast. There had been months of stasis, months of nothing, and now this. Ms. Ella seemed to read Dawn's thoughts. She reached over and took her hand.

"Remember?" she said. "You wanted to hold hands with me. On the way back from DC"

"I remember," Dawn said. She did not look at their intertwined hands, but she did not pull away, either.

Years later, Dawn would have trouble pinpointing exactly how it started. There were little overtures, invitations. The hand-holding. Ms. Ella sitting a bit closer to her on the couch. Reminiscing about select moments, moments that only involved Dawn and Ms. Ella, and neither of their children. One day, Dawn would reflect on the timing of these overtures, see them for what they were. But in the moment, they affirmed her reluctance to leave Atlanta and Ms. Ella behind.

Together, they looked at one of Dawn's old Stillwater folders, with notes on the sculptor Edmonia Lewis. Dawn had done some studies of *The Death of Cleopatra*: the neck tilted backwards, the slight, smooth curving of the lips, the dimpled chin.

"That was one of the first things you worked on after school," Ms. Ella said.

"Yeah," Dawn said, remembering. "You had me drawing pictures while Amber was doing high-level research."

"And why do you think I did that?"

"I don't know. I was messy. Amber wasn't."

Ms. Ella closed the folder. "I gave you figures to draw, real art, because I knew you had the talent," she said. "You needed a vigorous creative outlet. Amber didn't think that way. Her intelligence was more precise and analytical. More fastidious."

"She was a better student."

"Not necessarily," said Ms. Ella. "You were always more interesting. She didn't have to deal with what you had to deal with, after your mother left. It made you strong. Fearless."

As August approached, Dawn continued packing in a state of dread and anticipation that she didn't know how to explain to Monty. Ms. Ella moved among the boxes, fierce and buoyant, her fits of energy vying with Monty's plodding, humorless determination, until even to Dawn it sometimes seemed as if he was the one with the problem, he the one casting his dark grudge over the house.

One of his regulars bought a farewell gift for Cheryl, a Humpty Dumpty toy with an egg-shaped body, a bow tie, and a small black hat. The toy had a special feature: when you dropped it, the Humpty Dumpty broke into pieces, but the pieces could be assembled again, like a jigsaw puzzle. Ms. Ella presented the toy to Cheryl by the low brick wall that separated their backyard from the neighbor's, and together she and Dawn chanted the nursery rhyme while Cheryl jumped up and down and clapped her hands. When they chanted the nursery rhyme again, for a second time, they let the toy drop right at the word "fall," and Cheryl let out a piercing shriek and burst into tears.

"Baby, it's okay, the pieces go back together, see? It's part of the game," Dawn said, crouching down to show her.

But Cheryl was disconsolate. At first they tried letting her piece it back together, and then they put it away in a box in the back of the cupboard, but Cheryl kept balling her fists and screaming, and so Ms. Ella took it out into the driveway, ran it over, packed the shards in a box, and buried the box deep in the soft earth under the dogwood tree in the front yard. At last, Cheryl wiped the tears from her eyes and allowed herself to be comforted.

That night, at dinner, Dawn and Ms. Ella took turns trying to tell the story to Monty, but each time they burst into laughter, and then Cheryl started laughing, too. Monty sat slouching and weary from work, trying to understand the hilarity that was pinging off around him like a busy switchboard. At last, they gave up.

The first time happened soon afterward, in the evening, after Monty left for work. He'd asked Dawn to finish doing the laundry. She was exhausted. She was sitting on her bed, looking at her unfinished drawing of Ms. Ella and Cheryl, shading in the lower halves of the water jets. Cheryl had been fussy all day, refusing to nap, and Dawn had finally given up and installed her in front of the television with a sippy cup full of juice. By leaning forward on the bed, she could just see the living room through the balustrade columns that lined the stairs, and Cheryl's tangled blond hair as she sat on the floor watching *Rugrats*. She sketched, wearily, angrily.

Ms. Ella finished a phone call in her bedroom, came in, and sat down. She glanced over Dawn's shoulder at the sketchbook and said, "The left fountain jet, that one there, is out of proportion to the rest."

Dawn clapped the sketchbook shut and put her hand over Ms. Ella's mouth. Ms. Ella raised her eyebrows but didn't move her hand away. Dawn let her other hand wander down to the hem of Ms. Ella's shirt, slid it underneath. A moment later, Ms. Ella's hands gripped her waist.

She had done it to make her shut up.

And Ms. Ella had let her, Dawn thought, years later. Had waited for her to do it, so that she would think it was her own idea.

The next day, when Cheryl was watching cartoons in the den, it happened again, in the dining room, Dawn peering around the corner every few minutes to check on her daughter. And then, two days later, in Ms. Ella's room, after Monty left for his night shift and Cheryl was in bed. From there, it became a routine. They did not need to discuss it out loud. They just waited for the right time. It was that simple.

Dawn thought she knew everything there was to know about Ms. Ella. But now there were new things. Surprises. The Milky Way pattern of freckles on her right shoulder. The startling muscularity of her upper thighs. The stories Dawn had never heard, stories about when Ms. Ella was her age, in the early seventies.

"I decided to be a vegetarian and it didn't make sense for me to do it if I wasn't going to be militant about it," Ms. Ella said, in bed. Her bedroom was sparsely furnished and austere, with books piled high on the nightstand. "No one around me cared. Everyone was fine with it. So I went with these guys I knew to a grocery store where they had a lobster tank and Evan distracted the guy at the counter while me and Reese took the lobsters out of the tank and put them in a mop bucket. They stunk up the car! We drove down to Pier 68 and threw them in the water, one by one. There were all these fishermen. They thought we were crazy."

She laughed, and her brown eyes crinkled just like Monty's. Each time Dawn was struck anew by their physical resemblance, it made her think of studying Edvard Munch's *The Scream* in an art book the previous summer, memorizing its harrowing orange sunset and the black river and the gaunt, black-clad, shrieking figure in the foreground, until she could describe all of its details and colors without looking—and then, a month later, stumbling upon a different version of the painting in a different art book, a version in which the river and the clothing were blue instead of black. That was how their resemblance was: familiar and estranging at once. There were nights when Dawn went from one of them to the other.

"Were you satisfied?" Dawn asked. "With the spectacle, I mean."

"Not really. I still went around preaching about it to everyone I knew." She propped herself up on the headboard and began to dress. "I was strong-willed. Like you."

As late August approached, Dawn began to sleep even later, sometimes not waking until Cheryl came in to rouse her, arms full of stuffed animals. Dawn would roll over on her side, look through the window at the muggy haze of morning, feel the slick sweat along her back and behind her knees. She had sudden fits of guilt, crying spells in the bathroom. She missed one morning shift at the coffee shop, then two. She sat listless in her robe while Ms. Ella played with Cheryl in the den.

"What's with you?" Ms. Ella asked, the second time she missed work.

"What do you think?"

"How should I know, if you don't talk to me?"

"All this." Dawn gestured at her mother-in-law, sitting on the hearth. "This can't go on. We both know it."

"No." Ms. Ella handed a block to Cheryl. They were both silent for a moment, watching her. "But it's nice, isn't it? The way it used to be. When he was touring."

It was nice, Dawn thought.

It was horrible, too.

As the departure date approached, Dawn spent hours poring over her favorite art book, the one with Paula Rego's *The Family*. She was gripped by the painting's stark, unrelenting perversity.

There was an adult woman, two younger women, and a young man who appeared to be a little older than the girls, although it was hard to tell. He was dressed in a green suit and striped tie, the girls in skirts and blazers; they were just returning from a formal occasion; something about the quiet beams of light made Dawn think that it was Sunday, but the mood of the piece was unholy.

The primary action of the painting took place in the left middle ground, at the foot of the bed. The young man was half-sitting, half-leaning back, over the footboard, while his mother helped to undress him. He seemed much too old for this. He had been shoved or pushed there and retained a posture of humiliated vulnerability. He faced the viewer, legs spread, right arm raised; his left arm was invisible, clutching the footboard for support, maybe.

Behind him, the woman held his wrist and tugged at his jacket. She had a pink bow in her hair, a white apron or pinafore over her green dress, and one knee behind him on the bed. Her face was candid and open, a half-smile curving her lips. Her brown eyes looked down into the face of the boy's sister, who stood with her back to the viewer, thrusting her pelvis into her brother's. This sister wore an orange blazer and white collar over a black-and-white checkerboard skirt; each checkerboard had a cross inside it; it was a dizzyingly bright and geometric pattern, aggressive amid the muted sepia tones of the room. Her reddish-brown hair was drawn back into a ponytail, revealing her face in profile. She had a brown, angular, muscular face. Her eyes bored into her brother's: her pupil was white, she was not smiling, and her left hand grabbed at his waist. His head was knocked back against the mother's arm; his mother's other arm covered his mouth; he looked down at his sister with an expression of horror; he could do nothing.

Dawn studied the mother's face as she looked down at her daughter. The description under the painting read that the mother was "kind" and "trusting," but Dawn thought the mother knew more than this description let on. In the mother's eyes, she saw permissiveness, even encouragement.

Eighteen years old and already a mother herself, Dawn knew about the little conspiracies that could pass between a mother and daughter, secret communions, entire, silent schemes that would never leave the eyes, never leave the lips to be told.

Already, Dawn knew the canny subterfuge of mothers. The feeble rage of sons.

Dawn worked her last shift on the busiest Saturday morning she had ever seen. Customers lined up for two hours straight, holding backpacks and purses and babies and gym bags and yoga mats. Regular customers who wanted to chat lined up with hungover customers who complained about the wait or retched in the bathroom. They filled the room with noise and pulled the neatly arranged chairs askew and left used napkins and coffee rings and pastry crumbs on the tables.

Dawn worked the bar. She steamed milk and pulled shots and called out drinks and at the end of the rush her apron was covered in stains and her nose was full of the slightly burnt, chocolatey smell of coffee grounds. She had so much to do to clean up the seating area that it took a few minutes before she felt someone's eyes on her and noticed the brunette seated in the corner, thin frame wrapped in an awkward floral dress that was too old for her, shoulders hunched forward.

"Hey," Amber said.

"Hey."

They hugged, gingerly, uncertainly. They had not seen each other since the fight at Peachtree High, three years ago. Dawn avoided the neighborhood of her old high school. Amber fidgeted and looked down at her hands.

Dawn nodded at the glossy brochure on the table.

"What's that? You going on a trip?"

"This?" Amber fumbled with the brochure. "No. Well, yes, but not like a vacation." She turned the brochure so that Dawn could see. "It's a rare books training seminar in London. Mr. Berman ordered it for me. The college counselor."

"I know who Mr. Berman is," Dawn said. "What is that? Like a college?"

"No. It's just a seminar." Amber talked rapidly now, in a shy rush of words. To Dawn, she sounded childish, overeager. "We talked about it, you know. What I wanted to do. I had to make an advising appointment with him last week, because this is my senior year. Anyway. He asked me what subjects I liked, and I said English and History, but when he asked if I would want to study them in college, I said I wasn't sure. I mean, I said I didn't know if I could be a teacher or an editor or a docent or whatever, because of the public speaking. So he asked me when was the last time I liked something, really liked something, and I said it was the time I saw the *Shadows* book."

"In DC," Dawn said. "I remember."

And she did remember, she realized: a moment, slicing cleanly through the haze of the previous weeks, of her and Amber standing in front of the *Shadows* book. It was the last time she and Amber were together, Dawn realized with a jolt of regret.

"So he asked me why I liked it so much and I said I liked how rare it was, and how the woman at the Library of Congress knew so much about it, and all the places it had been sold and the people who owned it. Anyway," she concluded, her face flushed, "he said that maybe I would like to work in an archive or an antiquarian bookstore or something, that you just go to seminars and trainings and do apprenticeships for that. No college. I guess Ms. Ella would probably be mad about that last part." She peered at Dawn. "You still live with her, right?"

"Yes, I still live with her. And my husband Monty. And my daughter Cheryl."

"Yeah. That's what Tracy said."

"How does she still know everything?" Dawn said. They both laughed.

"Tracy's sister got a job at the pizza place Monty used to work at. I think that's how she knew. She was in my history class last year and told me about it. But we don't really talk about it much. Stillwater, I mean."

Stillwater. The word made the past come back in a rush. Dawn felt a strange thrill at knowing Ms. Ella in ways that Amber would never know her, and at the same time a fierce jealousy that Amber had left Stillwater behind. For Amber, everything there had ended, in a swarm of loss and love and pain and reckoning; but Dawn was living it still, had found a way to live it in the most intimate recesses of her mind and body. Would continue to live it, she thought, even when she left Atlanta behind at last, even when she moved away from the noise and traffic of the city to the quiet blocks and drooping Spanish moss of Savannah. She would leave Atlanta, but she would never leave Stillwater or Ms. Ella, not really.

"I should get back to work," Dawn said.

"Right. Sorry." Amber looked embarrassed.

Dawn went outside to change the trash cans, without looking back.

Chapter IX

Madeira Beach, 2012

MS. ELLA finished her first chapter before Dawn was done with the Cassandra statue. She handed over the bundle of pages in the clearing and Dawn looked down at them, at the same old eager handwriting, the transcription of that voice that was always speaking in her head. She felt suddenly and acutely claustrophobic.

"I'd love your feedback," Ms. Ella was saying. "If this chapter works, then I'll send it as a sample, once I get my proposal together. That's the next step."

Dawn put the pages down on the Cassandra's base.

"Okay," she said.

She read the chapter by the pool that evening. While the writing itself could not be that old, she saw that the thinking behind it was the product of many long walks and research trips, of endless reflection. The chapter was a long account of early settlement in Madeira Beach. Dawn understood how heavily Ms. Ella must have depended on the Tampa public library in order to write it without the internet. Throughout were the little rhetorical flourishes Dawn recognized from her school days: prose that clopped along with verve and authority, swift quotes from relevant news articles, the crafty raising and dismissal of counterarguments.

Ms. Ella was waiting at the table in the kitchenette, a bottle and two cups in front of her.

"Sit," she ordered. She poured Dawn a glass.

Dawn drank, felt the sting of liquor at the back of her throat.

"So." Ms. Ella leaned back in her chair. "What did you think?"

"It's good," Dawn said.

Ms. Ella grinned. "And?"

"It's good because of the level of detail. The strength of the evidence."

"And?"

Dawn listed the virtues of the writing one by one like a weary spouse dictating a grocery list. Ms. Ella listened with greed. There would never be enough to say, Dawn thought, looking at the strange blank spheres of her pupils, those eyes that looked without seeing. There would never be words that would penetrate enough to satisfy her, no abasement too extreme to be a suitable homage, to fill up that drinking, rapacious flatness in her eyes.

"That's enough," Dawn snapped at last. "I told you it was good."

Ms. Ella collapsed into a coughing fit. She doubled over and hacked into a tissue until Dawn, alarmed, got up and began to pound her on her back. Ms. Ella's cough changed to a hoarse, raspy laugh, expressing a congested yet irrepressible mirth.

After a moment, Dawn laughed too. Together, they laughed at the thing that had just slipped away from Ms. Ella, at all of the pride and vanity that had seemed to erupt like a mucus her insides wanted to expel.

Dawn filled their cups again.

"Ah, I can't do it, watching my health go," Ms. Ella sighed. "But I can't bring myself to jump into the bay, either."

"Why not?"

"I can't be bothered to write a note," Ms. Ella said. "Or walk to the bay, for that matter."

Dawn giggled girlishly, feeling relaxed from the liquor and the lingering mood of the twilight and the sermon. Was this what it used to be like? All the while Ms. Ella was giving her a sly, sideways look.

"Ms. Ella," Dawn said finally, wiping her eyes.

"Here it comes. The reckoning." She drank.

Dawn began to speak, but Ms. Ella waved her into silence.

"I was wrong, I know that now. Knew it then."

"Yes."

"We could talk about all the things I was wrong about. Or we could move on. That was years ago, Dawn. You're grown now. I'm old. My son won't speak to me. But my granddaughter will."

"Maybe you're right. But I don't want to talk about it now." Dawn took the bottle from Ms. Ella and poured again. "Tonight, I want to drink."

"Do you remember that toy she had? The Humpty Dumpty."

"That broke into pieces," Dawn said with a stab of remorse, remembering the strange hysteria of her daughter when she received the toy. "She thought she might break into pieces too, if she fell."

"She screamed and screamed! We had to bury it in the yard while she watched. She thought it would come up again."

They talked, remembering: Cheryl's first word, *Mama*, said as Cheryl reached from her high chair beseechingly during an episode of *The X Files*; Cheryl's first steps, taken in the heat of a summer storm, toddling towards the window, attracted by the pelting rain. Cheryl at three, at the pediatrician's, with a pea in her nostril; Cheryl on the first day of preschool, wailing because she had to leave her ruler and pencils behind.

They talked late into the night, even later than the guests in the parking lot stayed up, as memories of Cheryl displaced the hostility between them. Cheryl, this child Dawn had had because of Ms. Ella, but who had become someone else entirely, a creature of her own. When they finished the bottle, Ms. Ella collapsed on the bed and Dawn fell asleep in an armchair.

She woke with a start in the early morning to a voice yelling outside, some guest at the check-in office. She could not recall her dreams but remembered, with a mother's uncanny sense, exactly what her purpose was. She was dehydrated and exhausted, with an aching head, yet she felt strangely cleansed. The alcohol had burned away something nasty inside of her, the same way chemicals could make a sink look shining clean.

She got up. Ms. Ella was still fast asleep on the bed. Dawn drank a few mouthfuls of bleachy Florida water directly from the faucet, wincing, and strolled outside. There was a faint mist in the air, the aftermath of an early summer rain. The elephant ears in the clearing were shining with dew.

It was time. Dawn went to the trunk of her car, found the mask and gloves, and reached deep into her tire well to withdraw the plastic package.

Chapter X

Atlanta, 1996

MONTY walked in on them a week before he and Dawn were supposed to move to Savannah. He had left, as usual, for his day shift at the recording studio, but then he parked the van somewhere down the street, walked back to the house, and came in quietly, his footsteps masked by the loud episode of *Teenage Mutant Ninja Turtles* Cheryl was watching in the den.

What made it obvious was that they were both undressed, and there was no reason for them to be in the bedroom together in the late morning. Monty wore combat boots and had grown out his beard; he still carried his backpack and keys, and he looked sharp in the small, crowded bedroom, like a focused figure in an otherwise blurry photograph. He stared at his half-dressed mother with intimate, lifelong, mutinous rage, a rage whose depth and history Dawn could never completely know.

"Get out," he said.

"Mon," Ms. Ella said. "This is my house."

"Was," Monty said. "It's in my name, now."

Ms. Ella stared in disbelief.

"Get out or I will physically throw you out," Monty said calmly. "Or I could call Susan, if you want. Or, if you'd rather, I could call Simmons and the *AJC*, give them a statement. See what that does for your campaign."

Ms. Ella finished buttoning her blouse and went silently to the closet. She appeared a moment later with an overnight bag and began tossing socks and shirts and papers into it.

"This is my home, and I'm not leaving it," she said. "I'll go to a hotel so you can finish your tantrum. I'll call you tomorrow."

"Don't bother," Monty said.

Ms. Ella pushed past him and went down to the den. Dawn heard a jangle of keys and, a moment later, the slam of the door.

"Daddy, where is Grandma going?" Cheryl called out. "Daddy. Daddy."

"Just a minute, sweetheart," Monty called out. "Stay where you are."

He looked at Dawn.

"It's not what you think," she said.

He scoffed. "What is it, then?"

He disappeared without waiting for an answer. He came back a moment later with a trash bag and began throwing her things into it, at random: her wallet, her barista apron, a sweatshirt, her address book. Dawn followed him.

"You're not serious!" she cried. "Where am I supposed to go?"

"I don't care where you go." He brushed her hand off of his arm.

She trailed him as he moved from the bedroom to the bathroom, hurling invectives, weeping. She was making herself ridiculous, she knew, but she feared his silence more than anything else.

When the bag was full, he stood in front of her again, thrust it at her, and said, "Get out."

"What about Cheryl?"

"You can see her tomorrow. Go."

She took the bag and walked to the bus stop, farther and farther from the sound of her daughter wailing.

Dawn spent the night at a nearby Motel 6, drinking alone in her room and listening to the sound of families—happy families—walking down to the pool or to the vending machines. When Monty called the next morning to tell her to come watch Cheryl, she checked out and took a taxi back to the house. He was wearing his clothes from the day before. He clearly hadn't slept and, in his pain, he struck her as noble and paternal and terribly erotic.

"She's napping," he said. "I'll be back in two hours and I want you gone again after that."

"Monty."

She touched his arm, but he flung her hand away and left.

She went upstairs to the bedroom, looked at Cheryl peacefully asleep in her *Rugrats* T-shirt. A few minutes after Monty left, she heard a key in the door and went downstairs. Ms. Ella was wearing a blue tie-neck blouse Dawn knew well. She did not look sleepy at all and was moving around the house, looking at the mail on the coffee table, checking the messages on the answering machine.

"You can't be here," Dawn said, uselessly; she was just as afraid of Ms. Ella leaving as she was of whatever would come next.

"This is my house."

"It was your house. Now it's ours."

"Is that what you think? That I gave up my legal claim to the house just because I let my son pay the mortgage? If you really believe that, you're brainwashed. This is my place."

"Ms. Ella, please," Dawn said. "This is where we live. Me and Monty and Cheryl. Think about her. She needs a quiet place to stay."

"Well, she won't be staying with you," Ms. Ella said. "Not since I told Monty and Child Services about your little temper tantrums, both here and back at Stillwater. He'll get custody, no question. That's right." She gathered momentum from the emotion on Dawn's face. "That time you broke the CD player? All your little fits? I was physically afraid of you."

"You didn't!" Dawn screamed.

"Didn't I?" Ms. Ella said.

She went on, in a speech laced with vulgarity, to list out Dawn's various episodes: the incident when she ran into the woods back at Stillwater, the crying jags she'd had sometimes on the fire escape, the outburst from the year before. She recited all the ways Dawn was a dangerous and unstable mother, repeating memories and feelings Dawn had confessed to her in strict confidence, in those moments when they were alone in the bedroom. She accused Dawn of invading her family, of ruining her relationship with Monty.

“He’s too afraid to tell you the truth, but he knows. We both do. My son and I just want to rebuild our lives after what you’ve done to our family,” she said. Even though her tone was menacing, her eyes were flat.

What followed this was another breakdown, worse than the old ones. Ms. Ella left Dawn on the floor, writhing, her arms clawed and bleeding, which was how Monty found her when he came home.

Dawn remembered little of what happened afterward. She remembered the alarm in his voice and his touch as he bent down to her, and the feeling of being led by paramedics into the back of an ambulance.

She woke the next morning in the psych ward at Grady Hospital, in a long corridor where patients lay separated from one another by long blue curtains. Someone in the bed next to her was moaning. Her limbs felt sunken, heavy, and her tongue was thick. They had given her something strong, Klonopin maybe. She saw a nurse in pink scrubs padding down the corridor and called out.

“My daughter,” she said.

The nurse listened to Dawn babble for maybe fifteen seconds before cutting her off: “No one’s going to take your daughter away from you. But you need to get some rest.”

She must have gone to find Monty, because he came in a moment later and sat by her bedside in his work clothes, dark circles under his eyes.

“Monty, where is Cheryl?”

“She’s with your dad, Dawn. She’s fine.”

“Please don’t take her away from me, Monty.”

“Take her away from you? What are you talking about?”

Weeping, she told him what Ms. Ella had said, or as much of it as she could remember in her distress. He listened until the end and shook his head.

"She lied," he said at last.

Dawn spent two more days in the ward, sitting for periodic interviews with the social worker, who wanted her to start counseling. After the two days of observation, she was finally deemed not to be a suicide risk, and Monty picked her up in the van early in the morning of the third day and drove her to her father's house. They had agreed, in the exit meeting with the social worker, that it would be best for Dawn to stay there for a while, to minimize the risk of seeing Ms. Ella again; they would work out a schedule for Cheryl to come stay with her there on alternating days.

Dawn spent that first night, and every night for the next ten months, in her old room, the room her father had long ago converted into a spare room for guests, as if to signal that his daughter was really and truly gone.

Lying in bed in the mornings, Dawn would look around and see how thoroughly he had scrubbed away her remains, plastering over the holes that she had punched or kicked in the wainscoting, repainting the walls a cool blue-gray color to mask the crayon and pencil marks she'd left behind. He had made the room as clean and spare and anonymous as a bedroom in a corporate housing unit. The white headboard matched the white armchair in the corner and the white shades of the lamps on either side of the bed. A burnished mahogany double dresser took up part of the wall across from her bed, and a flat-screen television hung on the wall above it, reflecting the shine from the windows. There were no knickknacks or decorations, save for an abstract painting on the wall above the bed, a black canvas with white loops that suggested a roller coaster.

Dawn would lie under the cream-colored duvet and listen to the familiar sounds of her father getting up before she arose and made her way downstairs. He would be finishing his breakfast in the kitchen. He was fully gray-haired now and recently retired; he spent most of his days puttering, building World War II models and doing household repair projects. On Sundays he still went to mass, and on some weekdays he volunteered for outreach events with his church. He accepted his daughter into her former home with a gentle bewilderment, as if afraid he would accidentally set off her temper again. He cooked fretfully and often, as he had done in those early days after Dawn's mother left.

Only once, during Dawn's first week at the house, did he ask her what had happened. It was after dinner, and Cheryl was settled in the den watching *Barney*.

"Monty and I had a fight," was all Dawn would say. "It's temporary."

"Is it money?"

"Just work. Working a lot. It's hard."

"I see."

He covered her hand with his own. Together, they watched Cheryl. One of the calicos slunk into the den, eyed Cheryl distrustfully, and continued upstairs. Dawn could feel Ms. Ella's absence creep through her body, chilly and invisible, a vapor.

Cheryl started preschool. She spent most days with Monty and most afternoons and weekends with her grandfather. Dawn found a new job as a cashier at the art store, Easel, and arranged her schedule so that she could pick up Cheryl in her father's car and drop her off at Monty's later in the evening. The Savannah plan was abandoned. Monty began to pack and donate his mother's things so he could put the house on the market.

For Cheryl's sake—Dawn knew that it was only for Cheryl's sake and not for her own—Monty was civil to her, limiting their conversations to the topic of their daughter and their daughter only, asking no probing or jealous questions.

Dawn would never be certain why he had staged his departure and return at that moment, at what point suspicion had changed to certainty, or if the certainty had been woven into their relationship from the very start, like a hidden, invisible pulse, as if he had known, that first day they met in the square, that they would part for his mother—that he was in some sense delivering Dawn to her.

She did not fully understand it herself. It was not only lust that had started it; of this she was sure, although both women had submitted to it willingly. There was more than that: Ms. Ella clinging, refusing to let Dawn leave or grow away from her; Dawn's inability to leave Ms. Ella and Stillwater behind.

The affair seemed to have taken place in a cartoon or a funhouse, a place where everything was oversized and distorted. Dawn was ready to step out of it and back into the reality of her marriage. One weekend, when Monty came to pick up Cheryl, she brought up marriage counseling, and he did not say yes, but he did not say no. He only shrugged and said, "We'll see."

She raised the subject again after a birthday party for a girl in Cheryl's class, when they were speaking to each other politely over tiny, ridiculous cupcakes. Again, he said, "We'll see," but Dawn was heartened by the fact that he never sent papers. If it was really impossible, if it was truly out of the question, she thought, standing next to her father and watching Cheryl climb backwards up a winding yellow slide in Freedom Park, then wouldn't he have sent papers?

She read in the newspaper that Ms. Ella had withdrawn her intention to run for school superintendent again. She knew better than to talk to Monty about that.

When Cheryl asked about her grandmother, one evening after a parent-teacher meeting, Monty said curtly, "Grandma's in Florida."

Dawn thought of fresh starts and orange groves, of calm Gulf beaches with clear water and crabs walking sideways on the sand. She was secretly angry. Ms. Ella was the one who had moved, who got to start over, and Dawn was left in Atlanta with the mess.

But she was relieved, too. Ms. Ella's voluntary departure seemed to slam a door, to bury something Dawn had been unable to bury.

With Ms. Ella out of the picture, Dawn tried harder with Monty. That July, a year after the discovery, her boss Tim told her about a furnished vacation camper for rent up by Lake Lanier, a camper owned by a friend of a friend, and she brought it up one afternoon at the house, when she was dropping Cheryl off.

"She'd like that," Monty said. "Why don't you take her on your next weekend?"

"I thought we could all go. The three of us."

"I don't think that's a good idea."

"Monty, it's not her fault." Together they watched Cheryl in the yard. She was squatting on the ground outside, peering at something, an insect, maybe, on the trunk of the dogwood tree. The yard was mown and tidy, the milkweed uprooted, the flower beds newly turned and blooming with pink azaleas. A few stray boxes of Ms. Ella's old things were lined up on the curb for the garbage collector, next to the realtor's FOR SALE sign. "She's never really been on a vacation, and she's old enough to remember it now."

"Yeah. Still," Monty said.

"We'll have separate rooms," Dawn said bitterly. "If it helps."

It took another week of convincing, and then Dawn's father offered to pay for gas and groceries, and that was enough. They stuffed Monty's van full of snacks and toys and drove up early in the morning on a Saturday, the city giving way to long stretches of forest, dirt roads, and billboards that advertised fresh cider and pecans. The camper was parked on the shore of the lake, on a knotty, rooted site surrounded by pine trees. From the fire pit, they could see the lapping water of the lake and the slow, distant movements of houseboats.

On that first afternoon, Dawn took Cheryl swimming while Monty moved around the camper, unpacking. When she came back, wrapping towels around herself and Cheryl, she saw that he had made up the pullout bed for himself and put Cheryl's things in the smaller bedroom. "I thought you could have the back one," he said, jerking his head towards the master bedroom. Dawn nodded. It had been a victory to get him here; she knew not to expect any more than this.

But on the second day, Monty came with her and Cheryl to swim, and that night they made cheese sandwiches on the grill and ate them in polyester camping chairs by the water. Cheryl squealed each time she saw the silver flip of a fish.

"I want to go in!" she cried.

"It's too dark out now, sweetie," Monty said. "Tomorrow morning, first thing."

Cheryl pouted but brightened up when Dawn brought out graham crackers and marshmallows. "Let me?" she kept saying. "Let me hold the stick?" The three of them stood together, Monty guiding his daughter's hand over the fire, his forearms strong, his fingers dexterous and calloused. Dawn's eyes met his twice in the glow of the globe lights that hung along the top of the trailer. When Cheryl was asleep, Monty came into her bedroom and reached for her for the first time since the separation. She held her breath as he touched her, afraid of waking Cheryl, afraid of disturbing something with too sudden of an exhalation.

Later, she would remember the two weeks at the lake as having a hushed, unreal quality, as if time and the normal world had been suspended, just for them. In the mornings she got up early and made toast and orange juice in the quiet light, looking out the window at the graceful herons picking their way over tree roots. After breakfast, they swam or took

Cheryl on walks to look at water bugs, to scan the horizon for eagles, or to point at geese and wild turkeys on the opposite shore. Every few days, they drove twenty minutes to a farm stand in Flowery Branch to buy fresh peaches and bottled apple cider with the envelope of cash from Dawn's father. When it rained, they stayed in and watched Disney movies on the VCR. It was a neutral space, this lake, a place to make things, just as the lake itself had been made by damming the Chattahoochee and creating a reservoir: a fake but entirely convincing natural habitat, like the ones at a zoo.

At night Dawn woke to the sound of screeching crickets and saw Monty's bare shoulder, the familiar Dead Kennedys tattoo on his upper back, and went into the smaller bedroom to listen for the sweet short breathing of her daughter, the swishing rhythm of her legs kicking in the bedclothes. She sometimes stood in the dark for an hour, afraid to breathe, afraid to disturb the perfect stillness of the camper. She did not draw, she did not paint; she only looked at her husband and daughter and felt the chambers of her heart ache.

On the Saturday before their departure, some of Monty's band friends came up for lunch and a late afternoon swim, whooping and yelling in the water, sending the herons and fish away to seek quieter patches of shoreline. Afterwards they all sat around the fire pit, wrapped in beach towels and hunched over guitars, regaling Cheryl with bluegrass songs about trains. Dawn watched their fingers flying across the banjos and guitars; her daughter laughing and crying out, "Again!" each time they finished a song.

"We go home tomorrow," she said, under the music, to Monty.

"We should get an early start," he sighed. "I have to work tomorrow night."

"What are we going to do?"

He was silent.

"I can't go back to my dad's house, Monty. I can't."

"So don't."

He got up and began clearing away beer cans, not looking at her.

The next morning, they packed their things in an unsettled silence periodically broken by Cheryl's tantrums. They had left more of themselves in the camper than they realized. Every time they opened a cabinet or a drawer, they found more of the debris they had made: the red swimsuit Cheryl had already started to outgrow, the Sue Grafton mysteries Dawn read by the water, the CDs Monty had accumulated by the stereo. The three of them were like the thick vines of kudzu that crept all over the state, overtaking telephone poles and abandoned buildings and even hundred-year-old trees, attaching themselves to any firmness. On the drive back, Dawn wept intermittently as they passed families headed in the opposite direction, towards the lake, with kayaks and canoes mounted on their cars. Monty looked ahead in silence.

That night, Dawn tucked Cheryl in and walked out to her car, which she had left in Monty's driveway. He helped her move her things into her trunk. Afterwards, he stood by the driver's side door in the twilight, his figure a long shadow. He started to say something, then stopped.

"It's okay," Dawn said. "I know."

That night, back at home, she ignored her father's hopeful questions and asked for the white pages. *Speese* was beneath a long column of *Smith* surnames, and the listing gave an address in Eastlake, not far from where Stillwater had been.

Amber answered on the third ring. Dawn imagined her looking at her caller ID, confused, hesitating before she lifted the receiver.

"What's going on?" Amber said. "Is everything okay?"

"Not really," Dawn said.

"Oh." Amber waited. "What happened?"

"I don't know," Dawn said. "It's hard to explain."

"Okay. Sure. Take your time."

Dawn listened to her father in the kitchen, emptying the dishwasher. He was putting the glasses away extra gently, she could tell: sliding each one slowly off the rack and setting it in the cupboard with the quietest of clinks.

"Actually," Dawn said, "can I come over and stay with you? Just for a few days?"

Amber was silent so long that Dawn thought the line had gone dead.

"All right," she said at last.

Amber lived on the first floor of a weather-beaten apartment complex surrounded by oak trees, near the Eastlake MARTA station. She answered the door in a lavender T-shirt and acid-washed jeans with holes in the knees, her long hair down around her shoulders, and invited Dawn in. It was tiny, a monastic retreat stuffed with books. Three tall bookshelves dominated one wall of the living room, and more books were stacked on the floor in the hallway, so that Dawn had to turn to the side a bit to pass them. Amber showed her the finicky shower knobs, the thermostat, how to get water out of the Brita jug in the refrigerator.

"I know it's not much," Amber said. "But I can afford it."

"I love it," Dawn said. "I won't stay long. I promise."

"There's a park two blocks away, for Cheryl." Amber hesitated. "Her name's Cheryl, right?"

"That's right."

Dawn wandered over to one of the overstuffed bookshelves and picked up a small framed picture. It showed Amber sitting on a sofa, dressed smartly in black-rimmed glasses, a green dress, and flats, next to a man and a woman who were both smiling and both similarly bookish-looking.

"Is this from London?" Dawn asked. "The rare book school?"

Amber nodded. "That's Alex, my friend who runs a rare and used store in Charlottesville," she said. "And that's Cora. She works at the Schomburg Center for Research in Black Culture, in New York. She's an archivist. We all met at the seminar last month. Best two weeks of my life."

Dawn moved over to the futon and sat down heavily. She felt a deep and terrific exhaustion. Amber sat beside her.

"Was it something with Monty?"

Dawn's eyes filled with tears.

"Sorry," Amber said. "You don't have to tell me anything tonight."

"Thank you," Dawn said.

"Or ever, if you don't want to. You can just stay."

"Thank you."

Dawn closed her eyes. A moment later, she was asleep.

And this was how Dawn found herself living with an estranged friend, helping her scour catalogues for inventory she hoped to include in her own bookstore one day. Dawn slept on the futon and worked at Easel and saw her daughter as much as she could. She cleaned and did the shopping and cooked elaborate dinners from recipes she found in one of Amber's cookbooks, as a way of making up for the little she could contribute to the rent. Together, they took Cheryl to the park down the street, and Cheryl started calling Amber "Aunty Amber" and asking to hold her hand. Dawn worked on her sketches and joined her father once every few weeks at his Sunday mass.

Gradually, the woman who had dominated her life for years began to fade, although her voice remained, like the voice of the Cheshire Cat in the stories Amber read to Cheryl at bedtime. Dawn never told Amber about the voice. Stillwater and Ms. Ella and everything to do with them still meant something different to Amber, something exciting. Dawn had already ruined one thing. She could not bring herself to ruin another.

By the time Cheryl was in first grade, the voice had come to bother her so much that she went back with her dad to the family counselor they'd seen when she was a teenager. The counselor referred her to a therapist she could see alone, an elegant brunette woman in her fifties who specialized in behavior modification techniques. Once a week, for a year,

Dawn sat on the sofa in front of a glass-topped coffee table, under a framed Matisse print, and pretended that Ms. Ella was sitting in the armchair next to her. Together, she and Dr. Cook imagined a variety of scenarios.

"You're going into the kitchen to make Cheryl dinner," Dr. Cook began in an encouraging tone. "You know what you're going to make her. She's sitting at the table, waiting for you. What do you hear Ms. Ella say?"

"Well." Dawn adjusted her posture so that she was angled towards the empty armchair. "She starts just by observing."

"*She* starts?"

Dawn forced herself to address the invisible woman directly.

"You start by just observing. You say the meal I'm making shouldn't take too long or be too rich, or else I'll spoil my daughter."

"Okay. Then what?"

"Then you look over at what Cheryl is doing. Cheryl's playing with her Megaduck. You say that Cheryl should be doing something more mentally stimulating. You say I should get her a book to read or something."

"Why? Why is that? Why can't Cheryl just play with her game?"

"Well, because games are bad for your attention span."

"Okay," Dr. Cook said. "Let's do some reframing. You just said games are bad for your attention span. There is some truth to that claim, especially if your child plays them all the time. But does Cheryl play them all the time?"

"No, no. Just when I'm cooking or on the telephone and can't watch her. But—" Dawn's voice faltered.

"But what?"

"You're right, Ms. Ella," Dawn said to the chair. "Cheryl should be doing something more educational while she waits for me to cook."

"Listen. You can't be everywhere at once. You just told me last week that you take her on play dates, you draw with her, you take her to the park. At some point, you have to give yourself a break. Don't you see that?" Dr. Cook turned to the armchair and addressed it directly. "Ms. Ella, can't you see that you're making Dawn miserable?"

It felt forced and strange at first, but after a few months it started to work, and her breakdowns, her fits of panicked emotion, began to subside. Dawn found that she could sometimes silence the voice when it started up its cruel, gnawing chatter. She could imagine Ms. Ella sitting at her kitchen table and talk back to her, telling her to be quiet.

Sometimes Ms. Ella seemed too present, too loud, to banish. Once, when Amber went to sit down, Dawn exclaimed, "Don't sit there!"

Amber stood confused, dinner plate in hand, looking at the empty chair. "Why? Is there something wrong with it?"

Dawn shook her head. "Nothing," she said. "Just that the leg is wobbly."

When she and Dr. Cook were about six months into the therapy process, Dawn stopped thinking so much about the voice and started thinking about those moments after school at Stillwater, how Ms. Ella had understood about Dawn's own mother, how she understood her art, how she'd been the first person to see, really see, Dawn's sketches. She tried to explain these memories to the therapist.

"Well, of course it wasn't all bad, or you wouldn't have kept coming back to her," Dr. Cook said. "Don't you see? That's how these cycles work. If it was all bad, you would have left. But since there were cycles of good and bad, and the good ones were so good, you held out through the bad times, hoping for the good ones again."

"But were they good moments for her too?" Dawn asked. "Or did I just think they were?"

"There's no way to know," Dr. Cook advised. "You know that you loved her, deeply and for a lot of years. But you can't ever know what she felt."

"So it was all a lie."

Dr. Cook sighed, arranging her scarf. "Narcissists don't love like you and I love. But they love you in their own way."

That had addressed the feeling more fully, had filled in the blank spaces between the different clinical terms they discussed, terms like narcissism and negative narcissism and codependency and empathy. She grappled with all of it for months and the voice subsided a bit more, but she lost something too.

She never quite felt that same intensity about anything afterwards, not about her art, not about her new life.

It wasn't a bad thing.

It wasn't a good thing, either.

In those early months, Cheryl still asked about Ms. Ella frequently. "When's Grandma coming back?" she would say, as Dawn and Amber pushed her on the swings or leaned over to cut up her pancakes into child-sized bites.

"Maybe not for a while, honey," Dawn would say. "Remember? She's down at the orange grove with her cousin. Helping to sell the fruit."

The first time she said this, Amber looked at her curiously over Cheryl's head, but Dawn ignored her.

A month after Dawn moved in, Monty's attorney sent divorce papers to Amber's address by way of a courier service. Amber was at work and Dawn was making tacos for dinner. She answered the door in her apron, the stereo blasting one of Amber's Blur CDs, and signed the papers with the Atlanta Cooperative School pen her daughter had left during her last visitation weekend.

Chapter XI

Madeira Beach, 2012

THE ABSOLUTENESS of Dawn's solution to the Ms. Ella problem had been easy to settle on, because it was the only option. It was only the means to the end that she struggled with.

She was an artist. She would not do it in a conventional way. And Ms. Ella would not want a conventional way, if she could choose, if she could give directions. But this was not about Ms. Ella, Dawn reminded herself; this was about Cheryl, about protecting her from Ms. Ella's influence. It was too late for Dawn. But not for her daughter.

In this mood of perverse benevolence, Dawn began her research. At first, she told herself she would only find out if the book still existed—the *Shadows* wallpaper book, which along with *Agamemnon* had helped to start the whole thing. She looked through Amber's catalogues and databases. She used her miniature painting series as an excuse to stay in the store at odd times, when Amber wasn't there.

The book did exist. Eight copies total, all but two in museums. The remaining two were in rare bookstores in London and Virginia, to be sold only to museums, archives, or professional dealers, not to ordinary customers. Serious inquiries only.

It would have to be Virginia. Dawn thought about it for an afternoon, a few weeks before her departure, as she walked along the bike paths near Freedom Parkway, the hazy Atlanta skyline rising above an ocean of maple trees, forming a massive prism, flinging hot beams everywhere in shimmering, distorted flashes. What was in Virginia? The residency that she had already refused a few weeks earlier, in a fit of pique.

The gallery owner, an old contact from the MARTA mural project, was surprised to hear from her. "I don't care about the stipend," Dawn said before he could begin his stammering explanation. When he offered his guest room, she said, "That's okay. I want to spend some time in Old Town Alexandria." She then hung up and booked a budget motel near the interstate.

She arrived in Alexandria on a Sunday night, tired and restless, and spent her first three days at the gallery earning thirty hours of residency, so the second half of the week was free.

Then, she drove to Richmond and staked out Lee's Books for three days, sometimes from an outdoor table at a neighboring café, sometimes from across the street, striding back and forth on the cobblestones, pretending to read the historical plaques mounted on the buildings.

She studied the rhythms of the store. Every day at ten, Lee pulled up in his old Honda hatchback, unlocked the doors, fed the cat, stocked the shelves. At eleven, he wheeled the carts of paperbacks out onto the sidewalk and turned on the sign, an electric owl with glasses and a book that said OPEN across the front in neon red lettering. She watched him through the large display windows as he lovingly wiped the shelves down with a cloth.

Dawn's heart ached for him. How kind he was to everyone who came in the store! He knew people. Knew everyone. The customers came in specifically to speak with him, to catch him up on their lives. They listened while he talked and often brought him gifts: cards in pastel envelopes, tins with baked goods. Dawn understood that he was going through something. He had lost someone. Or was losing someone, maybe. Maybe he was sick, but Dawn didn't think so, not with the way he still lifted boxes of inventory and bent down to wipe the lower shelves, the way he still made his way easily through the narrow aisles, talking to customers, making recommendations.

He was too present, too alert, too solicitous. It would have to be the girl.

She came in the afternoons. She was a few years younger than Cheryl. High school, Dawn thought. Purple hair, lip piercing, bloomer-style pantaloons worn awkwardly over square-heeled boots. She was the most colorful and active shape in the store. It was easy to spot her as she flitted around the dark shelves, disappeared down the stairway into the basement, or rocked from one foot to the other in the side alley between the store and the café, vaping, a large grey cloud of smoke forming above her and above her only, a solitary thunderstorm. Alone at the counter, she hunched over her phone, the device glowing between her thumbs, giving off a light that made Dawn think of her own daughter coming to her from the yard when she was younger with a live, winking firefly cupped in her hands. The customers found the girl rude, Dawn saw, but she understood that the girl was not rude, merely terrified of people. She masked her terror underneath an adolescent sauciness that even the girl herself, clutching desperately at her device, feared might crack at any point.

Dawn went into the store at three in the afternoon on the second day. At this time, the store was empty save for the girl and the cat and a couple of idle browsers who paused briefly at the sidewalk carts and went on. The girl was behind the counter and did not acknowledge Dawn. The cat basked on a cat tree high in the back corner between two shelves. Its tail was a long, white, feathery plume, like something from a cabaret costume, flicking back and forth lazily. Dawn browsed the titles in the glass case, looking for the sober green cover. Nothing. She checked again. Still nothing.

Panicked, she strode through the store, her eyes racing over the shelves, and nearly tripped over a footstool with a bright sign that read EMPLOYEES ONLY. The cat stood up and arched its back, rebuking her sudden movement.

This motion, this arching of the back, was what drew her eye to the book. It was perched on a shelf high over the cat tree, on the highest shelf in the store, wrapped in plastic and adorned with a sign that read DO NOT TOUCH. ASK FOR ASSISTANCE. It could be seen from any point. Its visibility made it invisible.

Dawn paced underneath the volume, eyeballing the distance. The cat yawned and began cleaning its front paw. Dawn thought quickly and went to the display case in front, where she pointed at an old green-covered edition of Charles Dickens's *A Christmas Carol.*

"That one," she announced.

"Will that be all?" The girl looked at Dawn's hands, avoiding her eyes.

"That's it."

Dawn paid with her credit card, the last good one. On the way back to her hotel, she stopped and bought a box of plastic wrap. It was a half-hour's work to bind the book in plastic, wrapping and wrapping it until the title was hidden by a few artful crinkles.

The next afternoon, she returned to Lee's Books at the same time, three o'clock, the wrapped volume snug in her purse.

"Afternoon," the girl said without looking up when the bell above the door jangled.

"Afternoon."

Dawn made her way to the back of the store and dragged the footstool over to the high shelf by the cat tree. The girl was on the phone now, in the midst of a heated exchange.

"What do you mean?" she cried. "What do you mean, she didn't mean it? She said it right to my face!"

Dawn stepped onto the footstool. The cat's gaze followed her. In the nights to come, she would dream of that cat's eyes, of the black spheres of the pupils, the frank green irises. She swapped out the books, replaced the sign, and dropped *Shadows from the Walls of Death* into her purse.

Twenty minutes later, she was on I-95, heading south for Madeira Beach.

Dawn took the *Shadows* book out of her trunk now. She donned the mask and gloves, carried it over to the clearing, and unwrapped it. The paper was stiff and powdery as she mixed it into the final coat of clay. Dawn admired the texture of the grey material: mottled, the little bubbles of oxygen giving the clay a tropical, spongey look, like something from the bottom of the ocean. Patches of the pattern emerged from the strips as she slicked them on to the dress: a little sprig of red flowers by Cassandra's left knee, a patch of repeating diamond shapes near her ankles, a motif of beige leaves along her lower back, toxic green blossoms bursting along her hemline.

She finished the statue in early afternoon, when the leaves in the clearing were dry and shining and the palm trees tossed their heads proudly in the breeze off the nearby ocean. It would take a day to dry fully, but no matter.

She cleaned her materials from the clearing and burned the remainder of the book on the fire pit, still wearing her mask and standing upwind from the blaze.

Yuri came by with his broom and dustpan, later than usual, in camouflage pants and a T-shirt from one of the lobster restaurants on the Pass. He whistled at the statue.

"All done, huh?"

"Just about."

"You giving that to Ms. Ella today?"

"Yes. It still needs to dry."

"It looks good."

Dawn grabbed his arm.

"If something ever happens to her, I want you to get rid of it."

"Why?"

"Because it's no good."

He stared at her. "We all feel that way sometimes," he said, "but it doesn't mean you just throw everything away."

"Please just do what I ask. Promise me."

Without moving his eyes from hers, he said, "You coming to chapel this week?"

It is mine to revenge, I will repay, Dawn thought. But also: *And behold if the plague be in the walls of the house.*

"I'm not really religious, Yuri." Her voice was muffled in the mask; she slipped it down around her neck. "I told Maria and Caleb that I don't go to church."

"You don't have to be religious to think that something is spiritual. I don't care about botany or know about botany," he said, pointing an elephant ear spotted with dragonflies, "but still, I know that plant is spiritual."

Dawn was silent.

"Let me get this straight. You mean to say all this past week you've been sitting and sculpting with this woman who loves the history of this place more than anything, and hanging out with Maria and Caleb, who go all around here trying to help people who don't have anything. Helping people get to recovery. Helping people get the books and groceries they want. All around you people are talking their hearts out and you don't see anything in it at all? You don't think there's anything greater than us?"

"I think that there are people who believe that."

"That's why you'll only ever make grisly statues and things," he said. "Because you can't fathom that there's anything out there bigger than humans."

He studied the finished Cassandra, examining her squat, gesturing form, her open mouth, her fierce, torrential expression.

"She looks like you," he said, and left.

Ms. Ella was still passed out, snoring loudly, when Dawn moved the statue into her room. She left her sketchbook and Ms. Ella's notebook behind with it, along with a note. "Keep this for me," she wrote. "Good luck with the book. You may call Cheryl. You have my permission."

Ms. Ella was still asleep an hour later, when Dawn gathered her art supplies, packed her things, and checked out with the grumpy, harassed-looking woman at the office.

On her way out of Madeira Beach, Dawn stopped for one final look over the bay from the boardwalk at the Pass. The first faux-pirate boats of the day had just departed from the docks. Dawn looked out at their black cannons. A group of kids in pirate hats waved up at Dawn from the deck, and she waved back. On the pier, tanned waitresses moved back and forth among their busy sidewalk tables and gulls swooped down onto the boardwalk to snatch dropped fries. Skee-Ball arcades lit up; kids shot at targets with water guns, trying to win T-shirts and stuffed animals, while bored, acne-scarred teenage attendants in visors watched from behind counters.

She expected to feel a sense of triumph, but instead she felt defeat. Probably, she would succeed in killing the woman. But she would never kill her voice, not completely. Already, Dawn could hear it, that invisible, Cheshire Cat apparition that still spoke to her even as she stood alone by the water.

It followed her back to Atlanta and into her black, dreamless nights.

Why did you do it? asked the voice.

I had to, Dawn replied. For Cheryl.

The voice launched into a long speech then, about Stillwater and *Agamemnon* and the history of Tampa, and Milton's Lucifer. The voice spoke under a phantasmal pair of flat eyes. She crammed her pillow against her ears.

Morning came. Dawn started to dial Dr. Cook and stopped. She felt wild, unleashed, and feared what she would say to her, to anyone. If she said what she'd done, it would be the end for her. If she saw Dr. Cook. If she went back to the hospital. If.

Dawn felt another attack coming on, worse this time because she knew it wouldn't be the last. Still, she stayed home. Still, she crammed the fabric of her pillowcase into her mouth and waited.

By the third sleepless night, she made the choice. So I will go first after all, she thought calmly.

Just before sunrise, she got out her art book and studied *The Family*. She felt an uncanny and monstrous swell of recognition. She was transfixed by the grotesque funhouse shape of the bodies, the brooding sense of mutiny in the mother and daughter's eyes.

This time, she paid more attention to the other figure in the room, the other girl—another sister?—who stood in the light of the window and looked greedily upon the struggle. Her hands were clasped together in front of her heart; she was praying, maybe, or cracking her knuckles as a threat.

Dawn noticed, for the first time, the strange carving on the wooden cabinet between the bed and the window: a pelican crouched over a supine animal—a baby bear? A fox? The pelican was driving its beak into the animal's mouth, either feeding it or piercing it; Dawn couldn't tell. The light coming in from the window, the drawn curtains at the top of it, all gave this cabinet the brimstone mood, but not the sanctity, of an altarpiece.

Dawn returned to the mother's expression. She thought of a driving force that both pierces and feeds.

But now there was Cheryl, also eighteen, and just as talented as she herself was, and new. Dawn wept to think of her, and felt glad, and swallowed the pills, and went back to her painting. She looked at the light that came in through the open window, the unholy blaze that bathed the two figures on the bed. She stayed alive just long enough to see the sun of her own world rise like the one in the strange faraway room where the awful sisters stood, awash in violent sunbeams, ready for the slaughter.

Chapter XII

Atlanta and Madeira Beach, August 2012

IT WAS LATE SUMMER, the days humid and thick with haze, when Yuri called Amber at the bookstore. The air conditioning was broken, and Amber had propped the door open to admit a still wall of air. But no customer dared to enter that day. The sun beat through the glass windows and turned the store into a greenhouse. The books seemed to shrink in the heat.

Amber's mind was deep inside a wilting cinnamon fern that sat behind her cash register. She had been examining its woeful, forward-curving fronds, wondering what kind of care would lure it back from its defensive slumber, when the phone rang. She struggled back to the sound of Yuri's voice, alien and far away in its urgency.

"She died in her sleep," he was saying. "Maria and Caleb handled everything with the ambulance and the doctor. They found Monty's number in one of her notebooks. But no one could get in touch with him."

"He's on tour again," Amber said. "Amsterdam. He'll be back next week."

"I would have called you anyway," Yuri said. "Maria tried calling Cheryl, but her voicemail box was full. Ms. Ella wanted her to have the Cassandra statue. She didn't leave a will, but she told me she wanted Cheryl to have it. She said you told her about something Cheryl wanted it for, an art show. I was hoping you could give us her address so that we can ship it."

Amber stood up so quickly that her stool toppled over.

"I'll come get it myself," she said.

She closed the store, filled her gas tank, and drove down to Florida that same afternoon, arriving in Madeira Beach just after ten. It was quieter now that tourist season was over, and there were few guests in the hotels. Amber rolled down her window. The ocean crashed in the distance, lonely and threatening. The hotel pools were flat, blue, still. Bartenders leaned against countertops, staring at televisions. Bored waitresses sat outside and smoked or hunched over their glowing phones.

There were only five cars in the motel lot. In the pool area, a deeply tanned man in a polo shirt paced back and forth, growling into his phone. A sullen young woman in cutoffs sat in a chaise lounge, listening to headphones and staring at the water. Amber recognized neither of them.

Yuri was in the far corner of the pool area, smoking. When he saw her, he put out his half-finished cigarette on the ground and slipped it behind his ear.

"Long drive," he said.

"Thanks for waiting."

"Maria and Caleb wanted to come, but they had a ministry tonight. They send their condolences."

He led her to Room 126 and opened the door. The room was tidy, clean and bare. All of the debris was gone, the bedclothes and curtains removed. The room had been aired out and sprayed with pine-scented freshener. The walls looked bigger and cleaner without the crowding sheets of paper, the tiny handwriting.

"Trash or Salvation Army," Yuri said, reading her thoughts. "She was funny in the end. Started letting people in after all. She gave away a bunch of stuff and Maria and Caleb moved out the rest. She smoked right up to the last minute. Sat out by the pool talking to people about Humpty Dumpty. Wasn't making any sense."

"Maybe the lung stuff got her," Amber said cautiously.

"The drink, more like," Yuri said. "That's usually what gets em."

He led her over to the alcove where the Cassandra stood. This time, Amber was prepared for the ravaging gaze, the poisonous tunic. She stood for a moment, admiring the clusters of red carnations, the brown pinecones, the rows of white hexagons that still shone faintly after more than a century of shedding their toxic dust. The Cassandra's eyes looked back. Amber imagined that they looked more serene, more satisfied, than when she'd last seen them.

"What's this?" she said, pointing at a black object underneath the table.

"That's a sketchbook Dawn left," Yuri said. "We found it in the room, with Ms. Ella's papers. We thought you would want it. You need help with the statue?"

"I'm good," Amber said.

She donned the gloves she had bought and wrapped the Cassandra carefully in a plastic trash bag, holding her by the base. Yuri followed with the sketchbook and set it on the passenger seat of her car. She placed the wrapped Cassandra on the floorboard, head resting against the seat, like a smuggled relic.

"Take good care of it," Yuri said, tapping her windshield before she drove away. "You never did send me a picture. So I took my own."

"Please keep it to yourself," Amber said.

"What else would I do with it?"

Amber drove down Gulf Boulevard towards St. John's Pass. During the drive south, she had thought and thought about the location. Anywhere near the beach or the bay had to be avoided at all costs; the public thoroughfares, too, were off-limits, and the empty lots would all flow downhill, bringing the statue's poison into the sea.

She had finally decided on the site of a former car repair shop, because its ground was already poisoned. The lot was three blocks away from St. John's Pass, and she could hear a bar band doing Jimmy Buffet covers as she brought out the statue, then the concrete, the sand, the jugs of water. Working quickly, she made a hill on the far side of the lot, on a stained slab of pavement that had once been home to leaking cars, their insides seeping daily into the concrete. When the hill was about six inches high, she buried the Cassandra in it and added more concrete and sand to the top. Cassandra's face and her bright dress disappeared under the thick mixture.

Briefly, Amber allowed herself a moment of anger. Somehow, she was still in Dawn's shadow, even after her death.

But she had Cheryl, she thought.

Amber spent the next two days in a fit of hysteria, visiting and revisiting the lot. The first time she paced back and forth, pretending to make a phone call; another time, she rented a bicycle and went gliding by on the sidewalk. Each time, the little concrete mound sat dumbly, an eyesore on an eyesore. The sun beat down. Traffic glittered by.

On the afternoon of the third day a thunderstorm raged and pelted the concrete with rain. Afterwards, as the sun came out again, a few seagulls perched on top of the mound, squawking and chattering. The sight of these common birds populating the spot reassured Amber somehow, and she drove back to Atlanta at last.

On the night before Dawn's memorial show, Amber wrapped the sketchbook Yuri had given her in tissue paper, packed it in a pale blue gift bag, and drove to Peachtree Collaborative.

The gallery was tucked away in a residential neighborhood close to her childhood home, across from a convenience store and a municipal fire station. It was a one-story glass building with doors and shutters painted red. Large windows revealed walls of brightly colored canvases.

In the front of the gallery, along the left side of the walkway, was a brick courtyard built under the leafy arms of a white ash tree with branches low enough to sit on. Wrought iron benches with ivy scrollwork alternated with wooden planters full of hostas and lavender. Bamboo torches blazed the mosquitos away.

Amber took a seat on one of the benches. Cheryl appeared on the walkway a moment later. She carried sleeves of plastic cups in either hand. Her hair was dyed strawberry red now, a hue that brought out the freckles on her cheekbones.

Aliyah, her new girlfriend, followed behind her, holding a plastic bin filled with name tags and markers. She was a tall, stylish Black woman with a pink streak in her short hair and a lip ring. She was also a photographer, one of the artists in residence at Peachtree Collaborative. Amber, with the fierce kinship she felt for other introverts, liked her immediately.

She presented the bag to Cheryl.

"What's this?"

"It's the sketchbook your mother was working on when she died," Amber said. "I found it in the bookstore when I was cleaning. We can still show the bookstore paintings, but I thought you could display some of these too, if you like."

Cheryl sat beside Amber on the bench and opened the sketchbook wide. Firelight from the torches danced on the pages.

The sketches were all done in pencil. The first one was of Yuri standing in front of the pool, grinning, flanked by palm trees. A brilliant flash glanced off his cross and radiated outwards, as if to drag the viewer into the faith that it promised.

Aliyah leaned over Cheryl's shoulder and studied the picture.

"Was your mother religious?"

"No. I mean, my grandfather is Catholic, but she was an atheist." Cheryl lifted the sketchbook up, peering at the little details: the ripples on the water, the salamander clinging to the side of a planter. "It's funny," she said, after a moment. "She wasn't religious, and she wasn't trying to be. But still."

"Still what?"

"Still," Cheryl said.

Amber watched while Cheryl and Aliyah studied the rest of the sketches, one by one. There was a sketch of a cat's eyes, with the largest and strangest irises Amber had ever seen. There was an illustration of the clearing where Dawn had created her statue, surrounded by palm trees and elephant ears. In the foreground, a dragonfly hovered, preternaturally large. The final sketch, the most detailed one, depicted a hurricane tearing out of the sea, spinning up whorls of salt water, breaking the land violently into fragments of shore.

The water now would be moving restlessly against the timber. Seabass and redfish would be gliding in the current. Above them, on the boardwalk, the vibrations from hundreds of human footsteps would send the gulls and herons flying out over the Pass. Further inland, the mutely prophesying mouth of the Cassandra would harden in concrete, carrying forever and invisibly the unuttered anguish of the dead.

Acknowledgments

MY DEEPEST THANKS go out to the following people:

Christine Neulieb, Amanda Thomas, and Feliza Casano at Lanternfish Press. It is an honor to work with such a smart and thoughtful team.

Kevin Beverage, Sarah Starr Murphy, Alison Fisher, Yume Kitasei, Valerie O'Riordan, and Sara Crowley all read early drafts and provided helpful feedback and encouragement. I wouldn't be here without you.

The Fiction Forge has been a supportive, lively home for writers. Thank you, John Haggerty and Yosh Haggerty, for hosting this community!

To friends who have lent their support and companionship, and from whom I have learned so much about art, writing, and thinking: Stephanie Trainer, Casey Patterson, Karl Nykwest, Kait Nykwest, Sera Mathew, Karen Dwyer, Kirstin Hanley, Chris Girman, Colleen Hooper, Geoff Peck, Heidi Pennington.

To all Diamonds, Macks, Vogelsongs, Smays, and Zellers! Thank you for your support.

Librarians and independent bookstores: you are the best.

To the authors who took time to read and blurb this book: thank you.

Lisa Smith and Jake Smith, for reading, support, and trips to the boardwalk.

To John Zeller, for everything.

About the Author

BARBARA BARROW is the author of *The Quelling* (Lanternfish Press, 2018), which was selected as a Gold Winner for Literary Fiction in the Foreword Indies Awards. Her short stories have appeared or are forthcoming in *Faultline*, *Southern Humanities Review*, *Raleigh Review*, *Cimarron Review*, and elsewhere.

You might also enjoy...

The Quelling
by Barbara Barrow

Dreams Under Glass
by Anca L. Szilágyi

Witches' Dance
by Erin Eileen Almond